Slipping Away from Milford

To Joanna
best wishes
Rob Watson

for Sharon

Slipping Away
from Milford

Rob Watson

seren

seren is the book imprint of
Poetry Wales Press Ltd
Wyndham Street, Bridgend
CF31 1EF

© Rob Watson, 1998

ISBN 1-85411-181-7

A CIP record for this title is available from the British Library

*The publisher acknowledges the financial support of
the Arts Council of Wales*

Printed in Plantin by
CPD Wales, Ebbw Vale

'We won't be going far,' the man said, already striding off across the sand.

The boy, finding himself deserted, experienced a strange sensation of hovering untethered. His parents were nowhere to be seen, he had no recollection of arriving at this place, and, as he glanced about, he saw no evidence outside the walls of his sandcastle that he had made any mark on this world, which was now a wilderness.

Another thing they would say, once he was big enough to be abandoned in the house for an hour or two, was 'We won't be long'. That made him anxious too. They always returned, of course, and perhaps were never really very long or very far, but he couldn't judge distances and lengths of time with their easy minds.

The boy patted more sand against his walls, then wondered what he was building a castle for – he had no memory of starting, let alone *why* he'd started. There'd been no plan and no one suggested the idea. Everything was strange. The sky drifted along all in one piece, without a breath of wind. Nevertheless it was re-assuring to see and feel the thing he had made, and smell his sand-stained hands while waiting.

He was proud of his castle and would remember it as long as he lived. So long as he lived nothing could ever break it. And they were coming back, after all, as good as their word.

ONE

'What would you do if you could do what you want?'

Bob Ryman had had his first ever win on the pools, so naturally the conversation kept turning fanciful. It didn't matter that he'd only won seven pounds.

Peter Walker spat and watched his spit till it hit brown water. 'Get rid of the missus,' he grinned mischievously.

'Kill her?'

'Buy myself out. Buy my freedom.' As he said it the fantasy seemed to blossom and his grin changed to a kind of fearful yearning. Like everyone else he forgot, for the moment, that he was happily married.

'What then?' Bob pursued. Bob Ryman was a bachelor and the attitudes of men a decade older always intrigued him. For a policeman he had a touching sense of wonder, but it was grounded in ignorance and protected by prejudice. He meant well, though.

Peter Walker shrugged, almost a form of thought with him. 'Get drunk when I want,' he said. 'Stay out when I want.' He paused, wondering why there wasn't more, then rounded it off smugly: 'Go where I want.'

The reporter, Mal Mabey, was as inexperienced as the police constable. He too assumed Peter had meant what he said and although he laughed along with the others he was perplexed and hurt. Most weekends, especially in springtime, he covered weddings, and he loved them – adored the brides and bridesmaids, whose attire promised limitless luxurious bliss. He wanted to believe in a future as gorgeous as a good wedding implied. He also wanted to be a famous reporter. Mal wasn't cut out for big things.

'What about you, John?' Bob Ryman asked, detecting a dismissive grunt.

'I do what I want,' John Eakins said plainly. 'Don't we all? Why would a fortune make a difference?'

'That's true,' Mal came in eagerly. 'We've got everything, living here.'

But if it had been anyone other than John Eakins suggesting that a steady job and life on a council estate couldn't be improved on even Mal Mabey might have wanted to puncture the sentiment. John Eakins had the authority, somehow, and when he said something po-faced it still came across as a well-balanced truth. He'd seen more of life than the others. Been in the war, for a start, and hadn't been born in this area. Originally he came from

Monmouthshire, the valleys, mining stock. And he'd lived in London. Despite that, John wasn't as much an outsider as, say, the professional people who'd moved in – teachers, doctors, priests, solicitors – they were outsiders wherever they lived. John Eakins had a proper man's job, and men liked him on sight. For over ten years he'd been on the trawlers. He was courageous, strong and reliable. So when he pontificated no one tried to laugh him out of it.

Peter Walker spat in the sea again and kicked the stone wall: 'My old lady's all right,' he corrected himself unhappily. 'I wasn't meaning nothing.'

'If she walked out on you, Peter, you'd soon know what misery is.'

Bob and Mal listened to this needless moralising like foolish children. They didn't want to let on they'd taken Peter at his word. It didn't seem manly to be guileless.

'I wouldn't mind getting a new sidecar, though,' Mal Mabey said, 'and hey, if I come into *real* money, I could own my own paper! That'd be good.'

'You could start your own fleet of trawlers, John,' Bob Ryman risked.

'Aye, fair enough, there's nothing against a windfall.'

'I wouldn't leave Mrs Walker,' Peter continued. 'I'd take her on holiday, somewhere she's always wanted to go – Morecombe.'

'I'd buy land,' Bob Ryman said. He'd been waiting to say it. 'I'd buy property an' all. Then I could make sure no one would come in and ruin the place. If I owned everything here I could keep it like it is.'

John Eakins smiled at him: 'You really think these speculators are coming, don't you?'

'No doubt in my mind.'

'And they'll turn us into Sodom and Gomorrah?'

'Gambling,' suggested Peter Walker.

'Casinos and bright lights,' said the ace reporter.

'Dens of vice, showgirls, blackmail...' Bob couldn't bear to visualise the possibilities.

They all stared up the Haven, past the busy docks, on to the quiet town, and wondered why anyone in his right mind should want to alter it.

'I know a man who had a fortune,' John Eakins said, to lighten their gloom. 'Pal of mine. Right near the end of the war, this was. Europe nothing but rubble.' He lit a Woodbine, nodded in the direction of the road back to the pub, and they set off together.

'Me and Phil was digging around in some old cathedral, like, and we come upon this solid-looking box. Small it was – so big – heavy, but easy enough to shift. What d'you think? *Coins*, boys, solid gold. Hundreds of 'em.'

'Property of the Church,' Bob Ryman pointed out warily.

'That's what I said,' agreed John. 'Lost property, old Phil claimed. Now I never went along with him, mind, but I never disputed it, neither. He couldn't very well carry it with him, not for long, so he found some ground and buried it. Marked the spot. Reckoned he'd leave it safe till after the war, see. Anyroad, the war ends, me and Phil haven't seen each other in a while – this is a few months after we was demobbed: I runs into him in London. Same old Phil, taking his chances, liking a laugh. And in the end I remembered our find and asked him if he'd gone back. Y'know what he said?'

'Some other bugger got there before him,' Peter Walker reckoned.

'He couldn't find the spot,' Mal said, 'or they'd gone and built buildings on it.'

John Eakins enjoyed shaking his head. The story was reviving pleasant memories – he hadn't been to London or seen Phil Thomas for more than ten years. They were hurrying along Old Dock Road now, between rusting sheds and boarded-up houses that hadn't been in use since the thirties. There was a sharp cut to the wind, too, though it had been pleasant enough out on the point. Redundant roads had a despondency of their own. Eakins shivered at an imagined resemblance to the torn towns deeper down in his mind.

'He hadn't been back yet,' John told them. 'He was sure it was still waiting. He hadn't forgotten about it or lost his nerve or nothing. He just didn't need to go and collect it. That's Phil, see. That's how to handle a fortune.' He felt easier again as they scrambled up a bank into the sun.

'In the parable of the talents...' Bob started.

'Never mind that,' John cut him off. 'There's more than one way of looking at it. He had it there in the back of his mind, see, the knowledge of it. He was carrying on with his life the way he wanted, so he didn't need nothing more than knowing where he'd hid it. Probably still there.'

'Somewhere over the rainbow,' Peter Walker half-sang as they pushed into the pub.

'Not really *his*, though, is it?' Mal Mabey insisted.

John Eakins was disappointed. They were all in work, and there were few better places to live. Talk of pots of gold was idiotic. Peter joked it was Bob's round, since he had seven quid to squander. Bob grinned and said Drinks for everyone. The barman and his dog were the only other potential customers. John Eakins stayed with his friends through a daft discussion about pots of gold and how much a solid gold coin was actually worth, and where in France was it, exactly, that his pal had found this fortune? Like kids, he thought, missing the point of the story completely. It wasn't even greed – they wouldn't have grabbed shovels even if he'd been able to tell them. They just wanted to know so they could salivate with some precision.

His own thoughts fell back to London and a time before Rachel and marriage. Good days, and some very fine nights. He hadn't been miserable before he settled down, and it would have been hypocritical not to enjoy old memories. He'd never do anything to put his family at risk – Rachel and Foster meant the world to him – but in a way he understood Peter Walker's outburst. That was why he'd curbed it, and he felt mean now.

'Penny for your thoughts,' Bob Ryman intruded suddenly.

'A penny, Bob?' he laughed. 'I'll keep 'em to myself.'

What he wanted, though, was to keep them *from* himself, because they were obviously worthless. He was the man he was by choice. If he wanted to cut loose he'd have done so. He wanted what he had, needed nothing more. When he was at sea, physically active, no thoughts disturbed him. Inactivity was troublesome. His trawler was being overhauled, and that had left him with a few unexpected days at home. Rachel worked all week. The boy was at school. Odd jobs about the house were only absorbing if they were worth doing, and he'd finished the main ones. John Eakins wasn't built for sitting idle; something in his head would start to dance; something in his heart would want to follow. Resting was for dead men. He needed to pit himself against waves and winds, not fill out the afternoon playing cribbage. His foot tapped impatiently.

TWO

Aniseed balls four a penny, big gobstoppers a penny each; a stick of barley sugar wasn't essential, but you had to have some black-jacks and an everlasting stick of toffee to tug and suck through the main picture. Aside from sweets you needed something to cover comics, plus admission to the Astoria, without which Saturday morning would be nearly as bad as Sunday. Petey bought the *Dandy* and *Beano*, Colin the *Beezer*, *Wizard* and *Dandy*, Dewi the *Eagle* and the *Dandy*. Foster Eakins wasn't allowed a comic because his mam said they were bad for him. He bought sweet cigarettes and flat slabs of chewing gum for the pictures of famous film stars. Sometimes he had enough left for a toy from Woolworth's, and they'd rush up before the flicks started.

Foster was the moral conscience of the gang; at least, he thought so. Not having comics distinguished him from his friends, meant he came from a superior home. His mother had a full-time job and most mothers on the estate weren't allowed to go to work. They had to clean the house every day. Foster went to chapel every Sunday morning, followed by Sunday school. Most Sundays his mam took him back again for the evening service. Petey, Dewi and Colin were usually able to play out, on the green or down the woods. Foster would have preferred to be with them, but not if it meant having parents like theirs. All their parents were rather vulgar, according to his mam. His dad wouldn't agree with her, but she knew best.

While kids were yelling at friends, bouncing on their itchy-plush seats, and aiming pellets at enemies a few rows away, Colin turned conspiratorially and held out his hand to display several packets of the brittle chewing gum with collectible film star cards in.

'Have 'em, Foss – I don' collect 'em.'

You didn't know which film star was on the card until you opened the packet. The chances of finding another as lovely as Belinda Lee must have been infinitesimal. Foster hadn't seen her in a film yet, but he idolised her, along with Brigitte Bardot and a woman called Betty Page, whom he'd seen in one of Colin's uncle's American comics – two blondes and a brunette, all with nice smiles, sympathetic eyes and expressions that reached out directly to him from a world he hadn't yet developed much of an interest in, promising they'd be his friends.

Colin urged him to accept the gift, and Foster really wanted to, only he knew Colin had just stolen the things so he was torn between desire and self-righteousness.

'After,' he hissed, settling back as the Astoria's lights dimmed.

He just had time to catch Colin's look of bemusement turning to scorn, then spent the next couple of hours wondering how badly God would punish him if he accepted the cards by convincing himself that he didn't actually *really* know Colin was a thief. Being convinced that God was privy to his every thought ensured misery quite often, and Foster sometimes envied boys like Colin, even though they were bound to get it in the end. At least they did what they wanted for the time being. And had comics. And free Sundays. Colin was big for his age, too, so the fact that he was stupid didn't matter – he was still regarded as the leader of the gang. Foster was their strategist, but the job of moral conscience and superior being could be boring.

The day Foster Eakins accepted five stolen slabs of stale, inedible chewing gum and five photos of Jack Hawkins, Dirk Bogarde and Stewart Granger was the day he decided to throw prudence to the winds. Unfortunately it was also the day Constable Bob Ryman decided to buy himself a flute. (After a few seconds' chat with the proprietor of Bandy's Music Shop he realised that all he wanted was a penny whistle – just something with a little more scope than my police whistle, he joked stiffly. An urge to make music seemed to him to conflict with his size, his work and his rugger, so he was embarrassed and edgy.)

The boys examined sheet music taped to the yellow peg-board. Some skiffle still, and a song called 'Hook, line and sinker', which sounded mysterious and American though they lived in a fishing port and went fishing themselves often enough. If it had just been 'Hook and line' they'd have got it, but what was a sinker? A misprint, Dewi thought, should have been stinker. Petey wondered if it was a man who couldn't swim. Dead, bullet heavy. That made Foster remember a grisly scene from *On the Waterfront*, where Terry found his brother hanging on a wall, and it wasn't clear if the big hook went through his neck or just his coat.

Foster noticed who else was in the shop, and even noticed PC Ryman, because he was hard to miss, about six-four and broad with it, but his mind was on other matters: the useless chewing gum cards in his pocket, the possible meanings of hook, line and sinker, bodies hanging up in dark dockland alleys... He slipped the 78 record under his windcheater and started to leave before his three friends were prepared. He was nearly at the door when Colin shoved past, closely followed by Dewi. Bob Ryman grabbed Foster's arm.

'What's the hurry, lads?' he asked.

Foster trembled. Petey came to stand beside him. Colin and Dewi were nowhere to be seen. Foster couldn't meet PC Ryman's penetrating eyes. He reached inside his windcheater and brought out his prize.

'I'm sorry, Mr Ryman,' he said. 'It's the first time, honest.' He realised that poor Petey was going to suffer with him, and that wouldn't be fair. 'It was only me,' he pleaded. 'Petey never saw, nor the others. Let Petey go, all right?' Foster wasn't trying to be a hero. The words came naturally, with years of chapel behind them.

After a good long stare at the smaller boy Bob Ryman told him to hop it and thank his lucky stars and watch out in future. Then he gave Foster all his attention.

'I'm surprised at you, boy. What's your dad going to say? And your mam? I'll tell you what they're going to say. They're going to be astonished. Heartbroken. You're a disappointment.'

'Will I have to go to jail?'

'Mr Bandy has to decide if he wants to press charges. He's within his rights to. This is a serious offence, Foster. You'd better run along home now and tell your parents exactly what's happened. I'll have a word with Mr Bandy, and you can say I'll call at the house this evening. I will call, and there may be charges, so don't think you can hide until it blows over. You make sure you tell them.'

'Yes,' Foster muttered miserably. He glanced at the proprietor. 'I'm sorry, Mr Bandy.'

'Sorry, is it? Stealing my records! What next? It'll be the crown jewels before you know it. You need a good thrashing, that's what you need. I hope your father takes his belt to you. *And* you're banned from my shop from now on. And your friends – tell 'em from me. Go on, bugger off, thief! If I see you in here again I'll beat the living daylights out of you.'

Mr Bandy was no taller than Foster, and in any other situation a threat like that would have been outrageous, because anyone threatening Foster would have had to deal with John Eakins. But Foster had catapulted himself outside his father's protection. He had done wrong, and been caught, and suddenly was acutely aware of how secure his life had been until now. What would they do? His parents would probably disown him. When he met his friends by the bridge he tried to put a brave face on, but felt as if he'd been hit by a lorry and wanted to get home and cry.

'You shoulda settled for these,' Colin grinned, bringing out a whole box of gramophone needles with a flourish.

Foster could hardly believe it. Colin must have gone right up to the counter without anyone seeing. Was he invisible? His talent was awesome. And he didn't even have a gramophone. He threw the needles off the bridge. He just stole for the fun of it. Foster had taken the trouble to find a record he really wanted, 'Don't', by Elvis. Of course it was plain to him now that he should have heeded the title.

'I never expected *you* to pinch from the shops,' Petey said, and Foster felt there was no end to the weight of sin: now he'd lost his position as moral conscience, was no better than Colin after all.

'The funny thing is,' he lied, 'I was only playing. I was going to go back and pay for it. Look, I got the dosh in my pocket.'

Petey wanted to believe him, and Dewi didn't care. Colin smirked.

Foster headed for his house in torment, wondering whether to be blasé or crawl through the door and grovel on the cold kitchen lino. I'll kill myself, he decided, then they'll be sorry!

THREE

Rachel Eakins was trapped in the world view of her neighbour, Beverley Walker, who had given her a couple of lobsters in a tin bucket. The lid had been tied on because the lobsters wanted to escape. Beverley said they tasted scrumptious and would be a real treat even if John wouldn't normally eat fish. Peter, her husband, swore by them, and little Petey said lobster was the only tea he ever ate that tasted nearly as good as a bag of sweets.

Rachel smiled repeatedly and said thanks several times, but couldn't get away. She hated talking across the fence, loathed the way neighbours would simply come into the kitchen without knocking, couldn't adapt to the community no matter how many years she lived in it. Rachel wasn't a snob but she did value privacy. Bev Walker could go on nattering for half an hour quite easily. What she didn't take into account was that she was standing on her concrete path, just outside her back door, whereas Rachel had to stand on the vegetable patch. In slippers. Holding a bucket of lobsters in one hand, her billowing skirt in the other. She was glad when Foster ran up the path behind her and disappeared around the corner and into the house.

'I'd better see what he wants for lunch,' she sighed, as if it was a nuisance to be dragged away, but a mother's lot.

'He's back before our Petey,' Bev observed. 'I expect he'll be coming in next. Do this, Mam. Do that, Mam – always rushing. Never a moment to call your own.'

'That's very true,' Rachel sympathised, stepping back. 'Thanks again for these, though I'm still not sure I...'

'No, they're easy. Keep the water boiling away. Put it on now and they'll be ready for tea.'

'Right. I'd better get started, then. Ta, Bev. Ta ta.'

Rachel smiled again, hoping she appeared confident. None of the women except her seemed to have qualms about cooking anything, and she wouldn't seek advice because they'd have more ammo to criticise her. She already knew they distrusted her for working with her brains and not being as common as them. If they found out her potatoes were often underdone and her meat tended to come out a bit blackened they'd think that proved something. If only they knew the sad state her cakes were in, coming out of the oven and immediately sinking in the middle like volcanoes!

Rachel didn't have a big enough saucepan, so she put water in the tub normally used for boiling shirts. When she untied the lid of the bucket the two lobsters seemed to gasp and take an interest. A few attempts to get hold of one failed. She just couldn't. The solution was to pick up the bucket and empty the things into the tub. They appeared to like that too, and Rachel assumed they'd settle down in the water and drop off to sleep as it got warmer, dying peacefully soon after. She went outside and found the lid of the tub so she wouldn't have to watch them cooking.

Foster had thought seriously about packing a bag and leaving home for a few days, giving time for his parents' anger to change to concern, but he'd abandoned that idea because the nights were cold and they might not allow him to come back again when it suited him. He expected his father to be more severe than his mother. Most of the time he took their love for granted, but they didn't go out of their way to make him feel wanted, and it was disheartening to realise that he didn't know for sure how deep love went, or how much wrong-doing it would cover. He considered the earlier plan and decided to give it a try.

Foster had no direct experience of killing himself. As little pain as possible, ideally. He tried holding his breath. Didn't work. Knocking himself out – hurt his forehead on the wall. Then he thought of the sewing machine, which was at the bottom of the stairs, between the front door and the living room door. Along with pins, needles, bobbins, scissors and cotton reels, a screwdriver was kept in the left-hand drawer. Foster reckoned he should be able to end it all with a screwdriver. In the pictures the baddies nearly always clutched their tummies to show they'd been killed. Goodies had to be wounded in the shoulder, where even women could sometimes endure a nasty arrowhead. You didn't die from that. But a sword or a bullet in the tummy would make you clutch it with both hands, stagger around and fall down dead.

As silently as possible he pulled out the drawer and rummaged for the weapon. It wasn't a big screwdriver, like those his dad kept in the shed, but solid enough. Foster pulled up his shirt and examined his tummy. The belly button looked like the easiest point of entry, a ready-made bullet hole. With the delicacy of a surgeon or a child slipping a worm on a hook for the first time he eased the head into the cavity and winced when it tickled. By bending forward he found he could let go the handle and resemble someone with a screwdriver embedded in his guts. That was pleasing and he wished he could show his pals. His mother was singing in the kitchen. She often sang, but her voice sounded strained, too high and slightly off-key. Foster took a deep breath, held it, and pushed the screwdriver slowly in.

Disappointingly, his stomach moved with it. He had to at least break the skin. Probably once you got under the surface you could shove it in more easily, and then suddenly you'd touch whatever it was that made you die. He wondered if it would hurt very much. It could hurt a bit – he wanted to experience pain, within reason.

Foster extracted the screwdriver from his navel and used the head to scratch away at the smooth skin of his tummy. He saw it redden slightly, but before long accepted defeat. Drowning in the bath was bound to be easier.

Before he'd reached the bathroom, however, his mother screamed. She was not in the habit of screaming, so the sound terrified him. She screamed again, his name this time. Foster had visions of implausible kitchen catastrophes – she'd hacked off her hand with a breadknife, burnt her face hideously on the gas ring, would be writhing on the floor in bloody frenzy...

The commonsense reaction, to pretend he hadn't heard and hide in his room till Dad came home, lasted less than a second. Foster had to go to his mother's assistance, regardless of any ability to help.

She was standing in a dismayed posture, hands up to her face, staring grimly at the cooker. Tears streamed from her eyes. Foster looked at her to satisfy himself that no limbs were spouting blood. Then he thought he could deal with anything.

'What's wrong, Mam?' he asked.

'Hark at them,' she stammered feebly. 'They're crying with pain!'

Quickly he leapt to her side, seeing the tub on the gas, horrible antennae and eyes peeping out between rim and lid. There was a noise, high-pitched like a whistling kettle.

'What is it?' he grimaced.

'Mrs Walker said they'd boil easy. Lobsters, love. They want to get out of the boiling water.'

The lid rattled. They'd push it off soon. Rachel was at a loss, because it was obviously far too late to stop and put the poor things back in the sea. Despite hard shells they had flesh, and the flesh had been boiling for some time. It sickened her to imagine it, and sickened her more to know she was responsible. Foster was just as sensitive, though he hadn't taken a good look. How could anyone torture any living creature? And then enjoy eating it? Rachel wanted to throw up already. The humane thing might have been to empty the tub out back and crush the lobsters quickly with a shovel. But Rachel couldn't bring herself to do that, because the lobsters would still be moving, and they were so ugly anyway. She sent her son racing out to the rockery to bring a few heavy stones. She helped him place the stones on the lid. Then she went to the top of the garden, Foster with her, and waited for the end, well away from the lobsters' rattles and hisses.

In some ways it wasn't the ideal time for Foster to say he'd been caught stealing. Rachel stared in disbelief. She didn't yell, didn't hit him, didn't do anything for a while. Then she simply stepped away sideways, leaving him isolated. From a safe distance she scowled. 'Your father'll deal with you,' she assured him coldly.

Foster wished he'd persevered with the screwdriver. What use was a mother who wouldn't even put in a word in your defence?

One perplexed lobster appeared in the doorway and expired there, glowing accusingly until the sun went off the back of the house.

FOUR

John Eakins tuned in the wireless and settled back in his favourite armchair to listen to the shipping forecast. Tea would be on the table by the time it finished. These few minutes were his alone.

Foster drifted in and hovered awkwardly as if he wanted to say something. John didn't mind that. He liked to hear what conditions were like in areas where friends were filling their holds with herring, but he also enjoyed the novelty of father-son intimacy. In some ways he hadn't yet familiarised himself with the role of father; in some ways he was still too young, and too independent. Evidently Foster needed him to act the part though, so he did, feeling more like his own father, or some more distant composite of a stern authority figure. He turned the volume down.

'What is it, Foss?' he smiled receptively.

Foster grinned, fleetingly imagining he could do the whole thing as a bit of a joke; then he came over nauseous again. What he wanted was to be on the far side of this: after punishment, usually, came clumsy affectionate tenderness, a sort of renewal of cautious warmth.

His father was remembering that when he'd come in, just a few minutes ago, both Foster and Rachel were tense. Then he'd trodden on a bubble on the lino, which meant something hot had spilled from the cooker again. No smell of burnt meat, though, so whatever had gone wrong it wasn't his tea. Perhaps Foster had been engaged in some daft experiment, sanctioned by Rachel.

'It's all right, Foss,' he coaxed, rather proud of his power to subdue his family without force. 'What's happened?'

'After the flicks we went in Bandy's,' Foster said in a rush, 'and there was this Elvis song I wanted. I'm ever so sorry, Dad, I won't do it again.'

John Eakins sensed the shortcomings of complacency. As a mark of warning he switched the wireless off. Foster saw the yellow light fade fast – he retained a residual superstition that something small but living animated the wireless, and every time it was turned off felt disquieted, as if bereaved. His father suddenly seemed a lot more forbidding. If only they could talk about the lobsters, he thought, but instead he submitted himself to a full and contrite confession, and although his father glowered impressively, took it personally as an assault on his local reputation and made scathing remarks about his son's irresponsibility, he didn't hit Foster. For Foster that was an important realisation: his dad had the power, but was never going to use it, at least not on him. Other boys' fathers hit them as a matter of course, even for minor transgressions; Foster's dad was tougher than any of them, he let his son see how far he'd fallen short of a son's function.

Foster gulped. This was worse than crying. It was as if God Himself had found him wanting.

Tea was an ordeal. Actually the gammon and vegetables had been done to perfection, and no reference to the wrapped and binned lobsters was made. But no one spoke. Often on Saturdays they'd go to the pictures in the evening. Foster guessed that no such excursion was conceivable for the foreseeable future.

Bob Ryman turned up, and it was obviously a formal visit because he knocked at the front door. Because he had such a high regard for John Eakins he felt as awkward as everyone else. His sergeant, Archie Flynn, had trained him in giving stiff warnings to the parents of delinquent children, and the prepared words were some help; even so, he could see he was humiliating a man he admired, and what he wanted to say was all kids do something out of character once in a while – no big deal – they wouldn't be kids if they didn't get up to mischief. It was true. He couldn't relax and admit it, though. The best he could say was he'd persuaded Mr Bandy not to press charges, and that was somehow as galling as it was welcome. As if the moral health of the Eakins's trembled at the whim of a shopkeeper with bad breath!

Later Rachel told her son he'd got off lightly. He knew he had, and said he'd thank God in chapel tomorrow. It was true he felt lighter than before, only the sensation was unpleasant, caused, it seemed, by the jettisoning of small but necessary weights which had once connected him to security.

John Eakins went over the bridge to town, met friends, talked, drank, didn't make any reference to the incident. His mind was waterlogged with it anyway. He brooded heavily: Foster could have bought the record if it meant so much. Why steal? What made men so anxious to win the pools or find a fortune, when they lived good lives and needed nothing more? His son was all right, he knew that, and this shock would ensure he never stepped out of line again, but it would get around, men would talk behind John's back as if he was the one who'd dropped from grace. Fatherhood, family life... at sea you suffered none of that, you took your livelihood from it but risked death every time. It was a fair, clean fight, and whatever you got you had a right to. There weren't the same tensions on land. Nobody knew why they did anything, and too many elements could interfere. What a mess, he thought, downing another pint and hoping Mr Bandy wouldn't look his way.

FIVE

Rachel Eakins lay on her side staring at a long strip of pale night sky between her winter-weight curtains. The moon was above the house, a gleam on the white window sill. She wondered if lobsters knew when they were in the sea and when they were in a bucket of tap water, wondered if fish brought up in a trawl net realised what was happening, experienced the alarming draining away of their element, an undreamt of weight as they poured into the swelling hold. The bedroom was too stuffy.

John didn't stir when she got up to open the top window and feel cold air trickle on her face. Normally a light sleeper, he would sink to the deep after making love, and stay there till morning. Soon it would be time to take down the heavy drapes and replace them with summer curtains, translucent, freer. Lovemaking was still more than a duty, but Rachel accepted that it was less than a rainbow. She didn't blame anyone, didn't think of it as an issue that could be talked about. They made love in the dark, always, and somehow it had become too respectable, too low-key. The explosive passions of their courtship had been bound to taper off in time, with increased familiarity – everyone understood that. Only the darkness did not actually bring increased familiarity. Almost the reverse.

Occasionally she wanted to suggest leaving the light on; occasionally she thought it would be exciting if John came to her in his jeans and allowed her to unbuckle his belt and seduce him. But sex didn't really fit into their lives. Even at night it was almost furtive, not to be lingered over. Besides, it was hard to get into the mood after a day's work, an evening's cooking and ironing, knowing she'd be up early again getting breakfast, getting the boy to school and herself to the office. The weeks had a steady, respectable rhythm. Sex broke into it, upset the regular balance of life.

Her husband rolled. 'Everything all right?' He sounded concerned but sleepy, not knowing how much time had passed. He feared he'd made her sore – sometimes she suffered with cystitis, and he blamed himself. Women's problems were mysterious and usually depressing. Sex couldn't be an uncomplicated joy.

'Fine,' she reassured him. 'Go back to sleep.' But he already had. Rachel smiled. A good man, basically, willing to want to understand, never deliberately mean. But no more rainbows.

Rachel left the bedroom. In the kitchen the moonlight was bright enough for her to see everything. She gazed out at the garden, could even see a few lights from the docks. I'm not unhappy, she told herself. It was an odd mood she was in, yearning for something too vague to identify but anyway out of reach. She liked living where they lived, enjoyed her work, had no complaints about life, yet she was dissatisfied.

Mild spring days were coming early to the Haven. When John was away she and Foster listened to the shipping forecast together, but didn't worry as they'd worried through the winter months.

One Sunday Rachel wore a light summer dress, white with red dots and a red plastic belt, high heeled sandals. She carried her Bible in lacy-gloved hands. Men, and some women, glanced her way in chapel and she knew they disapproved, though the full skirt and tight bodice made her feel as clean as God could possibly wish. Some of the men were severe elders in dark threadbare suits that looked as though they'd been handed on for generations. Farmers. Silent, pious old men accompanied by grown up sons who were always bigger than these deadly fathers. She felt as vulnerable as a flower, but it was her chapel too, and she even took a Bible class with some of the children.

When she returned home Foster wanted to change and go out to play right away. She was about to change as well, but John asked her not to. He stopped to admire her.

'Haven't seen you in that in a while,' he murmured gruffly, and Rachel realised from his tone and the shy look in his eye that he was aroused.

'I wanted to feel summery,' she explained softly.

'How about if we lock the door?' he said, taking her waist in his strong hands.

'I'd better get out of this, then,' she said, almost hoping he would complain and take her a little more forcefully, passionately anyway, just as they were.

He wanted to, but thought she'd be appalled. Chapel dress, Bible there by the sink. And it wasn't simply the dress, it was Rachel wearing the dress that refreshed him. He didn't know how to say it without sounding like a pervert. By the time they'd gone upstairs, closed the curtains and undressed, separately, a large part of the impulse had withered.

John Eakins remembered post-war London and the kinds of girls they had there then, impatient and ready, same as you were, a doorway after the dance as good as anywhere else. Intensity then, and fun, but no commitments either side. More predatory, was it? More natural? In some ways he wished he was young again, uncertain and alert, less respectable, more himself. Freer, anyway.

'On a Sunday afternoon!' Rachel risked commenting.

'Aye, that's a first – sorry about that.'

'No, I don't mind.'

It was strange, they thought to themselves, to be embarrassed about making love in the afternoon. On the other hand, it turned out much the same as making love late at night. Rachel's rather blurry dissatisfaction returned. John found himself brooding about lost possibilities, the way his life had improved yet dulled.

SIX

Mother and son emerged from the last show, feelings still carrying the experience and making them reluctant to break the spell. Both had seen big Eli Wakefield, the simple Kentuckian, as an idealised version of John Eakins. True, Burt Lancaster was bigger, more famous and considerably more expressive, but as a backwoodsman radiating integrity and ultimately unbeatable strength he was, essentially, the same sort of man as John. And Rachel could see how in some ways she resembled the woman who wanted to tame big Eli, except Rachel thought she gave John more room to be himself. Foster had identified with little Eli, the boy who loved his dad and the free life of the woods, who went through hell when he had to go bury the hunting horn and attend school and try to become civilised. He never actually went hunting with his dad, and he wasn't allowed a faithful dog either; nonetheless the film seemed to him a miraculous reproduction of his life, or the way he wanted much of it to be.

While they'd been inside rain had fallen, so now the salt air was rich with the smells of greenery and soil from the headlands.

'We'll give him a few minutes,' Rachel said.

Usually John was there to meet them. He had no patience to sit for hours watching soppy films and, after seeing Rachel and Foster as far as the ticket office, would spend the evening with his friends. He didn't like films any more than the theatre, or reading, or listening to music, and nothing could be done to change him.

Foster thought of the scene where little Eli was being bullied. His throat throbbed as he remembered how big Eli, who'd been sorting tobacco leaves or something, jumped down and came to the rescue. Then the villain started using a bullwhip, which was unfair, and big Eli was getting beaten until the wheel trapped the end of the bullwhip and big Eli got a fair fight and of course trounced the villain easily.

'We'd better start walking,' Rachel said, noticing that everyone else had gone and the cinema's lights were going out. If John had arrived they'd have gone up to the chip shop and then sauntered home eating faggots and chips while Foster excitedly described the best parts of the film. But the chip shop was slightly out of their way, and John would probably bring some home with him a little later.

'That was a nice picture,' Rachel said as they came out below the square and could see the docks and the dark Haven and the lights of Hakin, where home was.

Foster held an imaginary Gabriel horn to his lips and blew a sort of hunting call. His mother smiled indulgently, but although Foster was glad to be with her, although he felt snug and close to her, he also thought she didn't really understand – she was too like that woman who'd tamed big Eli and all but shut out the woods and the roaming spirit. If only his dad could have watched the film, and Foster could have whispered that it was his favourite film ever – something like that – then his dad might have understood the bond between them. It couldn't be spoken, and too often didn't really seem to exist, however ardently Foster pretended. At bottom he wasn't sure his father loved or even noticed him much of the time. John Eakins lived in John Eakins's world, and no little boys figured in it. And yet, Foster felt, it could be different, if his dad would only take time out to take him fishing, hunting, or just walking up the garden.

'He looked horrible when he had his hair cut,' Foster said suddenly, remembering the distasteful scene where big Eli was humiliated into a smartly dressed buffoon, hoping his mam would agree.

'I thought he looked nicer with tidy hair.'

Foster gave up on her. Women, he thought grimly, just don't get it.

John Eakins didn't catch them up. Nor did he arrive with a parcel of faggots and chips soon after they reached home. After half an hour Foster went to bed, and after another half hour Rachel did too. She wasn't exactly concerned, because John was not the sort of man to whom anything untoward could happen and if, as occasionally happened, his friends kept him talking that was his affair – he wouldn't make a habit of it, and she was not the sort of wife to tie him to her apron strings. Even so, she was annoyed.

John hadn't planned on being late. He'd spent most of the evening with a couple of pals in one pub, and just dropped into another for a few minutes on his way down to the cinema. Unfortunately Fred Knight was there, having one of his turns. Fred was a gentle giant of a man, a pretty good boxer back before the war, known for resilience in the ring and meekness outside it. The side of a house had fallen on him in London in the blitz. As a consequence he wore a steel plate in his skull and would sometimes, for little reason, get dangerous.

'Thank God you've turned up,' a grateful barman said to John. And he didn't have to say any more because John could see Fred threatening two scared men in suits, while a third lay unconscious and bloody under the dart board. A couple of tables had been overturned and the floor was littered with glasses and bottles.

'Tried to get Bob?'

'Aye – can't find him.'

'Up Lord Nelson's – was a minute ago – just left him.'

'All right, but Fred's boiling over. . .'

'Aye, I got you,' John agreed reluctantly. It would have been better to wait for Bob Ryman, but in five minutes there could be two more men with broken limbs and an unpredictable tip of pub debris. What he had to do was stop Fred without hurting that great fragile head of his.

Stepping gingerly across the broken bottles on the floor, John came around wide, allowing Fred plenty of time to see him. Then he approached slowly, as if it was an ordinary quiet evening, and asked the two nervous strangers what they were doing in Milford. One of them – the one who wasn't in the process of being seriously throttled – tried to reply casually. He said something about developing the Haven, but sounded as if he was trying to talk rationally while attached to a roller coaster by his braces, and John nodded quickly and then caught Fred's eye and grinned in feigned surprise.

'How's it going, Fred?' he asked, though Fred's unfocussed look had already told him: Fred just didn't know who he was, and although Fred was terrifying at times like these John understood it was even worse for Fred himself, staring at an inexplicably alien world full of probable hostility. 'It's me, John Eakins – we're pals,' he said soothingly.

Fred couldn't absorb the information, so instead took a swipe at John's head. In better days he'd have come at it more subtly. Nimbly, John ducked and danced around. The two strangers – Londoners, the sorts Bob was always fretting about – backed off as far as they could, leaving their companion to bleed for the time being. Fred Knight frowned, crouched into position, fists under his chin, and began looking for openings. Even crouched he was as tall as John Eakins, who glanced at the barman to be sure he had the bat. Fred connected with a couple of body blows, but John managed to throw decent if ineffectual counter punches. When Fred went for a knockout John was ready – it caught his ear but he was already wheeling and continued, grabbed the cricket bat the barman kept handy, took it in both hands as he spun to Fred's side and swept down to hack poor Fred behind the knees. The plan was that Fred should then drop promptly and neatly, without injury to his head, but he left the ground and tackled John as he came back heavily to earth. John Eakins overbalanced but still wanted to save Fred's fall and in the confusion he threw out his right hand to take their combined body weights. That instinctive move was fortunate, since John was left-handed, but there wasn't a lot of immediate comfort.

A pint glass, split off top to bottom, stood waiting on the floor, and only an inch from it stood the base, and several jagged inches, of a beer bottle. John's open hand plunged for support.

'Oh, bugger it, Fred,' he exclaimed, taking in the damage, if not the pain, instantly, and accepting the probable loss of a hand with neither panic nor regret. 'Look what I've gone and done now!'

Fred looked, and saw, and snapped out of his trance at once.

'Bloody fool, John,' he growled in confused concern. The speed at which the blood poured out was chastening. 'You need a turnykit, mun.'

The barman and Fred did what they could to cut off the blood supply to John's right hand, the barman all the while thanking John profusely for stepping in at such short notice, and Fred apparently agreeing.

Rachel Eakins threw on a dressing gown when she heard Bob Ryman calling upstairs – he'd let himself in the back way, which was usual. John had suffered a bit of an accident, he explained, cut his hand. He'd been rushed to the hospital out by Haverfordwest, and if she wanted to be with him Bob would drive her in his new car. They were trying to save the hand, and hoping to save all the fingers, but it was a bad one.

Rachel's first anxiety was what to do with Foster, who'd remained asleep.

'Leave him,' Bob said. 'He's not a baby.' Rachel thought the young constable knew best – she didn't claim to know a great deal about boys and their independence, and everyone else on the estate seemed to know it all. So she left Foster alone in the house, hoping he'd still be asleep when she got back. She couldn't believe John had been brawling again. She was disgusted. When Burt Lancaster fought Walter Matthau it was justified, unavoidable and heroic, but that was in a film. Grown men should know better. What sort of example was it for Foster, to have a father who got into fights in public houses? Bob Ryman found himself attempting to explain to Mrs Eakins how highly regarded her husband was, precisely because of his willingness to wade in and help when the situation warranted it. John had saved him the job, he said – he was on the side of law and order, so it couldn't be called brawling. Rachel understood, but understanding wasn't the same as condoning.

'Sorry I missed you after the flicks,' John said weakly, failing to prop himself up. He'd lost pints of blood.

Rachel wanted to slap him, hug him and cry at the same time. 'Daft old bugger,' she whispered, kissing his cheek.

A couple of days later Fred Knight called at the house, carrying a bouquet of roses for Rachel.

'How's the old man?' he asked humbly. 'If there's aught I can do, like, just ask, and it'll be done.'

'Thank you, no,' Rachel replied rather stiffly. 'We don't know yet if the hand will ever be of any use to him.'

'Aw, Duw! My fault, all of it! He's one of the best, your husband, missus, and you can tell him I said so.'

'Thank you, Mr Knight.'

She wouldn't invite him in. He was not a friend of the family, just a boozer whose body gave off an unpleasant odour. He had tears in his eyes, and Rachel thought it right he should suffer. These men! She hated their camaraderie. The barman had praised John to the skies, insisting he'd saved the pub and could have free drinks whenever he wanted. Bob Ryman had thanked John for doing his job for him. The men John had saved from a beating had left a note of thanks with the barman. Fred Knight blamed himself. But the only man who was going to lose out was John Eakins. Even if his hand healed fully he'd lose a month or two's wages, and none of his friends was going to make that up.

'You go in like Ivanhoe or something,' she complained to him several times, 'and everyone cheers. And now look at you!'

'It's not as if I had a choice,' he pointed out sheepishly.

'Next time, and there'd better not *be* a next time, think about your family first.'

'Aye, aye, cap'n,' John said. When she was cross he felt especially proud and protective of her. Rachel wasn't a limp tepid woman. She still had that limber quickness he'd been drawn to from the first. 'You know, I can't shift position very easy, but – is Foss out playing? – you could come and sort of... I know we haven't tried... What I'm saying is, it's supposed to be possible with you sort of... on top, like.'

Propositioning his wife exhausted him and he closed his eyes in defeat, expecting her to storm out. She did leave the room for a while. But when she returned she had a bowl of soapy water and a cloth to bathe him, and she'd changed into her dressing gown and had nothing underneath, and she chuckled nervously and asked him to keep his eyes shut while she got on board. It wasn't even the afternoon. Mid-morning. Praise to his injury!

Foster played in the woods like little Eli Wakefield. He walked taller than ever amongst his friends, because his father had tackled

Fred Knight and all the men still talked about him as a hero. The botched record theft was forgotten, at least by the other boys, and Foster was again the moral arbiter, son of big John Eakins. The woods rang with their playing and grew thick with leaves and blossoms, and it was paradise that spring.

SEVEN

Wedged in the rocks around from Hakin Point the body could have remained undetected for days. Could have fallen off a ship and been heaved in on a wave; just as easily it could have tripped over the cliff and tumbled into position on the drag of a receding tide.

The gales that had been battering the Haven most of the last week had ceased sometime during the night and now the sky looked as if someone had frozen it before it had time to adjust for this new serenity. Thin trails of white vapour stretched in long motionless smears overhead, copying the general inland drift of the fjord's broad waters – more than twenty miles of navigable water, according to the advertising put out by the Chamber of Trade, a paradise for yachtsmen. It should have been, too. It was a beautiful inlet, low hills either side, unspoilt, barely accessible beaches. Apart from trawlers, the only competition yachtsmen might notice would have come from a flying boat – a fleet of old wartime Sunderlands was tethered a few miles in from Milford, and occasionally one would be allowed to skid off for exercise.

Yachtsmen hadn't made the Haven their Mecca yet, though. A few naturalists came on holiday, took boats out to the islands to study gannets or seals, and sometimes they stopped in the town, but no one was pouring money into the area. This disappointed hotel-iers and shopkeepers but didn't bother the trawlermen, who unloaded about a thousand tons of fish every week.

Trawlermen looked westward, to the open sea that began visibly at the mouth of the Haven. They weren't concerned with what lay behind them, which was the rest of Wales and all England, and most of them would have been amazed to learn that the future was not going to come in at them from the sea, face to face; it was going to sneak up behind, from that disregarded backlot, England. The dead man was an emissary from London.

Usually people didn't die in Milford Haven. A schoolteacher had recently gassed himself, but he'd been cracking up for months anyway, and was from Cambridge. Nobody got murdered. People only died of extreme old age, and so were barely noticed. If there was a bad winter it was possible for a few trawlermen to die heroically in the North Sea. Nobody ever just keeled over on the rocks. The body awaiting discovery between the Point and Hubberston Fort was something without precedent: a mystery.

The first boy who saw it imagined he was looking at a water-logged bundle of old clothes. He didn't think it especially remarkable that a bundle of old clothes should have washed up on the rocks. Only last week, before the onslaught of the gales, playing in the woods near the estate where they all lived, one of his pals had found a stocking and a brassiere. These items were snagged on a bush and seemed to be in perfectly good condition. And Dewi found a pipe once, half filled with tobacco. Colin himself had found a nearly new pair of daps on the path. Petey once picked up a ten bob note, and swore he'd found not stolen it, under the seat at the Astoria. Another time, climbing over the rocks, they came across a little Scotty dog, wagging its stumpy tail, and there was no way that dog could have been where it was, and then they all risked their lives saving it and carrying it all the way to the RSPCA man's house, and didn't even get in the paper, didn't even get a sniff of a reward. Anything could turn up anytime, and no one ever thanked you.

So Colin took aim and threw a rock about the size of a cricket ball, and it was a good shot. It hit the bundle and stayed there.

'Bull's-eye!' he crowed, blinking with surprise.

Petey and Dewi started chucking stones as well, quick to adapt to any new test of prowess. The blue sky was motionless, but gulls were wavering on the unfelt breeze or sitting on the water and bobbing in and out of sight as rapidly as the little whitecaps. The water was never flat calm like a lake. It was sheltered, but it was part of the sea nonetheless, so it couldn't stop moving. The boys had grown up with it and with the same nature.

Foster Eakins was the one who yelled a warning.

None of them wanted to go much closer to the target; the rocks were sharper near the water, you could feel points through the soles of your daps, and if you slipped and fell on your hands you could get a nasty gash. At the base of the cliff the rocks were rounder, and coloured differently. The boys had discussed the possibility that rock might not be one thing, that there might be as many makes of rock as there were bikes or roller skates. Foster had promised to look it up in a book to settle the matter, but he hadn't and the subject had passed. There was air, water, rock and earth; somewhere between rock and earth was sand. There was fire, grass, insects, birds, cats, dogs, other animals and people. There was coal, too, and possibly iron, steel, diamonds, gold and Bakelite. Foster had planned to compile a list of the basic things of the world, then ask his teacher if there was a common denominator, something to prove that God had made it all as an interdependent, functioning, adaptable whole. But he hadn't got around to it yet. So many things to do! Anyway, he claimed the bundle of clothes was a dead body, and that meant they had to investigate.

A few yards away they stopped. Close enough, since whatever it was, it was probably revolting. Not that they could smell it. The air was rich with the tang of the sea. But the look of the thing was bewildering, like a dream whose details are almost exactly right, yet just off enough to bring on queasiness.

'That's not nobody's body,' Colin scoffed.

'I reckon it is,' Foster winced.

'You can't have skin that colour,' observed Petey. 'That mud down by that old sewer pipe's like that. I seen an eel that colour.'

Nobody much wanted the thing to be a human body, but it was wearing grey trousers, a filthy white shirt and a tangled grey rain-coat. The leg that wasn't trapped seemed to bend more than a proper leg should, and the one that was trapped had accommo-dated itself to the contours of a jagged crack in the rocks. The feet were bare and the boys could see they were indeed feet, not flip-pers.

'Our dad told us they pulled up a corpse in the nets once,' Foster managed to say. 'He said all its features was washed off and it looked like a monster from the deep.' He shuddered. 'It's being in water,' he explained, 'if you stay in too long.'

'Yeah,' Dewi said, recalling bathtimes, 'you can get prune-fin-gers.'

'Could be a creature from outer space,' Colin ventured. He resented the dead body. He was sullen. He'd thrown the first rock and he was wondering if he'd get the blame. It was the first time he'd murdered anybody, and he was anxious to protest his inno-cence, or just get away and forget it.

'Nothing we can do,' said Dewi, similarly wishing he hadn't seen the thing at all. 'Let's move on. Let's play around the fort.' He turned back and then, to show he wasn't a coward in a panic, bent to examine fissures for trapped treasures. You didn't very often come across coins in the rocks, but teething rings, tins of tomatoes or corned beef, wooden spoons, all kinds of magical objects would be thrown in by the tide, and even if you wouldn't give them a sec-ond glance in the house, out here they were finds.

'What do you want to do, Foss?' Colin asked, making it Foster's find, Foster's responsibility rather than his own.

'Tell somebody. Somebody better stay on guard. And not touch nothing. That's the main thing when you find a body.'

Normally they were inquisitive, and if it had been a dolphin or a seal they'd have prodded sticks into it, clambered nearer and laughed derisively, but something about its lost quality, the deadness of its human being, robbed them of the exhilarating fear that would goad them to outdo one another in brazen daring. They wanted to wait further back, right under the cliff.

No one else was likely to stumble around the Point, so guarding the find may not have been necessary. The very reason they'd started from the Point was to be in a place off-limits to all but the wildest adventurers. It was true, though, that a few relatively easy paths from the top of the cliff enabled fishermen to get out where the body lay and catch bass, and even tope sometimes. But the boys regarded those easy routes with contempt.

Petey and Colin stayed because Petey had a bottle of pop to sustain them and Colin was big enough to defend their territory in the unlikely event of the arrival of another gang of desperadoes.

'If he was rich we could have a reward,' Petey said, swigging his pop and wiping the top between swigs.

'I wonder what it feels like,' Colin said, 'dying, like.'

Petey swallowed a big mouthful and then passed Colin the bottle without wiping it. He clutched his stomach and staggered, groaning pitifully. Colin, belatedly, drew his finger and shot his friend in the guts, then blew the smoke from his nail and holstered it smoothly. They both cheered up a bit, having put the body in perspective, and started talking about the last Roy Rogers they'd seen. Nobody'd been shot in it, but galoots were lassoed and that looked more skilful.

'What would you do if he started to get up?' Petey immediately wished he hadn't asked.

'Did Foster tell you 'bout the time his mam tried to boil lobsters?' Colin asked nimbly, belching insouciantly. 'The lobsters that wouldn't die!'

Petey turned into a lobster, wiggly fingers at his temples. Colin started chucking stones at the empty pop bottle. There wasn't a lot you could do when you had to stand guard over a body you didn't want to think about. Picturesque views left both boys unimpressed. Rocks existed for climbing. If you couldn't climb them you might as well be sitting at home, going through your autograph album and wondering which of your favourite football heroes you'd resemble most nearly in ten or fifteen years.

'D'you reckon Foss found anybody yet?'

'Taking their time, aren't they?' Colin paused, stone in hand, bottle stubbornly unsmashed a few yards away. 'We should've just unhooked his leg and let the tide take him out to sea.'

'Yeah. It's a wasted afternoon now, isn't it?'

'Blame Foss. It's all his fault.'

EIGHT

John Eakins was rendered almost surly every time he encountered a new example of his uselessness. You start off with two good hands, he lamented, but you favour one and take the other for granted. You just never think an injury to a hand you hardly need is going to affect your left. Every job that came up seemed to call for a kind of steadying balance he was unable to supply. With a badly designed tool you could rail against its maker; John could only blame himself. He didn't work in his garden, couldn't mend anything in his shed. At one time he thought he could strip wallpaper in the living room, going at it like a swordsman, but after making a mess of one small area he abandoned it. Until recently he'd taken the view that you had two of everything so there was a spare available for emergencies. This was a sorry way of learning about the subtlety of the body.

He was standing in Sam Niblo's garden when he heard Foster calling his name. Sam kept chickens, and John had noticed a section of rusty net-fencing that needed repairing. He had the pliers. He just couldn't hold the pieces steady enough to tease and twist the wires into place. It was frustrating because the hand was mending: he could hold a tennis ball and apply mild pressure with two fingers and a thumb. With his left hand he could feed the chickens, and that was all he'd gone up there for. Even that wasn't necessary, since Mrs Niblo had always done it while Sam was at sea. It was a fill-in activity that failed to make John believe he was making the best of life. You can't disguise idleness, he told himself: you're doing nothing.

The chickens had clustered near the netting. They knew food was appearing on the dirt just there, but didn't seem aware of a human presence and John Eakins wondered how such idiot birds had ever survived in the wild. That caused him to reflect that a man with nothing better to do than fan grain at chickens which didn't even belong to him was in a miserable state.

He turned and brushed his left hand against his leg and gazed across the back gardens towards his own. Foster had disappeared inside the shed. When he came out he looked lost and hurried to the top of the garden to see if anyone was on the lane that led down towards the docks. John Eakins did what several of the men did: instead of following the path out to the front and crossing the open lawns he stepped over the first wire fence, crossed Bryn Gibson's garden, stepped over the next, crossed Peter Walker's, stepped over the next and strode up behind his son.

'What's the racket?' he asked softly, amused to see his boy jump. 'I's feeding Sam's birds,' he added, seeing Foster's disbelief.

'You wasn't in the house or the shed,' Foster still explained. 'I thought you'd gone down the market.'

Foster looked up at his father and right away had to fight back the urge to cry.

As he rushed his explanation, realising the rush was partly in order to assure his father he hadn't been caught stealing again, Foster started to feel physically lighter than before. Carrying the responsibility must have been a heavier burden than it had seemed. Passing it on made him feel noble, and again weak enough to cry.

John Eakins listened, then merely nodded and said 'Okay.' That was sufficient for Foster to be bathed in glory.

'Dad's by here,' he shouted unnecessarily as Dewi came running from the fronts and saw for himself. 'I've told him. It's all right now.'

'Colin threw a stone at him, Mr Eakins,' Dewi blurted out. He'd been holding that information in his head, the one detail he wasn't going to share with any adults because a gang was supposed to stick together in a crisis. 'But he never knew it was a man, like, else he wouldn't have.'

'How do you feel, both of you?' John inquired. They sounded over-excited and he had half a bottle of brandy indoors. But they were kids and he wasn't sure they were shocked enough to need it. Finding a body, though, that could turn anyone a bit green.

'If we got to lift him, like, carry him up the top...' Dewi paused, contemplating the unpleasantness of cold contact and not wanting to be that close to death just yet.

'Left Colin holding the fort, is it? All to himself?'

'Him and Petey.'

'I'll go down,' John decided. 'We'd better get a hold of Bob, too.'

Bob Ryman only lived across the green, but was more likely to be up in town – the boys would get to the station-house faster than he could, and he surmised they'd be happier doing that than returning to the rocks.

'What about the doctor, Dad?'

'Aye – Bob'll know who to bring along. If he's not available, if Flynn's on the desk, say you're my son, Foss. Archie Flynn can be a bit slow on the uptake.' What he meant was, sergeant Flynn thought children were mischief-makers. His rule of thumb was that every kid in the neighbourhood had gone bad because of Bill Haley and Jerry Lee Lewis. There'd been riots wherever rock 'n' roll films were exhibited. The kids all had switchblades under their jumpers and a firm intention to rob and maim on their minds. The only hard evidence to date of this distressing epidemic was that Flynn's nephew had been caught stealing a cauliflower from the greengrocer's and kicking it along Hamilton Terrace in broad daylight. *Don't Knock The Rock* had been to the Astoria without a single seat being torn from the floor. Archie Flynn distrusted the young and lived with a mother who distrusted him.

After the boys had hurried away on their mission John remembered his son's shame in Bandy's Music Shop. More than likely Bandy had talked about it, so Flynn might tell Foster to go back and bring him the body before he'd do anything. But they'd locate Bob. The boys were bright and Milford wasn't that big.

May sunshine, John Eakins grinned wryly as he mounted his bicycle and wobbled off one-handed, it fools you every time. He was thinking about the moods of the sea, but at least his despondency had lifted. Now he had something to take a look at, something to do – I'm as bad as the boys, he thought. Need a little adventure. Anything. And because of the mildness in the air and the unchanging brightness of the blue sky it didn't seem as if pedalling to the cliff to examine a corpse was morbid. He only hoped it wouldn't be anyone he knew. He changed gears with his thumb. Even that was painful. Good job the back brake was operated by his left hand. He hoped Bob would give the boys a ride in his car, make the day worthwhile for them. There were only three cars on the estate. Bob's was being paid for over several years. John Eakins and the older men were dubious about such arrangements. If you can't afford something, don't get it, that was the prevailing attitude. Bob Ryman was a decent man, but he had that reckless streak and was considering getting a television set and an enormous gramophone with a built-in wireless and cupboard space for storing records, all on the H.P. He'd regret it, John reckoned. If men didn't live within their means there'd be misery all over. And it wasn't as if anybody actually needed unbreakable records. Bob said this machine had four speeds, which was one more than John had on his bike. It would still play 78s, but could handle 45s too. 45s were only smaller 78s, though. Then it would run at 33 revs a minute, for Long Playing Records, which had about five songs each side. Where was it going to end? Bob wasn't clear what 16rpm had to offer, but he looked happy about it. It's ready for the future, he said hopefully. Not a backward-looking man in every department, not when it came to personal comfort anyway. John Eakins shifted gear again and scowled. It wasn't civilised to have new gimmicks coming along all the time. You needed things that would last, things you could get familiar with.

Cycling past the cluster of prefabs he nodded to a man who was cleaning his windows and it occurred to him that although he often assumed he knew everybody in Hakin and Milford this was not the case. He didn't know that man. The people in the prefabs were presumably quite poor – the council houses on the St. Lawrence were grand by comparison, but you didn't have to be wealthy to live in them. First time he'd taken Foster past the prefabs Foster had asked if they could move. John Eakins smiled at his son's innocence – the prefabs had been intended as temporary accommodation and should have been done away with years ago. Foster had thought they looked cosy. Kids, John Eakins thought, don't know when they're well off. He liked the little picture-book two-foot high picket fences, and didn't notice how near the prefabs they were, how small the gardens were, how restricted life would be if a whole family was stuck in something that size. Foster's way of looking at the world was bizarre, John thought, and that was as much effort to empathise as he'd ever given his son.

It surprised him how often his unchecked thoughts ran in the same groove – money, basically. The subject didn't consciously interest him. An honest day's work, a decent day's pay, a clean, comfortable council house – he had it all, or enough to settle for. But the prefabs – that was money, or lack of money. Bob's desire to buy the latest gramophone – money.

Being off work was a bugger, though. Showed up large dull areas which hadn't worried him before. Made him wonder if there was more to life than taking each day as a success if nothing dramatic happened.

He dismounted and walked his bike across the rough waste ground towards the edge of the cliff, leaving it propped against a bush. It was safe enough. Nobody was going to steal a bicycle. Everything was safe in Hakin. The place was too small and cut-off from the world to have hiding places, and that was one of the things he liked about it. Even if it wasn't strictly true, he behaved as if it was, as did everyone on the estate – you never bothered to lock anything, you trusted your neighbours and you weren't let down. Another thing he liked, he thought, breathing deeply and gazing towards St. Ann's Head, was the big sky embracing endless sea and just waiting for you to steam out and forget your cares.

NINE

'Where was you when they give out brains, Colin?' he asked as he joined the two boys on the rocks. He didn't say it nastily, more like a well-worn refrain.

'Off sick, Mr Eakins,' Colin replied cheerfully, not yet knowing what he'd done wrong this time, but so engrossed in aiming at bottles he'd forgotten to feel guilty about the body he was guarding.

'If you throw stones at bottles you'll end up with smashed glass,' John pointed out. Colin and Petey could have told him that: they'd finally made Petey's pop bottle explode after about a hundred goes, and were flushed with pride. 'I ought to give you a good clip round the ear,' John continued. 'Our Foster got glass in his foot last year. This hand – that's glass again.'

'The tide'll wash this lot away, Mr Eakins. You'll be all right here.'

'Just in case it don't I want you two to pick up all the pieces you can find. And don't cut yourselves doing it. PC Ryman'll be along shortly.'

They grumbled off and did as they were told. They weren't rebellious, these boys, they just lacked imagination. John Eakins watched them a few moments, then made his way out to the body.

Water was beginning to wet the bubbled seaweed on the rocks but it would be a few hours before the body was under again. At the mouth of the Haven he could see a ragged black knot, a few trawlers on their way home. Half an hour and they'd be mooring in a line outside the harbour. Two hours before high tide they'd be let in. He wished he was out there instead of examining a man who couldn't be helped.

John Eakins had seen plenty worse in the war, and knew not to look for remnants of human dignity. All death could do was ridicule the illusions of the living, if you let it. Everybody wound up something you'd rather avert your eyes from, and this one wasn't too bad close up, despite a battering from several high tides. The free leg had snapped at thigh and knee, and the trapped leg looked grotesque because of the way the baggy trousers had settled. The ankle had locked into part of the fissure; another protuberance held the knee in place. Otherwise the body could move with the water. It didn't look like a sailor or a local man. Possibly he'd made his way on to the rocks, trapped his foot and then felt the water rising till it drowned him, but dressed like a tax collector expecting rain why would he have wandered so far from town?

The trawlers were not appreciably nearer. Water splashed John's sock. He crouched and strained to lift the shoulders, just to find out if the body would be easy to extricate when Bob came. Something clattered. He grunted and heaved at the torso, revealing the man's arm. 'Well I'm damned!' he wheezed softly. Of all things, a pair of handcuffs, one bracelet tight around the wrist, the other part locked but unattached. Puzzling.

John Eakins stepped away to consider. His first thought was he'd found a criminal or a detective, whose companion might be washed up elsewhere, missing a hand, perhaps. Then he remembered that men sometimes cuffed themselves to cases containing important papers. Or money.

Colin and Petey were still dutifully collecting broken glass in the shade of the cliff. He considered calling them over to help in the search, but finding anything was too unlikely and one of them might slip into the water and make a fuss.

He dropped into a shelving shingly inlet, feet sinking in soaked pebbles, and turned to climb out again immediately, his sensitive right hand touching leather before he'd even looked. Simply balancing on a shelf at eye-level, waiting to be swept out to sea, the brown briefcase looked as if it had wanted to be found.

When he reached up to lift the case its handle came up in his hand, the break explaining the locked handcuff neatly. So he climbed up and sat beside the find and grinned, pleased his hunch had proved to be exactly right. I'll tell Bob, he thought, and Bob'll say I ought to be a copper. The handle had bust and the cuff had slipped off. This didn't explain why the man was dead, or what he'd been doing on the rocks, but it was a bit late for all that anyway.

The trawlers seemed suddenly to have drawn much nearer. Almost opposite, yet not close enough to discern figures – he did not know all the ships. There were more than a hundred and fifty altogether. Foster had been amazed when he told him, because the boy had assumed the dozen or so he saw at any one time constituted the fleet. At least that many diesels, John had laughed. His trawler, like all the older ones, was steam-driven. Those coming in now were steamers, too, gulls following hopefully as usual. He missed work. Flexed the bad hand instinctively, resentfully. Couldn't even help load the trains that went out every night to deliver fish to markets and shops right across Wales and England. Couldn't do a damn thing.

He fiddled with the catch until it sprang free. The case was so heavy he'd expected it to be full of water. But it wasn't. Nor was it packed with documents. Just plastic bags. He tugged at a corner and pulled one out, and that was when he first felt the chill of a reckless impulse. For a few seconds he waited, undecided, then curiosity led him to open the plastic packet and begin counting, turning notes with his left hand, the other good enough to hold a stack of lost money. Soon it became clear that he was totting up a wad of at least a thousand pounds, and there must have been forty or fifty waterproof packets stacked in the briefcase. The realisation that he was sitting on a rock with a fortune beside him made John Eakins nauseous. Although he hadn't done anything wrong he felt wretched and oddly adrift. The best thing to do was carry the briefcase over to the body and wait there with it. Not merely the best thing, it was the obvious thing, and if the situation were repeated a hundred times it was what John Eakins would do ninety nine of them. No question.

The boys were looking rather forlorn when he approached them, their cold hands gingerly cradling piles of glass they didn't know what to do with.

'I don't know,' Eakins sighed irritably. He peered all over, saw a deep thin fissure no one would be able to get stuck in, and suggested they empty their collections there. Then he made a different suggestion, as if he meant to give them a break. 'You could have yourselves in the paper,' he said, 'pictures an' all – the boys who found the body. Be local heroes.'

'Cor!' Colin gasped.

'That'd be good,' Petey agreed.

'Aye – trouble is, old Bob won't bother fetching Mal out for this. You'd have to get to the newspaper office, tell 'em yourselves – have to be quick off the mark, too, coz we'll have to shift the body before high water, and if it's gone when Mal gets here he might not be bothered.'

'Are you staying, Mr Eakins?'

'Oh, aye, I'll stay. And I'll ask Bob to wait as long as we can, give you a chance to fetch Mal. You mind you get our Foster and little Dewi in on it an' all, mind.'

He smiled encouragement. Colin and Petey took off, scrambling urgently and not caring about minor grazes any more. As soon as they'd gone around the Point he returned to where he'd dropped the briefcase. No time to fret about the rights and wrongs, or what he'd say if he met Bob on the way up to his bike. Desire had simplified matters, removing the moral perspective entirely.

On the back of John Eakins's bicycle was a deep wooden box he'd made, not quite deep enough to take the briefcase out of sight.

So he shook off his jacket, squirmed out of his jumper, stuffed the jumper around the protruding case and didn't hang around worrying that everyone would take one look and wonder why he'd wrapped a briefcase in a woolly. He left his bike leaning into the bush, innocuously visible, and scrambled down the track and out to the rocks, only hurting his hand once, while too cleverly getting into his jacket during the rapid descent.

He looked at the dead man's clean toenails, not out of curiosity, just to fix on something neutral.

What have I done? he asked himself. I must be mad.

At the same time, though, he knew he couldn't step away from his madness. He was excited by the awareness that it was folly, that somehow, by letting himself recognise folly and still go ahead, he had regained old youth. He was excited by the imminence of danger and, curiously, it seemed a purer kind of excitement than he had experienced in storms at sea. Deliberately, yet for no reason, he had put his good character at risk, his reputation, everything he stood for in the community. It was exhilarating.

Part of John's mind still worked rationally, preparing a bluff excuse: Course I wasn't thinking of stealing it, Bob! You know me better than that! Just didn't want the boys doing nothing silly. What would I want with so much money?

Nobody on the St. Lawrence estate could turn rich overnight and not get arrested by morning. Obviously he was doing it for a gag. He'd never broken the law in his life. And that was stamped in his nature, because he wasn't one of these timid men who would if they could but simply lacked courage. He was strong enough to lead where others followed, independent enough to live whatever life he wanted, and the life he wanted was clean and true. He had a wife, a son and the kind of unquestioning loyalty that kept men like him in jobs like his forever.

While John Eakins was proving that he couldn't in any circumstance do what he had just done his old friend Phil Thomas entered his mind. Phil, a reluctant but dogged soldier, had no malice in him and took every dismaying situation in his stride, shooting if he had to, but mostly just enduring the weariness with resigned common sense. But one afternoon a German sniper surrendered to them, quite undramatically, and without warning Phil walked up to the poor fellow and shot him in the head. For John it was one of the most shocking moments of the war, being not only unnecessary but unprovoked, also absolutely out of character. Later Phil just said he must have been holding that in for months. That was all. And no one would ever bother him about it. Men were getting blown apart every day. Phil could live with what he'd done and, much later, John Eakins realised that Phil would have cracked up if he hadn't expressed himself just that way.

Suddenly he tore at the dead man's clothes, peeling the sodden material until he found the inside jacket pocket. The wallet. Identification.

It wasn't theft exactly. He pocketed the wallet without glancing inside. Didn't want the money, if there was any. Wanted the man to stay a stranger, a floater maybe, washed in from the open sea. Bob Ryman wouldn't be on the lookout for a briefcase until he found out who the man was, what his business had been. Perhaps no one would ever know, if the wallet was gone.

John Eakins sat on the rocks and watched the trawlers slowing into a line to await the tide. The sky hadn't changed all afternoon, but he felt further away from everything, as if he too were a stranger, seeing the Haven and its beauty for the first time, stunned by its loveliness.

TEN

Mal Mabey measured out his life in column inches, waiting for the big break that would throw him into the embrace of the *Western Mail*, or even the *Manchester Guardian*. He travelled around Pembrokeshire in a motorbike and sidecar, wearing a leather helmet and goggles, leather gloves with sleeves like wings, and a double-breasted leather frock-coat, imagining he was Biggles.

'So why wasn't you in school today?' he asked the smaller of the two boys, pencil poised, notepad open. Didn't miss a trick, Mal.

Petey, hair up in arms, eyes watering from the exciting sidecar journey to the cliff, gulped guiltily.

'Our class is off today,' Colin helped, frowning and wishing he'd paid attention when they were told why they should stay away. 'You can ask anybody. We're not mitchin', honest.'

Petey nodded, finding concentration difficult. A lot of fuss about nothing, he thought. A complete waste of what should have been a great bonus of a day. There was nothing diverting to look at down below now, just half a dozen men, plus Foster and Dewi, hunting for the dead man's shoes and socks. What was the point? The really galling thing – though he wasn't going to mention it later – was that when they'd shifted the body they put it on a canvas stretcher between two wooden poles and two of them carried it over the rocks and around the Point as if they were strolling down the lane. That made him feel smaller than he was. Climbing around the Point and not plummeting to your death had been a major daring feat, and those men took the body that way because it was easier than bringing it up the track. He smoothed his wayward hair, but it refused to stay put.

'Funeral,' he said suddenly.

'Funeral?' Mal Mabey queried.

'Oh, aye,' Colin remembered, 'that's it – one of our teachers was having his funeral today.'

'It's a mark of respect,' Petey said solemnly.

Mal Mabey couldn't quite see how he was going to use this information, but it added another layer to the brief story in his mind: Boys off school on sad occasion of schoolmaster's funeral find mystery body. It was – what was the word? – it was ironic. Could you put irony in an inconclusive piece about an unidentified corpse?

'Odd bloke,' Colin continued. 'Used to weep in assembly.'

'Wept in registration one morning,' Petey confirmed.

'Not much cop as a teacher.'

'I can't write that,' Mal told them. Kids – no sense of decorum. Possibly the angle was too subtle. Whatever he wrote he wasn't going to stop readers turning to Garden Tips first, not unless the dead man had relatives in the area. The snippet Bob had given him was better. Apparently floaters didn't come up the Haven, and this was the first body they'd ever found on the rocks. The Haven wasn't like the Gower. A pal of Bob's had said you couldn't get a peaceful day's fishing off the end of the Gower on account of all the floaters the sea coughed up.

'When we gonna have our picture took?' Colin asked.

'I've taken your names. You probably won't be photographed this time.'

'Can we cadge a ride home off you then?'

'I want a few more words with PC Ryman and John Eakins. After that, maybe.'

'That's your name, innit? Maybe?'

'*Mr* Mabey to you, boy. And get away from there. What're you doing?'

Colin had noticed the blue jumper in the box on the back of Foster's dad's bike. He was curious to see what bulged beneath it. But not excessively. He moved back obediently in case Mr Maybe went and told Mr Eakins he was snooping. For some reason Colin had imagined there might be a couple of loaves of bread in there. He was a bit peckish.

'Here comes trouble,' Bob Ryman grinned, seeing Mal come sliding down the cliff with his goggles on his forehead and his earflaps flapping. 'A regular bloodhound. Tell him about the hand-cuffs, John. I bet he'll solve the mystery for us.'

'It'll be like you say,' John Eakins muttered, 'some foreign detective off of Interpol, outwitted by a criminal mastermind and thrown overboard.'

'Reckon that's plausible, is it?' Ryman asked sceptically.

'Not if I'm being honest with you, Bob, no. But if it's not nobody from town it must be somebody's come in from outside, so he's either a birdwatcher or one of them buggers who wants to open us up to new industries. And he wasn't dressed like no bird-watcher.'

Bob Ryman nodded and tried to look wise beyond his years, squinting hard at the town he loved. Over the last twelve months or so there'd been more visitors than normal, men in suits, money men. There was talk of a transformation, Milford Haven becoming a huge oil refinery – big ships, new jobs, money like confetti, unimaginable disruption. He liked the Haven the way it was. When you've got paradise on your doorstep you don't try and make it any better.

'If it wasn't for those cuffs...' He trailed off, irritated by a detail he couldn't make sense of. 'My guess is he was carrying something important. I only wish we'd found it. I wish he'd had something in his pockets, too.'

Mal Mabey had joined them and was pretending not to be straining to overhear the conversation. 'No chance of a murder, I suppose?' he put in.

'No reason to think so. Yet,' the constable told him.

John Eakins wished he could help. It upset him to see Bob so mystified and tentative, and he could have said he'd found the briefcase as soon as Bob arrived on the scene. Too late now – not the sort of thing you could pretend you'd just remembered. Men continued searching amongst the rocks, though they didn't know what they were meant to find. Only he and Bob knew that, and he alone knew they weren't going to find it. Foster was helping. John Eakins tried not to be aware of his son's eager scrambling, or how it would look if one of the boys on top of the cliff suddenly held up the briefcase.

The only solution to the bind he'd put himself in would be to take a dinghy out after dark. He couldn't row yet, but as long as the water stayed reasonably calm he could scull well enough to get around the Point and drop wallet and case over the side. If the objects sank Bob wouldn't be helped at all, but John couldn't help that.

On the other hand he could emigrate.

'It's possible our man was a gangster,' Bob ruminated. 'Print that, Mal, and you're on your own. Off the record, Archie had some stuff on some London boys who might be wanting to lease some of the headlands – enquiries about Hubberston Fort, planning permission to make a club of it. That's only the beginning.' He looked at John and Mal, neither of whom appeared particularly convinced. 'Failing that,' he added, 'I wouldn't be surprised if he was sent from some ministry, in mufti, like, coz they won't admit the scale of what they're wanting to do here.'

'What you on about, Bob? Dens of vice again?'

'Mark my words. Suez. Nasser. I'm serious. Nobody heard talk about oil till Eden went, and sterling collapsed. It's all connected.'

'Bob, you're nutty as a squirrel's picnic,' John Eakins chuckled. But he was uncomfortable. His friend was no visionary, and rarely

44

concerned himself with anything outside the Haven, but this one theme obsessed him and was beginning to sound realistic. If the dead man hadn't been wearing handcuffs he wouldn't have fitted the plot half as well. Bob was floundering out of his depth, but he wasn't completely stupid.

Just then a hoarse yell came from the rocks and John Eakins chilled, as if he'd been found out. Astonishingly the noise had been made by his son, who loped towards them triumphantly, waving a sopping brown brogue.

'Well done, Foss,' his father said. 'Your mam'll give you what for if you catch a cold, though, and I'll get it in the neck an' all – better get off home now, right? Well done.'

Constable Ryman concealed his disappointment and noted the shoe size in his book. Then he sighed, stepped away from the splashing tide, called the others to stop, thanked them for their efforts and dismissed them.

'Can I give you a lift, John?' he asked.

'I've got the bike, ta,' John said, and thought: I've got the bike and more money than you've ever seen, and in a few minutes I'll know if I've got away with it.

The immensity of the wrongdoing hadn't yet got through to him. So far he felt mainly like a liar whose son's trust was causing him anguish.

The trawlers were still waiting on the tide, the sky still holding trails of frozen cloud in its brilliant blue grip. More chill came off the water, but the gloom wasn't felt by anyone else. John Eakins was glad when Foster said he'd rather ride home in Bob's car than walk alongside the bike with his dad. Everyone went. Eakins slowly pushed over the waste ground to the road. So easy, he thought, yet there was no thrill to it.

ELEVEN

Upstairs three bedrooms, lavvy, bathroom; downstairs living room, dining room, kitchen; an airing cupboard on the upstairs landing, a wedge-shaped broom cupboard under the stairs; pantry in kitchen, plus some cupboards, and wardrobes in the bedrooms.

Where, in a house whose every space was used, could a man conceal anything from his wife and child? The spare bedroom was Rachel's office overflow. She handled household bills, tax returns, anything requiring brains and patience, and filed them all in that room. John was intimidated by it, felt a dunce just taking a cup of tea in to her. To sneak in when Rachel was out was unthinkable; besides, obviously he couldn't hope to hide his briefcase in any part of the house she'd made her own. And that, it surprised him to realise, was all of it. Even Foster's box of a bedroom was Rachel's domain, because she still changed his sheets, put clean clothes in his drawers, gave him permission to stick photos of film stars on his walls when John thought he should stay faithful to Cardiff City and Manchester United. Rachel's presence was everywhere, John's nowhere.

It was strange, he thought, because she was not domineering and he was hardly self-effacing, but here he was for the first time in his married life with something to hide, and he was starting to resent Rachel for looking after the place so efficiently.

The garden shed, however, was his. It housed their bicycles, various gardening tools, his seagoing waterproofs, hammers, mallets, chisels, planes, saws, set squares, screws, nails, seedlings, several old torches and a few lazy old spiders. He could probably dump the briefcase under a piece of sacking in complete safety, without padlocking the door.

The wallet bothered him more. To have someone else's wallet in your possession was harder to explain than a briefcase you'd picked up. More deliberate, more personal – well, frankly it was theft. Eakins's scalp froze. He dropped the wallet on the dusty surface and refused to go through its soaking contents. He wished he'd had the sense to chuck it straight into the Haven.

'When you coming in, John?' Rachel suddenly called.

She couldn't see him. She was at the kitchen door. The shed door was ajar but she didn't need to step outside the house.

'Oiling the mower,' he called back. 'Be in now just.'

He hefted the briefcase into the far corner, behind the lawn mower and the spades, and covered it with stiff old coal sacks.

Then he reached in and flipped the wallet behind the briefcase. As he straightened and it crossed his mind that he was now a very wealthy man, he wondered if time would ever convince him that wealth could be fun for all the family. He knew the answer, though, and intended to dump his fortune as soon as possible. Maybe in a few years he'd be able to tell people, laugh about the episode. Maybe not.

Rachel was putting out the dinner – stew again, to be followed, again, by rice pudding with a well-burnt skin on top. Before her job they wouldn't have had the same dinner two nights running, and she sometimes apologised. Other times John got the impression she blamed him, as if he should have taken over, but he hoped she understood how unrealistic that was. He wouldn't have known where to start. It was funny, though, because you always had a man in the galley cooking everything at sea, and you didn't find that unnatural. In fact it would be ludicrous to put a woman in that situation. But presumably when old Dicky Dolan was home he stayed out of the kitchen and stuffed himself on whatever his mam and his two sisters set before him.

'Stew,' John observed quietly.

'Sausage and chips tomorrow,' Rachel promised.

'Good day?' he asked, hugging her from behind, his left hand reaching for a breast to squeeze gently, his lips planting a kiss light as a soap bubble on her neck. When he was that close he could easily believe there was no significant world beyond them, that his impulsive lapse really was very trivial. The faint distinctive smell of Rachel's neck meant more than all the news in all the newspapers in Wales.

'How about you?' she answered, swaying against him, taking his wounded right hand in both hers to cradle like a fallen bird.

'Foss tell you?'

'He doesn't seem too upset by it.'

'That's kids, isn't it?'

They didn't say a lot. They were sure of each other and happy with the way they lived. Rachel knew her husband hated his enforced idleness, though. He wouldn't read and there wasn't enough to occupy him around the house. She was glad he hadn't slumped into drinking and betting, like some of the men who got injured. John, she thought proudly, had more character. She felt bad about the stew. She also felt bad about earning more than he did, but because she dealt with their accounts she was able to keep quiet about that. He knew, of course, but pretended not to, and that was the best way. Men were shaky with anything sensitive.

You had to pamper them, because their work was dangerous and deserved to be appreciated. It was daft you could earn more in an office, embarrassing. John assumed being a secretary meant taking shorthand, typing letters. Rachel practically ran that company.

While they were eating Foster said something about the dead man – Bob Ryman must have been airing his potty theories in the car. Foster wanted to know how life would change if new industries came into the area. He wanted to know if they'd be rich and if there'd be new cinemas, new shops, if there'd be a dance hall and a bowling alley and a funfair and a skating rink. It was bewildering to hear a child you thought you knew spilling out his cheap fantasies as if he truly believed every one of them was about to come true.

'He was just a dead man on the rocks, Foss. You're babbling, boy.'

If his father called him 'boy' like that, scornfully, Foster usually shut up. Ignoring the warning could result in the threat of a smack. Foster couldn't remember the threat ever being carried out, but storms made him anxious even if he kept dry. He swallowed a swab of bread and stew and checked the atmosphere before pushing his luck.

'Constable Ryman said there'll be so much dosh coming into town in ten years we won't recognise it.'

'Dosh?'

'Money, Mam.'

'I'll bet Bob Ryman didn't say dosh. Nor should you. It's slang.'

'Everybody says dosh, it's just speaking.'

'Foster, I'm dealing with wages and dockets and orders all day long, and no one uses that word.'

'Constable Ryman did.'

'Then he ought to have his bottom spanked,' Rachel said. She was aware of the comical aspect, though, and Foster liked it when she only played at disapproving of everything.

'He was talking down to your level, boy,' his father explained. Foster didn't like that at all. Just nasty for the sake of it. 'That doesn't make it all right for you to talk ignorant.'

Rachel glanced surreptitiously at the ceiling. Her husband's support was not as essential as he assumed.

'When Bill Haley and Frankie Lymon and Frankie Vaughan fly over, maybe they'll come here, if we've got a big dance hall.'

'I think you'll find Frankie Vaughan's already English,' John Eakins said, not absolutely certain, not really caring one way or the other, simply hoping to put a stopper on Foster's exuberance.

'Never! He sang 'Green Door' – that's rock 'n' roll.'

'Perhaps so. But that other one – Donnie? Lonnie, Donnie? – he was English. The point is, in ten years the music will be different and you'll be interested in something better. Anyway, the Haven isn't going to change. I don't know nobody who wants it to, so how can it?'

'Constable Ryman said we wasn't really looking for that man's shoes. He thinks he had something else on him, like plans or a suitcase full of dosh, and he could have been a foreigner, from abroad.'

'Why would he think that?' Rachel asked.

'It's rubbish,' John Eakins scoffed. 'I don't want to hear any more of this. Bob's got a bee in his bonnet since those coppers from Glasgow came here last summer and laughed at him for thinking he had a proper copper's job. The only foreigner you're likely to see is the Johnny Onion man.'

'I saw a man in a turban once, didn't we, Mam?' He'd been walking into town with her. They'd crossed the bridge and were passing the dock gates when they spotted a turbanned gentleman inside a telephone kiosk, attempting to get out and being blocked by someone intent on keeping the door shut and crushing his leg if need be.

'That's right,' Rachel agreed. 'A drunk was assaulting him.'

'Are we going to have pudding or not?' John asked testily.

Tactfully his wife and son abandoned their reminiscences. Later, after Foster had gone to bed, Rachel asked her husband what was worrying him. Nothing was, he growled.

'Is it Foster? Has he done something he shouldn't and you don't want to tell me?'

'Nothing's wrong at all. I suppose I'm fed up with this blummin' hand. And old Bob feeding Foster these crazy ideas. Why can't things be let be? Everybody wants something more than they've got. Peter Walker's talking about getting a deposit together, buying a house. Bob says he's been wondering if that's the next thing to do an' all.'

'You haven't rowed with Bob and Peter?'

'Course not. Don't you think they need their heads banging together, though? Bob's too young to remember, but Peter's nearly my age, and he goes on about buying a house for security, an investment.'

'I'm sorry it was stew again. I meant to pop in the butcher's on the way home, but...'

'Rachel, I wish you'd give it a rest, honest.'

He felt desperate. He couldn't tell her he was angry because he had a case full of dead man's money in the shed. He couldn't say he wished he hadn't taken it because sooner or later Bob would have to come and arrest him and then Foster would have a common criminal for a dad. He could barely even face it himself that he'd been inspired at least partly by his son's attempt to steal a record – the brooding afterwards, the struggle to comprehend such a senseless impulse.

John thought it reasonable he should be in a rotten mood, and not too much to expect a bit of forebearance from anyone who loved him. He might have guessed Rachel would immediately sense the change in him, but she didn't have to press so relentlessly. A man had a right to *some* privacy.

'Been thinking,' he said, 'I wouldn't mind seeing old Phil Thomas again, just to see how he's doing.'

'Phil Thomas? The one you were in France with?'

'That's him, aye – old Phil. While I'm off work, like, I ought to pay him a visit. Won't have another chance, will I?'

'Has he written?'

'Not since Christmas.'

Phil sent a card every year, always too risqué to put on display. On the basis of his Christmas cards Rachel disliked the man and distanced herself from her husband's association to the extent that she was now deeply suspicious – she'd convinced herself that John had never really cared for Phil Thomas.

'But where does he live?'

'I'll find him.'

'By going to that place in Soho?'

The cards advertised a club. Phil Thomas worked in a place that had striptease dancers and jazz music. She loathed him.

'I'd only be gone for a few days, love. A week or two at the outside.'

'And this is something you want to do, is it?' Rachel thought she was controlling her fury pretty well. She may have sounded like a prim schoolmarm, but John wasn't behaving like Big Eli Wakefield. He must have been planning this move for days, furtively. 'You're missing him so much all of a sudden?'

'He was a good pal. He was all right. If we can't afford the fare, all well and good, but Phil's always inviting me, and saying it won't cost nothing to stay. And here I am good for nothing for weeks on end – what's so wrong?'

'He works in Soho, John. I'm not stupid. And you've never bothered with him until now, so what is it? What's happened?'

'What, because he works in a club I can't never see him, is it?'

John sounded aggrieved, though fundamentally he shared his wife's reservations. What he couldn't share with her was his somewhat irrational idea that being in London with Phil would enable him to sort the money problem, make it disappear. 'You think I'd be tempted by exotic dancers? Think I'll fall into wicked ways? Give me some credit, Rachel! Who do you think I am?'

'I think there's something you're keeping from me, that's all.'

'If there was there'd be a good reason,' he pointed out.

'What is it, John?'

'Nothing.'

A whole evening's worrying had shifted the proportions of his life. The house was comfortable but far too small for him to breathe freely. The community was friendly but far too inquisitive. It was necessary to break manacles whenever you felt them hampering your movements. He'd been a soldier, and was a trawlerman – he wasn't a weedy little fellow like that shopkeeper, Bandy. He needed scope for his energies. The money should belong to him, he should be able to feel it was his. Anybody could have found it and kept it. No one knew of its existence. He didn't even want it, particularly. He wasn't greedy, didn't crave it, but just on principle, he thought angrily, he ought to hang on to it. And Rachel had no right to stop him visiting an old pal like Phil. What's the good of being married for years and years if you won't trust your husband the one time he wants to go off somewhere a bit unusual?

Saturday, he decided, like it or not, I'll go.

That should give him enough time to bring Rachel on to his side, he hoped. He wanted to leave with a clear conscience.

TWELVE

It was raining on Saturday morning when the two tough guys from London turned up. They must have stopped overnight in Haverfordwest, someplace not too distant, because they were clean-shaven and didn't look at all crumpled. They came in from the Haverfordwest road anyway – there was no other – and parked close by the Baptist chapel.

The gaunt one stopped to read a plaque that informed him of the town's history, its association with Nelson, its foundation by Quaker whalers from Nantucket. Rain dripped off the brim of his trilby until he straightened and looked across the Haven at the misty gusts of drizzle and shrugged his shoulders.

'This is going to be fun,' he grumbled to his partner, who also wore a trilby and a plain green gaberdine. His partner was not gaunt, though. He looked as though he could open a safe by sitting on it. 'What the fuck's a Quaker whaler from Nantucket?'

'Christ knows, but if it came here and thought this was an improvement, that rubs Nantucket off my must see list. What is this place, George, it's all bloody water!'

They strolled into town, and out the bottom before they'd realised that was all there was to it. Strolled back, rather disdainfully, and located the newspaper office. There they identified themselves, plausibly enough, as reporters from the London *Evening Standard* anxious to follow up on Mal Mabey's story. No, they said, they weren't prepared to hazard a guess as to the identity of the dead man, but they were working on a hunch. Yes, they said, they'd certainly be calling at the police station shortly, but they'd hoped to have a word with the little lads who'd found the body, if Mal Mabey had the names and addresses on file.

Mal wasn't in the office, but it was no secret where the boys lived – down past the docks, across the bridge into Hakin, and if you followed the road to the right, past the woods, you'd see the St. Lawrence estate above you on your left. They all lived there. Found the body just around the rocks, beyond the jetty. You'd see the jetty, Hakin Point, as you walked down towards the docks. Funny old thing, though, wasn't it? Him with handcuffs on, and wearing a suit like he was a tax inspector or something. No evidence it was murder, like, and no clue as to why a stranger would get himself trapped on the rocks like that. Most odd. So a London man, was he?

'Don't miss a trick, do you, mate?' George, the gaunt one, said.

'If we turn anything up we'll let Mabey know,' the other promised cordially, winking at his sour partner and heading for the door.

Outside he paused: 'What's that bloody awful racket?'

'Seagulls,' George told him. 'That's the sea over there, so it must be seagulls. We get seagulls on the Thames. They're not rare.'

'When was the last time you saw the river? Bloody starlings, I know bloody starlings. They're bad enough, but at least it's not all fucking day.'

'You probably get used to it if you have to waste your life on the arse-end of Nan-fucking-tucket.' George didn't think highly of Milford.

'I'd mow 'em down,' the big man said. His name was Aidan Gentle, but hardly anyone knew that. To associates he was known as Gently, and most assumed that was a witticism, since his methods were notoriously uncouth. 'What we going to do if these kids don't know about the money?'

George shrugged: 'Let's get a drink first. Get out of this lousy air, away from this filthy bloody racket.'

'You don't like it either?' Gently was pleased. 'Beginning to think you had a side I didn't know about.'

'You saying I haven't?'

'Don't be touchy, George.'

'I'm not touchy. You're the one who thinks we can find forty thousand quid by offering some kid ten bob. If you're wrong we've come on an errand any prat could do. Look at it – whole town's not worth what I've got in my wallet!'

Their mission was to assess the mood of Milford. The front-man had been a solicitor, and perfectly respectable except for the somewhat unusual task he'd been given, and the large amount of cash he'd been provided with. George and Gently were to find out, tactfully, if the solicitor's unexpected death had awakened anything resembling suspicion. Much larger sums of money would be changing hands if conditions had remained favourable. But George was right – nosing around to see that further investments could probably go ahead was not a job for specialists in violence. He and Gently had come after the money, which their employer seemed prepared to write off.

They saw a pub ahead and ducked inside gratefully. A half-dozen smelly sailors stopped talking abruptly and stared at them as if they were gangsters.

'Reporters,' Gently announced quickly. 'London.'

The stares continued several seconds, but since he gave nothing more away and didn't look daft enough to buy everyone a drink the sailors went back to more guarded conversation about teeming portions of the ocean. The intruders found a sheltered table by a window whose green panes were thick as bottles.

'Any bugger can simply drop dead,' Gently whispered to George. 'It happens. But a man doesn't drop dead with forty grand chained to his wrist and then lose it. Those kids are probably buying out the fucking sweetshops!'

'We don't know it's forty. That's an approximation.'

Gently wiped a finger along the window, then rubbed dust and dead flies into an ashtray. Then he popped the finger into his mouth and licked it. He raised his eyebrows, not displeased with the flavour.

'That reporter mentioned the bracelets. Anybody who read that would know there's a case full of money around here somewhere.'

'Somehow I don't think so,' George said. 'We already knew. That's why we're here first. And if Mr Wary wasn't killed, if he just dropped dead on the rocks, I reckon the money's in the drink.'

'You're a pessimist, George. You've got to believe in gut feelings.'

'Yours, you mean? If Mr Wary had already contacted the right men they'll be shitting themselves at the moment. Now we turn up...'

'I'll protect you,' Gently said as if he was speaking to a cuddly baby.

George looked hard at him: 'Your mind's not getting around this at all, is it, mate? The money's a daydream. I'm humouring you. If you're right we'll share it. If you're wrong I'll brain you. Either way we're here to meet a few names, reassure the bastards, and...'

'Let's have some fun,' Gently cut him off, bouncing the table as he stood up. 'Let's find those boys.'

'Yeah,' George muttered, 'cutting kiddies down to size, that's going to take all our talents, that is!' He didn't believe in the money. Back in London it had sounded realistic enough, and Gently was hard to stop when he had an idea, but out here it was plainly ridiculous. If the money hadn't been lost at sea it would have been all over the town by now. It wasn't the sort of town that could keep good fortune under wraps. He also felt that he and Gently were exposed, just by turning up, and that made him nervous. In London every other bugger you met was a stranger, so you could slip in and out as if you belonged. Here it was like wearing a sign saying Shifty: Call The Cops. 'Just do me one favour, Gently,' he said when they reached the street. 'Don't get carried away – no blood, no noise. All right?'

'I can be subtle.' Gently sounded offended. 'I'm not stupid.' He gazed up and down the road and shook his head in amusement. 'On the other hand,' he added slyly, 'you and me could seal up this hole in a couple of hours, take everything they've got.'

George had to admit he was probably right: 'Wouldn't be worth the effort, though. So let's go with the low profile. It's not what Milford Haven is now that interests anybody.'

'Yeah, yeah – invest in the future.' Gently'd heard it all before, from the men who supposedly had the brains, and certainly had the money – the men he and George worked for, and resented, and were better than. 'Nan-fucking-tucket,' he scoffed. 'Las-fucking-Vegas! You see it?'

'We're not visionaries, Gently, we don't have to see it.'

'Let's go lean on the laddy who found Mr Wary, then.'

'Fair enough.'

THIRTEEN

Something had gone wrong with his parents. He hadn't heard them being unkind, but there'd been silences cold enough for icebergs filling the hall and the kitchen. Disputes were rare enough that a whispered debate was a dread sound, so when he heard murmurings late into the night he shivered under all his sheets, blankets and eiderdown. The voices hadn't risen above a drone, a tremor that coiled and recoiled monotonously, but Foster had quaked.

Last night when his mother had come in from work she'd immediately started preparing a big dinner, as if it was Sunday, and the boy's impression was that she was only doing it to make his dad wretched. His dad *was* wretched, too, all quiet and pained-looking. Friday night should have been fish and chips. So he was wondering if they were planning to give him away. His mam probably wanted to keep him, he thought, and his dad couldn't see the point. Maybe it was the other way round.

He sat in the greyness with his laughing friends and watched the first serial with no involvement. Colin was handing out sweets every few minutes. That was because his uncle had been so proud to read that story in the paper he'd given Colin half a crown in addition to his normal pocket money. With his mouth full and dripping Foster was still sulky. His parents had never threatened to give him away. He was often insecure anyway. His mam worked Saturdays sometimes, didn't dote on him. His dad was sometimes away at sea when the weather was bad (Foster listening to the shipping with his mam, not understanding the special language, fearing the worst).

The warm dusty smell of the cinema usually made him snug, but this Saturday morning he couldn't get in the mood. His dad wasn't supposed to be going back to sea yet, but he slipped into Foster's room while it was still dark out, kissed his cheek and said he was off. The bed was cosy and Foster nearly went right back to sleep, had to force himself to emerge into the chill dawn air of his room, sneak along the landing and strain to overhear what they were saying in the kitchen. Only murmurs again, then the back door.

'It'll be on now,' Dewi said excitedly, pushing Foster's arm to make him concentrate. 'How's he going to escape?'

'He'll be killed,' Foster said, repeating words they'd all spoken several times since last week's episode, which ended with Black Hawk unconscious in a wooden look-out tower that was about to explode.

'He can't be,' Colin hissed across urgently. 'He can't escape, but he can't get killed.'

They were smart enough to know the serial wasn't true, but adventure stories showed you how ingenious heroes could be. They'd been gripped by real anxiety at Black Hawk's plight this time. He was unconscious in the tower and the tower was exploding. He couldn't get out unscathed. The cartoon had ended. Foster was remembering a few hours ago, climbing on the lavvy seat and opening the window, peering out to see a grey strip of dawn light between heavy blue cloud and the long black roof of the dock market, staring down into the dark garden in time to make out his father's shadowy figure, the long white duffle on his shoulder, as he stepped over the fence and strode up next door's garden to the stile they'd built at the end. Everyone used it for a shortcut. He watched his father disappearing downhill. He'd definitely gone, definitely kissed his son goodbye, as if it were a regular departure. Foster knew it wasn't, and was too scared to ask his mam at breakfast, in case she yelled at him, said it was his fault, confirmed he'd never see his dad any more.

'This is it!' Dewi sighed ecstatically, wriggling in an impossible attempt to settle down.

Two minutes later the boys were appalled, too stunned to discuss what they'd just seen. Foster took it as absolute gloomy proof nothing could be trusted. He felt for his penknife, then silently pressed the point into the seat in front, scoring it slowly. The scratch he made was only a few inches long, but it helped express his rage at being conned by the serial and life generally. It wouldn't surprise him now if he returned home and found a note telling him to find another home and some new parents. Black Hawk had revived. Not only that, he'd found a rope, which definitely hadn't been there last week. So he'd abandoned the tower before it exploded. Yet they'd all seen it blow up with him unconscious inside. The boys were livid. If the rope had been there last week, if he'd shown any sign of reviving, they wouldn't have minded.

'What a cheat!' Dewi said glumly. 'That was stupid that was.'

'They couldn't think of a way out,' Foster said, level-headed. 'He ought to have died.' Until that moment he'd willingly accepted that heroes got out of scrapes their own way, but now he grasped a new and disturbing idea: stories were made up by people you never saw. Same with books – you were carried along by the heroes, not by writers who had nothing to do with them. Black Hawk had just stopped being a hero, turned into something even less than a character.

And it was raining heavily in the street as the boys headed back towards their estate. Gloomy rain, rain of disillusion, Foster reckoned.

'It's like when you read a book,' Foster had a go at telling his friends, though the revelation was too recent for him to feel sure. 'It's all made up by the writer. Films is just the same.'

'Everybody knows that!' Colin said scathingly, but he didn't really, and he frowned. 'What I reckon is, there was a bit missing last week, and they found it and put it in today, coz it makes sense if you think about it.'

At least the house wasn't deserted. Foster suppressed his relief, because his mother's presence, after all, was not a surprise to her.

'I haven't had time to get you lunch,' Rachel apologised. 'Have a corned beef sandwich if you want. Or are you not hungry?'

She often asked him that on Saturdays, knowing he'd been guzzling sweets all morning, but sweets never affected his appetite like she said they did. Foster started sawing at the bread, mildly incensed at having to do the job himself.

'Mam,' he queried, recalling the recent cinematic disappointment, 'if they don't think up what to do themselves, why are they the heroes?'

'I don't follow. Who are you talking about now? Oh, by the way, two men knocked on the door asking for you.'

'What!'

'An hour ago. They were going round the houses.' She smiled vaguely at her foolishness: 'Big men, they were. Gave me quite a start. I thought they were spivs, gangsters, whatever you call them. But it's all right, they're just reporters, following up on Mal's story.'

'Phew!'

'I know. It's Colin they want to talk to most, since he actually found the poor man first.'

'No he never! He never, Mam, we found it together. Colin's a big-head.'

'Here,' Rachel said, seeing the mess he was making of opening a tin of corned beef, 'let me, before you have your fingers off. We don't want two wounded soldiers in the family.'

'Is Dad's hand better now, then? Is that why he's gone to work?' Foster was pleased to have brought in the subject so naturally. His mother twisted the key off the sharp hinge and narrowly avoided getting slashed.

'He hasn't gone to work,' she explained mysteriously. 'Those reporter men are coming back in a bit. Next you know it'll be on the wireless.'

'I'm playing out, I don't care if it is on the wireless. Colin can stop in and talk to them if he wants. Why should it be on the wireless?'

'I don't suppose it will,' his mother said, perplexed by his attitude. She looked at the slices of meat, waiting for inspiration. None came. She put a slab of bread on top. Foster went to the pantry for the pickle jar, sighing too loudly, to let her know he didn't approve of having to do everything himself. 'Your dad's decided to visit an old pal of his, while he's off work and can't make himself useful.'

'Is he back tonight, then?'

'He'll be back when he's back. Now don't bother me now, that's a good boy, I've got some work to sort out upstairs. What shall I say if the reporters come back?'

'You can tell 'em we're down the woods if you like. Mam?'

'What?'

'In the film this morning, Black Hawk should've died, but they put in extra bits that weren't there last week.'

'You're not expected to take those serials seriously, Foss.'

'I don't, but I always thought the hero was the main one, who had all the clever ideas, but he's not the main one – the main one must be whoever made the film, the photographer.'

'I suppose that's true.'

She wasn't paying attention. How could it not matter to her? Foster thought he'd latched on to an idea that could make his whole life move ahead differently. If the main people weren't the ones you saw doing things, but the ones who *made* them do things, and you never saw them.... He ate his sandwich rapidly, wishing he had the ability to follow through with speculations like these. Colin could play being the hero, it didn't mean anything. Foster could be the one who really knew what was going on all the time, and if none of the others acknowledged his supreme importance he could just smile inwardly. It was like being God. No one ever saw you or suspected you were the main one, but you were. Foster's mood improved: he was getting a grasp of it now, he could feel what true heroism was – nothing showy – he liked it.

The reporters weren't in his thoughts. The body was days ago and not a subject to retain any thrill. His father, comfortingly, obviously, now, hadn't deserted him. His mother had gone quietly upstairs to work. Everything was perfectly all right. The cheap con trick of the serial was enabling him to gain a new perspective. None of his friends had enough brains to...Foster didn't complete the thought in words, but in a convincing if immodest sense of his enhanced intellect he swaggered through to the front room, gave the gramophone a couple of winds, screwed in a new needle and let rip with 'Green Door', yelling accompaniment and leaping on and off the settee until his mother cried out mercy.

FOURTEEN

When a car passed by its tyres sounded like sticking plaster ripped off skin; otherwise what was left of the drizzle was silent, unless you went under the boughs, where you could hear drips breaking continuously and a raspy sighing from soft undergrowth. The whooping of the boys didn't so much echo up from the lake as fan out and linger like a memory of some previous summer. They generally played at the bottom of the wood, because the ground levelled out and there was a broad footpath along one side of the little lake. As soon as you got into the trees you had to contend with half-concealed roots and awkward bushes – fine for hiding, but unless you had a full-scale battle in progress inconvenient. From the path you could shoot arrows vertically and try to send one over the highest branch; then you could stand there squinting up while it plummeted back to earth, and you could think about the stone-sharpened nail you'd fixed for an arrowhead, and would it be worse to be laughed at as the first to run away or hold your ground and get a nail through your eye?

But they hadn't brought their bows and arrows that Saturday afternoon. Petey had his brother's sheath-knife, and they practised throwing it tip first, none of them getting it to stick into a tree, or even into the wet earth. The balance wasn't right, Foster explained. The knife was specially made for hacking, not throwing, so it was-n't as much fun as knives in the pictures, which always stuck in. Petey hacked at some nearby bushes for a while, but they were too springy. Then, for a while, they played with Colin's spud-gun (he'd brought a couple of potatoes), but the little rounds of potato real-ly stung too much to be laughed off bravely, so they couldn't fire at each other and they couldn't find any stationary birds to aim at, and the satisfaction of shooting the water soon palled. They were at a loose end, irritated by the Black Hawk film that morning, unable to shift effortlessly into heroic roles. They walked desulto-rily down the path, which would eventually meet the lower end of the road, not far from the bridge. To avoid depressingly inconclu-sive discussion of the film they sang snatches of favourite songs, argued about who was going to play the washboard when they got their skiffle group going, and who was going to find a small tea-chest, a broom handle and a piece of string to make the bass. They all wanted to be lead vocalist, basically, except Dewi, who took piano lessons and said he didn't mind. Foster tried to prove him-self by imitating Elvis Presley, Fats Domino, Lonnie Donegan and

The Platters, convinced he sounded exactly the same and offended by the derisive hoots of Colin, whose Fess Parker, Tex Ritter and Chas McDevitt were gratingly bad. Petey, annoyingly, managed a perfect Frankie Lymon, and the only thing to say was that 'I'm Not A Juvenile Delinquent' just wasn't skiffle.

Foster carried a box of matches he'd picked up in the garden shed – there'd been a packet with a few of his dad's Woodbines, too, and if he'd been Colin he'd have stolen them, but he wasn't, so he hadn't. Near the end of the lake was a bush whose odd dead-seeming branches could be easily snapped into cigarette-size twigs. It had a mottled browny-white fluted bark, papery thin, and a kind of sponge stuff inside. They lit up and did their best to smoke. There was a burning sensation, not much flavour, though the main thing was holding the lighted twigs and feeling sophisticated and a few years older.

Two big men in trilbies and long raincoats appeared as if from nowhere. The boys fumbled to abandon their cigarettes. Neither man appeared to care.

'Are you the boys who found our friend the other day?' the bulkier big man asked, and he had that sticky kind of smile you sometimes received from grown-ups who wanted you to like them, the kind of smile that meant there was probably a bag of sweets about to be whipped out to win you over.

'Yeah,' Colin said, taking charge immediately, 'but he was already dead, and we never knew he had no friends, like.'

'It's a manner of speech,' the thin one said. 'He wasn't even an acquaintance. But we're interested in the story, any trifling details, really, anything Mr Mabey didn't put in the paper, perhaps. Which one of you is Colin?'

'That's me,' Colin gloated. 'You called round ours earlier, didn't you? I told our mam to tell you we'd be down by here.'

'So you did. And we'd like to ask a few questions. Is that all right? You saw him first?'

'Yeah,' Colin said quickly, taking a step towards the men in the hope of blocking contradictions.

'You others,' Gently said, brushing his fat hand at them as though he were wafting away a bad wind, 'buzz off, all right? Come back in ten minutes.'

Foster warned Colin in a murmur: 'If they give you anything we share.' He was angry, because by rights they should have realised he was the correct choice of interviewee, but he was too proud to say so and compromised by taking the lead in racing back along the footpath as if he'd thought of something miles more exciting.

'They was round ours an' all,' Petey grumbled. 'I don't see why it's always Colin. He makes out he's the leader just coz he's big.'

'Yeah, well let him come back and find us,' Foster decided shrewdly. 'We don't have to go back to him. Let's hide.'

At first that was a fine idea, only it wasn't easy to crouch behind bushes on a hill and not get a wet backside, and although the drizzle hadn't annoyed anyone before it soon became evident that crouching motionless was a surefire way of feeling every single cold drop that slipped off a leaf. And it was quite extraordinary how prolonged the unpleasant sensation from one little drop of rain could be. Foster offset his discomfort by turning it into a sort of scientific investigation: you could weigh a drop of water, you could look at it, you could spread it on a sheet, but whatever you did you'd never know what it was capable of until you'd felt it land unexpectedly on your neck, bore into the skin immediately, then trickle right down your back and be as searing at the end of its run as it had been at the beginning. It felt like being slashed with Zorro's sword. There ought to be long scars afterwards, that you could display unflinchingly. Foster wondered if scientists took this sort of research into account. He doubted it. He was probably the first person to discover the secret properties of raindrops. All he had to do now was come up with a use for his discovery. He could probably make millions, if he could think of something.

Colin didn't come looking for his friends. They waited impatiently, hooting carefully every half minute with their special hoot that anyone else would mistake for an owl or a bear, confirming to each other that none of them had changed positions, rather hoping that someone *would* move, then listening again through the screen of odd rustles and drips in the fading hope of hearing Colin's lonesome, aggrieved, apologetic, anxious, even diffident cry.

'Oh, no! Look!' Dewi groaned at last. 'I'm soaked now – it's come right through the seat of my trousers, and now it's come through my jerkin an' all, look, on both elbows, and down the back of my blummin' shirt – I'm soaked!'

'You been lying down?' Petey mocked, because he'd succeeded in remaining dry nearly all over. His socks were sopping, but Dewi's dismay let him feel like a natural born backwoodsman.

Hiding was abandoned. They stretched and stood about on the path, examining Dewi's elbows and trying not to laugh too unkindly when he admitted that he had been lying down, on his back. That was, he insisted, a method he'd read about in the Boys' Own Paper, or somewhere – you didn't always have to crouch, and in fact, if you were going to be concealed for a long time you'd cramp up if you crouched, whereas lying down, as long as you could see and not be seen, was a lot more sensible. He did have a point. But he was still sopping wet.

'Where's Col got to? You reckon he's gone off home?'

'He would, wouldn't he? If they gave him some dosh. I bet that's what he's done.'

'I saw it was a body before he did,' Foster asserted pugnaciously.

'That's true,' Petey agreed. 'You want to bash him one.'

'I will, one of these days. He'll push me too far.'

'He's big, though, isn't he?' Dewi reminded them sorrowfully.

In the flicks that didn't matter. The hero was usually big as well, but at times you'd get a baddy who was a monster, and the hero would still bash him in. In the flicks you only had to be right and then you were bound to win. It seemed reasonable, and proper. Foster's reluctance to fight Colin wasn't at all heroic, and he knew it. He was ashamed, more or less convinced he'd been born to be a hero but part of his character had been fumbled, and instead of total confidence he had to live with this tragic flaw, which was not exactly cowardice – more, he thought, an enervating sense that ultimately it simply wasn't worth it. He didn't really want to fight anybody.

Despondently the boys trudged down the footpath once more, no longer expecting to find Colin, but needing to confirm that he wasn't there so they could go home seething with justified anger.

He was sitting almost exactly where they'd last seen him, near the fag bush, huddled up on his side like a baby. Even Colin wouldn't have been daft enough to go to sleep on squelchy leaves, the others knew that, so they drew up to him warily, as if they thought he might go off like an unexploded bomb. The quiet whimpering, that made Foster shiver and glance at Dewi and Petey to see how startled they were, was way outside Colin's usual range of noises. This was worse than finding a dead body on the rocks. Colin might have been any one of them. Foster's tummy felt gurgly, just as it had once when he was vigorously jabbing a garden fork into the hard earth border, a little hand fork, jabbing it in under the leaves to break up the soil because his dad had promised him a shilling if he did it well, jabbing away enthusiastically, thinking of the shilling and at the same time pretending he was engaged in a swordfight – all thrust, no parry – when suddenly he brought the fork back out from under the leaves and he had a frog impaled on it, two prongs just above its hind legs and going right through its lower body and out the other side, the frog squirming slowly, turning its grotesque, nearly human somehow, head, and staring straight into Foster's eyes, as if *he* could help! He shivered all over, reluctant to get any nearer to Colin, who was simply too big to be curled up crying like a baby, and he remembered his horror, his sheer panic, his inability to do the obvious thing and hold the frog under his shoe while he withdrew the fork. He couldn't even bring himself to look at it a second time, but jabbed it into the earth, ran for a big spade, then plunged the spade over and over as near the fork handle as possible, until he had enough broken soil to load on the shovel and chuck behind the plants. It took a while to even out the border afterwards, and he left the fork for someone else to find. It shamed him. The frog's pitiful expression would, he feared, stay with him all his life. Even the shilling didn't compensate for what he'd done. It was like getting the twenty pieces of silver. He was Judas, though he loved wild nature. Foster trembled, and reached to touch Colin's shoulder.

'Hey,' he said affectionately, 'what's a matter, Col?'

Colin shrank away, failed to disappear entirely, and exploded in tears and snot. He was shaking so hard he couldn't complete a full word at first. Foster tried to help him to his feet but he kept squeezing his legs together.

'Was it those blokes?' Foster asked, sounding tough, ready to sort them out, as long as they were definitely well away.

Dewi and Petey stood tighter together, miserably unable to race for the safety of home just yet.

'He smacked us round the head,' Colin eventually admitted. 'Then the thin one, he showed us this knife, and then he....'

But no one had cut him. Through heaving breaths Colin recreated his ordeal, and if he'd been laughing it wouldn't have sounded nearly as sinister and scary. But he wasn't showing off, either, wasn't ever going to brag about this. Gently had held his arms and told him if he didn't remember what he'd done with that briefcase he'd be sorry. Colin had insisted, obviously, that he was sorry but he didn't know what they wanted. Gently had grinned at George and said they'd better make sure he wasn't lying, and then George had held the knife right in front of his face, before lowering it slowly towards his groin and proceeding to slice his fly buttons off. Colin had wet himself and they'd laughed at him.

The boys listened, spellbound, all their animosity to Colin gone. This was real, and disturbing in a way that the much more exciting adventures in the pictures had never touched. It was nearly a sort of joke, an embarrassing incident you could snigger about, but none of them felt a bit like sniggering. None believed Colin had deserved such a nightmarish come-uppance. It could as easily have happened to Foster, Petey or Dewi, and they shared their friend's humiliation and gliding terror – they'd all seen how tall the two men were, all heard them speak like typical grown-ups. Not men to kick in the shins and evade with merry laughter. Not at all. It seemed possible they'd even lied, which grown-ups weren't meant to do, and weren't really reporters. Mr Maybe was a reporter, in his silly Biggles costume, and he was soft and wouldn't ever cut anybody's flies off. In fact they had no experience whatever of adults behaving so viciously – a clip round the ear, or a belting, but that was always from your dad, and never without a good reason that you understood already. And Foster didn't even have that example, because his dad was the Big Eli Wakefield-backwoods-man-hero-type, who only fought to right wrongs, like when people had tricked him out of his Texas savings.

'We ought to find our dads,' Foster blurted out, gulping as he realised that that was precisely what he could not now do, because he'd watched his father leave at dawn. 'Or go round PC Ryman's, coz I bet it's against the law. I bet he'll go and arrest them for this, coz it's not right.'

Colin's eyes opened wet and wide and imploring. He begged Foster to forget it. The men had leered and promised they'd be back in the dead of night if he told anybody. He tugged out his potato-gun, jammed the end into one of his spuds, withdrew it loaded and fired into the earth. Petey drew his brother's sheath-knife and adopted a defensive stance, ready to take on all foes. Dewi, thoughtfully, picked around in the leaves until he'd collected all Colin's missing buttons.

None of them was willing to panic openly and make a break for the safety of the St. Lawrence estate, but the road between made each of them feel awfully vulnerable and all breathed a little better when the green was in sight, and all the houses in a crescent around the green, and there was no sign of two men who claimed to be reporters but looked like gangsters and behaved like rotten big bullies.

'We won't have no more trouble from them now,' Foster claimed sensibly. 'They wouldn't dare come near our houses coz our dads might be home and they'd give 'em what for. And besides, anyway, we don't know whatever it is they want us to know. And they know that now. So it stands to reason.'

'I bet they're cowards,' Petey said, his sense of fair play coming from the same Saturday morning curriculum as Foster's. 'Men who picks on kids got to be cowards, isn't it?'

'That's true,' the others concurred hopefully.

Closing the back door and passing your mam in the kitchen had never been such a massive relief before. Safe from harm. Home!

FIFTEEN

Leaving home before daylight John Eakins had felt dishonest and cheap in spirit because his wife, having no option, had made up her mind to trust him. Few things could check a man's eagerness as rapidly as being given permission to go wrong. Rachel's frosted trust made it like being married to Deborah Kerr in The King and I – instructive but a bit crippling. The ease with which she could get inside his mind and show him how inferior he was had long ceased to amaze, but he wondered if she understood how much this intimacy ironed out his love. Snooping, it was. Bad as going through a man's wallet, forever fretting at his conscience, forcing him to brood and go irresolute when what he needed was a bit of uncomplicated affection. She made him feel like he was running for cover, ashamed of what he'd done, and that wasn't the way John Eakins wanted to see himself, or be seen by others. Bloody Rachel, he'd thought right through the morning, has to be so naggingly *right* all the time! A good woman, his beloved, but inflexible – a man had a right to be wrong once in a while, a need, even, and Rachel never allowed for that. It was chapel made her tight. It was the sea made him easy. And as far as John Eakins went, the sea was a better moral arbiter than chapel, any day of the week. Errors were inevitable when the sea changed so rapidly. A man had to have a bit of leeway, now and again, else he'd seize up and be about as much use as a tory in the valleys, all his values haywire, every breath he took coming from elsewhere. A man had to have a touch of the outlaw in his sinews, and Rachel really knew that, deep down, knew she was going against what was basically good in him when she tried to steer him too close to shore.

All these fragments of guilty indignation had been aired throughout the morning, without clarifying anything. By the docks he'd cadged a lift in one of Fisk's lorries – the driver was a friend. There were stops then in Camarthen, Neath and Merthyr, so it had been a long and dreary haul, and although he found plenty to moan about, fairly unspecifically, he hadn't been able to convince himself he'd travelled any distance. Quite the opposite. To John Eakins it began to seem as if wherever he went it would be raining and Rachel would be suffering nobly, and the only end in sight would come with ignominious arrest, public humiliation and the predictable, inevitable loss of all his bright good luck and decent life. Yet he didn't consider slinking back home, or dumping the money. It seemed to him he had no choice but to play it through, even if there'd been no deliberation in the first place.

Eventually he boarded a train at Cardiff, heaved his long white duffle on to the string rack and sat opposite so he could keep an eye on it. He was hoping for a compartment alone, but for some reason there were always people with nothing better to do than travel to London, and he found himself sharing with a young mother and child, an elderly man and a youth. None of them appealed to him in the slightest, yet the old man obviously wanted to strike up a conversation. All John could think of was the unnaturalness of mixing with total strangers, who hadn't a clue what it was like to have a bad hand keeping you from the sea.

When they went into the tunnel under the Severn he felt miserable, isolated, hounded and ready to snarl. When they emerged his temper improved at once. England! Right across Wales rain had dropped incessantly. In England the sky was blue. But it wasn't only the brightening afternoon – he dreaded tunnels that went under the sea, had a not unreasonable horror of all that weight of water crushing him, an upside-down nightmare. He was a sailor who couldn't swim. He trusted boats. He reached for the leather strap on the door and unhooked it to lower the window by a couple of notches. The air had a nice acrid smell to it, but they were far enough from the engine not to be troubled by smuts. He lit a cigarette and settled back and stared at the metal-framed poster inviting him to take a holiday in the Isle of Wight. He was out of Wales, well on the way to London now, and felt the big space at last. The money was still in its sealed packets inside the briefcase, at the bottom of his duffle. Having got it this far, he thought, he'd saved everyone at home from potential disruption. It was like being a bomb disposal expert, removing the danger from your loved ones. He felt good.

'If you don't mind, old chap,' the elderly man said, 'your smoke's going in my eyes.'

John Eakins sized him up, but the old boy wasn't a troublemaker. His eyes were watering.

'I didn't think. Sorry.' He flicked his Woodbine out and leaned slightly towards the woman, indicating the window. 'I should've asked,' he said apologetically. 'Shall I shut it?'

'Oh,' she exclaimed, either stunned to be spoken to at all or confused by the complexity of the question. 'No, please, not on my account. It's refreshing.'

The old man coughed: 'Actually, perhaps it wasn't your cigarette so much as the smoke from the engine.'

'You want it closed?' John asked him coldly.

'If the young lady doesn't mind.'

She shook her head and reddened visibly.

'How about you?' John asked the young man, who was pretending to ignore this petty chat and read a book entitled *Declaration*. He looked up reluctantly.

'It's immaterial to me.'

Officer type, John Eakins deduced dismissively, remembering one or two of the twerps he'd taken orders from long ago. He looked at the tear-stained face of the old man and nearly relented. Then he wondered why he should defer, just because of seniority.

'I wanted it open, they don't mind and you want it shut,' he said. 'I been travelling since dark this morning, cooped up most of the time. I like a bit of air.'

'Obviously I can't force you,' the old man said pathetically. 'If you insist I shall have to move to another compartment.'

Again John Eakins nearly relented. It wasn't an important issue. The child whispered to her mother, then glanced back at John, who looked at the woman.

'My daughter would like it open,' she said.

'If it comes to that, so would I,' said the student.

John was surprised, and felt sorry that the old gentleman had been outnumbered.

'You want me to go along and see if there's a seat for you?' he asked.

The old man mopped his eyes with a handkerchief, shaking his head, defeated but determined to stay and make the others suffer his presence. After a few minutes John Eakins lit another Woodbine, then he moved and sat next to the woman.

'I think there are some No Smoking compartments further back,' he said pointedly.

'There are,' she agreed, accepting a cigarette from his packet.

It was childish, he realised, but undeniably delightful, this deliberate refusal to give in to the old boy. If anyone else had done it John would have taken the old boy's side. He couldn't, now. He and the young woman had colluded. That too was curious. Out of nothing they had quickly established the kind of rapport which might easily have led to something further.

'I've got a boy myself,' he found himself assuring her, though he hadn't intended to speak to anyone about his background. 'Maybe we should stand in the corridor to smoke these.'

The woman smiled and stood up with him. Her daughter followed them out and then ran up and down the narrow corridor, peering brazenly into all the other compartments, but not being a nuisance to her mother.

It was a long time since John Eakins had been anywhere inland without Rachel. He enjoyed chatting to a not unattractive young woman whose little smiles and mannerisms were so new. She was rather ordinary, he supposed, looked at objectively, and in most situations he wouldn't have noticed her. But close to, whenever she said something or responded, he got a kick out of it. He was flirting, and so was she, and it was harmless, just mildly beneficial – flattering, anyway, to be liked on sight by someone a good decade younger.

She and her daughter lived in the basement flat of her parents' house in Whitechapel. Her husband – there was an evasion – her husband wasn't really around any more. She was returning from a visit to her brother, who lived outside Cardiff – Llantrisant. Looking after the girl meant she didn't get out much, or have many friends. He listened and sympathised. She was such a nice young woman. It was a terrible shame when anyone became trapped in a role that allowed no freedom. Some of the best years of her life were being wasted in a basement flat. She was doing the right thing, devoting herself to her child, but there'd be no reward. She wasn't complaining, it was John, reading between the lines, feeling that as a man he ought to be able to help a decent woman like her. If he hadn't been happily married, of course... He frowned. He *was* happily married, and this was the first time he'd found himself in a strange woman's company, and already he was halfway to believing she could have been his wife as easily as Rachel. Did he have a deeper capacity for love than he'd suspected? Was he just letting himself be sentimental because he was on a sort of holiday? He didn't even have the girl's name yet. He knew nothing whatever about her. But he'd been attracted to Rachel without knowing anything, and they'd been married long enough now to know they were meant for each other. Maybe that only meant they'd been happy to adapt, and with another woman the same commitment could be made, the same years could pass contentedly, only the relationship would be subtly different. It was an odd thing to consider, especially considering how little he and Rachel actually had in common. Rachel was good with bills, tax returns, aspects of life that gave John a headache; she attended chapel regularly, by choice – he avoided it like plague; she liked going to the pictures... How was it possible they'd stayed together so amicably? He loved her in all sorts of ways, liked the way she dressed, the sound of her about the house, liked catching glimpses of her when his mind had been elsewhere. Even so, he supposed he took her for granted. And didn't know a great deal of what she thought. Except that she trusted

71

him as completely as he trusted her, until now with good reason.

He'd been telling the young woman that he was convalescing, and visiting an old friend he hadn't seen since just after the war. He'd been telling her he wasn't sure about his lodgings – he intended returning to the digs he used to have, which might not be available.

'Well,' she said, without coyness, merely being sensible, as one friend to another, 'if there's any difficulty you could kip on my couch. I think I can trust you. Shall I give you my address?'

He wondered why he wasn't flabbergasted. They'd been talking less than an hour, yet the offer was genuine and natural.

'That's very decent of you,' he said. 'I'm not sure it would be right, though. I mean, I don't know what my wife would say. I mean, I do. That's the point.'

'I could take offence.'

'Oh, no, please don't – I know there's nothing for Rachel to object to, it isn't that...'

'In London, don't you remember? People are a bit less hidebound about some things. Where I am, anyway, I don't think anyone takes any notice of who comes and goes.'

'Well, I appreciate the offer, but to be honest I'm looking forward to my old digs – nostalgia, you know.'

He'd hurt her feelings, though she pretended not to care. He hadn't meant to snub her, hadn't meant anything. Perhaps he shouldn't have allowed himself to get into a conversation in the first place. But what did that mean? Could he never risk talking to women, just in case a friendship threatened to come out of it?

'After I've seen about my digs, maybe I could pop over, for a coffee, or a cup of tea?'

'It isn't necessary. I wouldn't want you to think I'm begging for company.'

'No, I don't think that at all. I'm the one who's going to be a bit of a stranger in town.'

She brightened up: 'Well, I'll copy my address, but I won't mind if you don't make it.'

That's queer, John thought breezily when he left her at the station: I've made a date with a woman who knows I'm married. I need my head examined. But he wasn't taking a critical tone with himself. He was pleased as punch. An old married man, still able to wow the girls! He threw the duffle over his shoulder and walked with a swagger. What a tonic! And maybe she'd been pretty. Already her face was lost. All he had in his mind was how warm and alert he'd felt while talking with her. He took out her address just to see her handwriting. Her name was Bobbie, and that made him grin because it didn't sound like a proper girl's name, unless she was a Yank, chewing gum and listening to those loud songs Foster pretended to like so much. He went into the pub on the station and ordered a pint of bitter.

'Sailor, are you?' a man said, nodding at his long duffle bag, placing a hand on his shoulder.

'Aye, home from the sea,' John smiled.

'Looking for a good time?' He squeezed John's shoulder. 'I'll take you places where the girls are out of this world, Taffy. You're in luck tonight.'

John Eakins took several seconds to stare directly into the man's eyes.

'If your hand's still touching me when I get to the end of this sentence,' John said in a steady, rather definite voice, 'I'll make it look like this one I got here.' He showed the man his right hand. The man slipped away down the bar to bother someone else.

'I don't like being called Taffy,' John explained to the bartender.

'Fair enough,' said the bartender. 'How about Taff?'

John laughed and bought him a beer. What the hell, he thought, it's London and I'm carrying about forty thousand quid around: I'm a free man!

Sixteen

Despite a joke with Colin's buttons George and Gently were disappointed. They were going to have to report back to London that the money had been washed out of Mr Wary's grasp and lost in some twenty miles of navigable water. That was precisely what they had intended to report anyway, but they'd hoped to be lying.

'I still can't believe it,' Gently grumbled. 'Acts of God don't normally extend to a nice lump sum like that.'

'It's not meant to be our problem,' George reminded him. 'Business won't suffer, and that's all we were checking. Nobody's tooling up for a crimewave. This town's just lying back with its legs open, and it doesn't even know.'

'Yeah,' Gently smirked.

They'd just visited the last of their contacts, an estate agent with several small companies and undeclared interests. He'd met with Mr Wary. He thought there was nothing suspicious about the death. Wary had wanted to get a close look at the Haven – it still hadn't been decided which side to base the oil refineries, and there was talk about new bridges, access roads and so forth. As for the money, Mr Wary refused to let the briefcase out of his sight, and wouldn't trust his hotel's safe. He kept it handcuffed to his wrist, which was comical because the handle on the briefcase was faulty. So he collapsed on the rocks and the briefcase broke free and went out on the tide. Sad, but final. Mr Wary had been discreet about his business. He'd only spoken to men he'd been empowered to contact, so nothing had changed.

George and Gently had sauntered the length of the main shopping street on a Saturday afternoon. George had counted a total of eleven cars, and not many more shoppers. Oxford Street it wasn't. If all went well, in a few years there'd be casinos, limousines, prostitutes and all the rackets that made life worthwhile. He wiped his eyebrows and peered across the Haven. The sun was shining on the fields on the other side. He couldn't envisage the transformation, but that wasn't his business.

'That estate,' Gently growled. 'Why do people live in houses all the same like that? Grass everywhere. No privacy. No action. What a shower of shites, eh!'

'Yeah, well, we've done what we could. Shame about your hunch – I wanted to believe it, too.'

'Sorry I wasted your time, George. You're right, we should've let this be done by a couple of the boys.'

They turned the corner and were in the road where they'd parked a few hours before. The car was where they'd left it, but it had been joined by two others, both beyond it, both with men inside.

George didn't say anything to Gently. Gently didn't have to say anything to George. They approached their car unconcerned, Gently handing George the keys, George unlocking the boot and rummaging for something wrapped in a grey blanket.

A car door slammed behind him. George handed the keys back to Gently, who was facing one of the men who'd been awaiting their return. This man was known locally as Small Derrick Jones, in non-ironic reference to his want of inches. He bore a thin moustache that looked as if it had been applied with an eyebrow pencil, and for a skinny short man he had plenty of swagger. He expected his Italian suit and shoes, and the camel-hair coat draped across his shoulders to make the world step back in admiration.

'You boys been sniffing around our town,' he said, stopping far enough away that he wouldn't need to crane his neck too obviously. 'I'm here to tell you we don't need no cheap hoods from London peeing on our patch of grass.'

'Your friends afraid of getting splashed?' George sneered.

'Just there to show you – we don't have to get rough on your first visit, so long as it's your last.'

'You're warning us off!' Gently exclaimed, in mock-surprise. He was pleased.

'It's a small town,' Small Derrick admitted. 'We also control a few other places.'

'Haverfordwest?' Gently guessed.

Small Derrick Jones nodded shiftily, reluctant to give away anything important regarding his sphere of operations, but proud to imagine his network had been remarked in London.

'We wondered when you'd show up,' he boasted, 'after what happened to that pal of yours.'

George moved a step closer: 'What did happen, exactly? You meet him?'

'Nobody stays in Milford without us knowing his business.'

'You saying you had dealings with him?'

'Now I'm not saying we did and I'm not saying we didn't.'

'You're not saying what I want to hear,' George said, 'and that's a pity, because you look like a boy who likes keeping his clothes clean.'

Small Derrick grasped the threat quite soon, and his confidence suffered a hiccup. He glanced over his shoulder to be certain his supporters were ready to leap in punching and kicking.

'You're not here to question me,' he remembered. 'We're here to see you off. Sort of welcoming committee in reverse.' He snickered at his wit. 'You best go while the going's good.'

'George,' Gently asked his partner wearily, 'will you, or shall I?'

George flipped aside his gaberdine and revealed what he'd removed from the back of the car. It was a lovingly cared-for American tommy-gun. He only used the stock on Small Derrick, hacking it down where the man's shoulder met his neck. Then he pointed it towards the cars and enjoyed the spectacle of trapped men not knowing where to protect themselves.

'The money,' Gently said flatly.

'Did he have money on him?' Small Derrick whined. 'He just said he was thinking of buying up some property. Dunno what happened after that. All I heard was he died, dropped dead. Ticker give out, or something.'

'We talked to the kid who found Mr Wary,' Gently explained, bending so Small Derrick, on his knees in the road, wouldn't miss a word. 'That was all there was – Mr Wary's body.'

'I know. I know. One of my contacts was there when they was searching the rocks, so they must've thought there was something to look for.'

'Now I'm not happy,' Gently said, pressing a finger into the spot where George had hit Small Derrick.

The pain gave Small Derrick inspiration: 'My brother told me John Eakins was the first on the scene.'

'Eakins!' George snapped. 'His kid was one of the boys.'

'John Eakins,' Gently said. 'And who's he when he's at home?'

'Nobody. A trawlerman. Thinks he's hard.' Small Derrick rubbed his neck and wobbled to his feet, hoping to show there were no hard feelings in the criminal fraternity, and maybe they should band together and deal with trawlermen who waded in and stopped fights and were tough enough to laugh at him and his gang. 'I wouldn't be surprised if he found something. Sly bugger, he is.'

'Thank you,' George said. 'One more thing. I'm reluctant to put holes in your cars right now, and maybe it isn't absolutely necessary to hurt you either, but the fact is, we thought we'd done and now we'll have to conclude some more business before we leave, so what were you saying about seeing us off? Sounded to me like you might want to stand in the way of progress.'

'No, no,' Small Derrick said. He was thinking fast but couldn't come up with a revised and less reckless threat. Gently grabbed and frog-marched him to the first car. The men inside wanted to be mistaken for strangers to the area, especially when Gently smashed Small Derrick's head into a headlight. He allowed Small Derrick to collapse the short drop to the front wheel, then George strode up calmly and used his knife to slash Small Derrick's leg.

Gently wrenched open a door and leaned in.

'We mean business, boys,' he smiled. 'Is that going to be a problem?'

He was smiling because he liked few things better than the sight of men who'd considered themselves to be tough wilting like daffodils. He was also smiling because he'd remembered calling at the house of Foster Eakins before lunch, and speaking to Mrs Eakins. He thought he would enjoy calling on her again, making her watch what he could do to her old man. He was smiling because the money was afloat once more. It was his destiny to possess it.

'Things are looking up,' George said.

'Well, when I get a hunch take me serious.'

'When I see the money I'll take you any way you want, mate.'

'Pervert,' Gently sneered humorously.

'In your dreams,' George sneered back.

'Nightmares, more like,' Gently scoffed.

They had a good working relationship. That was as far as it went. They just did what they did. They waved at the departing cars, then George put his tommy-gun back in its blanket.

'John Eakins,' Gently murmured. 'Sounds like a thieving bastard to me.'

SEVENTEEN

Late afternoon Rachel washed her hair and clipped in the curlers, though she didn't expect to be going anywhere. It was a Saturday thing to do. When he was home John never took her dancing, but the walk up to the Astoria, then coming out after the film and finding him waiting, the three of them eating faggots and chips on the walk home, had a sort of reined-in romantic feel. She didn't fancy the pictures as much without the prospect of her husband as escort, and that wasn't to do with the safety of the streets. You make your moments where you can, she mused, studying her tightly-rolled and currently unflattering hair in the mirror. Foster would be disappointed, but he'd find something to occupy him. All day she'd been hoping John would reappear, having thought it over and realised he couldn't stay away when there was no sufficient reason. But he was a stubborn man, rarely completely selfish, but very determined when he wanted to be. And, objectively, he had a point: no reason why he *shouldn't* visit that old friend. Rachel wondered for a second why Foster had kept to his room all afternoon, not a sound from him. She pulled out a couple of curlers and looked for somewhere snazzier to attach them. You're not going to feel any better when it's done, she realised. Styling only worked if there was somewhere to go, and someone to go with.

She shouted to Foster, asking if he wanted to run round the local chip shop for their dinner – usually he did, because she'd let him keep the few pence change – but in a forlorn voice he called back that he wasn't hungry, wasn't sure he felt like eating. Rachel wondered what was wrong this time. Probably another fight with one of his pals – Colin, the oafish one. Foster was always on the brink of World War Three with him.

Obliged to come up with a meal when she was reluctant to cook anything Rachel peeled a few potatoes, put them through the slicer and heated oil – chips, like it or not. A couple of fish in the frying pan, without batter.

Foster said batter was the only good thing about fish. Serve him right for being so finicky. She boiled peas and a few runner beans. Called him down. He ate without complaint, without interest. Could have been a plate of cabbage. Rachel wasn't the first to hear if a new bug was making the rounds. Beverley Walker always knew, even before any children had fallen sick, it seemed, but because Foster was so healthy Rachel remained ignorant. He didn't look off-colour, but he was down in the dumps about something. She didn't want a sullen son for company.

'Chips all right?' she asked.

'Aye, fine.'

'Fish?'

'All right, aye.'

'You haven't finished your greens.'

'Full up, Mam.'

'Eat them.'

He had another go, his mother mildly disturbed at the feebleness of his protest. She didn't want to make him sick.

'You haven't got to finish if you're poorly. Are you poorly?'

'I'm all right.'

'What is it, then? Annoyed with me?'

'Nothing, Mam.'

'There's nothing good showing this week. It's an old one, *Blood Alley*, and I didn't go first time round because it sounds nasty.'

'I don't fancy the pictures tonight.' He'd been looking forward to *Blood Alley*. It had John Wayne in and sounded brilliant, especially if it was in colour.

'Still annoyed by that serial this morning, is it?'

Foster had put Black Hawk out of his mind. He shook his head. Rachel thought, It's hard going with John away. The boy wouldn't risk these sulks when his father was near.

'Rather play out again, is it?'

'Don't think I will, Mam, not tonight.'

Rachel wondered if she was a bad mother. Once you got them to the stage where they played outside they didn't need much mothering, not in the sense of showing affection. They cringed. They needed everything doing for them, of course, but then so did their fathers. Boys and men were the same, hopeless about the house. At one time she'd taught her son to iron shirts and darn socks, and he'd been eager to show off his skills for a while, but it was a phase and it passed. She wondered if she should get closer to him, establish more of a bond, but he was at an awkward age, not young enough to be uncritical, not old enough to be a pal. She felt sorry for the boy, with his dad away so much of the time. If he went up to his room he'd remain there all night. They had a television set in the lounge, and Rachel was happy enough to watch it for an hour, but Foster found it tedious. Rachel enjoyed variety shows – dancing, magic tricks – but she was alone in that. Her husband and son regarded it as her television set, no doubt of that, as if it were a kind of offering to propitiate her.

'I was wondering,' she said, having only just thought of it, 'if you haven't got anything particular planned, whether you'd like to help me with a spot of decorating?'

'What decorating?' Foster asked suspiciously. He hated having chores forced on him. Grown ups were all the same, thought they could cut right through anything you were doing and force you into something entirely different, like your own life meant nothing. Then they'd make out it was for your own good and get cross if you shuffled your feet. You only lived to be made use of, far as they were concerned. They never came and asked politely if they could help *you*; it was strictly a one-way deal. You couldn't interrupt *them* and tell *them* to do something different, because it was rude. All in all, though, he didn't have any specific objections to decorating. But it annoyed him that his mother hadn't somehow guessed what had happened to Colin. Unreasonably, Foster still expected parents to know what was going on. Two cruel men were out there somewhere, and only he and his friends were coping with the fear. That wasn't right.

Rachel reminded him that his dad had started stripping wallpaper in the front room. Foster had grown accustomed to the torn patches. They had new rolls of paper all ready. Wouldn't it make a nice surprise for his dad to come home and find the job done? They could easily do it between them, and if Foster was only going to sit up in his room dreaming of Belinda Lee and Brigitte Bardot he might as well make himself useful for once.

She didn't have to make a song and dance about it. He'd decided to help before the sarcasm. How'd she know I love Brigitte Bardot? he wondered. He only had one photo of her, and kept it in his satchel. He hadn't told anyone about her, because she was supposed to be French and naughty. He'd seen her in *Helen of Troy* and *Doctor at Sea*, but hadn't taken a great deal of notice. He'd only fallen in love since getting her photo. Foster's notion of love was touchingly chaste. He imagined meeting her and walking around town, telling her about films and rock 'n' roll, becoming best friends, possibly even kissing her briefly on the lips, as people did in films. Mainly he liked her grin, and he knew she'd get on well with him. He'd keep their love separate from school and from his other friends. Brigitte existed in a realm he only thought about occasionally, when he felt misunderstood and alone. His mother's casual amusement at his expense heated him up. She spoilt everything nice and quiet, everything private and lovely. Like after *The Kentuckian*, when she told him big Eli Wakefield was better with his hair cut. It was incredible how wrong her perceptions could be, and perplexing how powerful a shadow they cast over his dreams.

'I'll find some old shirts we can wear,' Rachel said brightly. 'You can put the plates to soak, if you will. Oh, and go out to the shed and see if your father left the bucket and the paste-brush in there. I couldn't find them under the sink.'

'Where's the torch?'

'Oh, Foster,' she chided him, 'use your loaf, boy! In the drawer next to the pantry, where do you think?'

He disliked being spoken to like that. Why should she assume he'd know where the stupid torch was kept? Besides, the point was not whether or not he knew where the torch was kept. The point was he'd asked for it as if nothing else was the matter. Those men could be anywhere, in the garden, even in the shed, and Foster hadn't let on he was scared. He'd just asked her where the torch was – if that had been in a film everyone would have been on his side, thrilled by his quiet courage, touched by the loyal heroism of his determination to confront the night without terrifying his mother. She didn't even sense that he was protecting her. Mothers were a disappointing lot.

Sighing heavily at the injustices and dull realities of life he rummaged for the torch and ventured outside. It had stopped raining and the soil smelled strong enough to make him wish he'd gone to the woods to play. He shone the yellow beam all around his father's shed, and found it rather eerie. No brush, no bucket. But she'd either send him again or, worse, traipse out herself and find the things straight away. So he ignored the shiver down his back and searched more thoroughly, eventually moving the lawn-mower and checking the corner.

The wallet was clammy. The skin over his shoulder blades went icy seconds before he realised consciously that this was not his father's wallet. Gingerly, Foster opened it on the rough wooden work-surface, setting the torch down close beside it. He could see there was money inside, and right away he guessed this was what those two men had come after. Presumably his father had borrowed it from the dead body – not stolen it, he wouldn't have done that – he must have removed it for safe-keeping. Something like that. Foster was confused and worried, remembering his father's sternness when he'd confessed to trying to steal: 'Don't'.

Then he wondered if other things were hidden in the shed and he quickened with an odd resentful kind of glee. Colin's uncle had a pile of nudie books he kept in an old coal scuttle inside his coal bunker. Petey's dad wore a surgical corset no one was supposed to know about. Dewi's mam and dad did rude business every Friday night with Glenn Miller records on. Adults couldn't be relied on just to be parents and heroes, but Foster still needed to think his were exceptions. Nevertheless, he scouted around, and was relieved to find nothing more furtive than three old torches and two old copies of *Picture Post*, with wartime photos.

It was hard to think what to do about the wallet, but if his dad had gone off without handing it to constable Ryman it was hardly up to Foster. He started fingering the notes, then feared ripping them and decided to replace the whole thing. Then he went outside and found the bucket and paste-brush round the back of the shed.

He paused. Saturday night. A clear moon, bright stars, clouds you didn't even see at first and then saw distinctly. Milk-light was shining all down the gardens, making the concrete fence-posts stand out like bright stiff figures, glinting on washing poles and wire fences, transforming the backs into a landscape as dreamy as the flicks; it was still, poised, magical, and at any moment might become an ocean of frigates, a battleground of lances and broken tents, a snowbound forest in the rockies... Foster stepped back just inside the shed to appreciate the silent prospect and not disturb it with his presence. He realised how easily you could lull yourself into believing you were miles away from any landfall, or anyway from your house and all that distraction of having to talk and be included when you wanted to be by yourself. Foster felt, for a moment, that he had become his father, standing there undisturbed and at peace. This was why his dad liked to escape in the evenings, pretending to mend things in the shed. Foster shivered with the pleasure of being a man under the moon, responding to serene nature. I'll have a shed when I'm married, he decided, so I can come here to smoke and look at the clouds around the moon before I go in and say goodnight to Brigitte or Belinda. I'll wait till they've gone to sleep, then go in.

Foster stepped away from the shed and took a few steps towards the house before he stopped and his heart flopped like a jelly rabbit from its mould. It wasn't jelly that came into his mouth, though, but sick, and the two London men re-entered his whirling fears.

It was a movement, or something, at the corner. He couldn't quite see down between the two houses, but had the impression that he *could* see what was just out of sight around the side of his. A big, burly, man-sized intruder. The fat one – had to be. Foster tried to squint quickly, to catch a glimpse and not be caught looking, as if he might escape so long as he didn't let them see him seeing them. It wasn't far to the back door, but far enough, especially carrying a bucket and paste-brush. Further than from the corner to the door.

The corner, and beyond it a moon-shaded part of the side of Petey's house, looked deceptively normal and still, and Foster could almost have changed his mind, because he couldn't actually detect anything specifically wrong. And then he could. A darker area of darkness – nothing more precise than that, and it wasn't even projected on the wall, just seemed to emerge there when he didn't glance directly that way. A darkness just off the edge of his house, not on Petey's, and there, suddenly, the tiny confirmation – a slide of darkness taking away the pale hairline glint along the top wire of the fence.

'John?' a deep voice called, whispering somehow, urgent and low.

Foster was startled and lost all power of volition. The darkness went away and a giant stepped out.

'Is it you, John?' Not frightening, the voice. Even so.

The boy's will was commanding him to run, but nothing happened and a moment later he recognised the giant as Fred Knight, not the London terror. He began trembling and wanted not to, because Fred was a friend of his dad's and wouldn't hurt him. Fred saw the boy and stopped, uncertain himself.

'Can I have a word with your dad?'

'He...' Foster stopped, reckoning it was unwise to tell anybody his father wasn't close by, just in case.

Fred Knight seemed to be swaying slightly, as if there were a breeze. Foster could smell the ale, a warm and manly smell, nice in moonlight.

'I'll go in and ask,' Foster added nervously.

Fred Knight nodded. He'd been drinking but he wasn't drunk. More importantly, a few pints never affected his power if it came to a roughhouse, and that was why he'd come to see John Eakins, to lend a hand. Fred had watched Small Derrick Jones get beaten up, and heard one of the Londoners threatening to go after John. He knew professionals when he saw them, and those two would outclass his friend. John Eakins was quick on his feet, one of the best natural southpaws Fred had come across outside the ring, but he wasn't a killer.

Rachel Eakins pulled the door in far enough to fit her head into the gap. She looked impatient, hostile. Fred Knight wanted to look at his feet. Women confused him, Rachel Eakins more than most. A smart woman, a tidy little woman, a bit of a lady.

'John can't come down,' she told him coldly. 'I'll take him a message.'

'Be better if I could see him a minute,' Fred grumbled.

'I'm sorry.' Final.

Fred sighed. She blames me for his bad hand, he reminded himself. She hates me. If John's poorly I'll keep watch all night.

'Is he sick, then?' he asked, needing a strategy. If John was too ill to pile in it would make a difference: Fred Knight was wondering who else he could call on. No one from Small Derrick Jones's gang, that was for sure – Fred liked going in their cars, but he wasn't heavily involved with them and he knew they disliked honest working men like John. Bob Ryman came to mind, but if John was mixed up in something shady he wouldn't want Bob finding out. 'I got to speak to him,' he blurted out. 'Please, Mrs Eakins!'

Rachel held her ground, but Fred Knight frightened her. And he wasn't going to go away. Like Foster she knew it was prudent to pretend her husband was at home; on the other hand no one was ever taken advantage of on the estate, and the big drunken layabout was a friend of John's.

'John's away, Mr Knight,' she confided. 'We don't want everyone knowing, like, but he went off this morning and he won't be back for a few days, or a week or so.'

'He's not here?'

'That's what I'm saying. He's in London.'

'London, is it? Duw, duw, well that's a relief!'

Rachel frowned: how could it be a relief when the man had something important to tell him? Men! Idiots!

Fred relaxed. If John was in London they couldn't touch him. Maybe he'd known they were after him. That made sense. John knew what he was doing. Should have guessed he'd stay one jump ahead.

'So do you want to leave a message?' Rachel asked.

'No need now. I'll be on my way.'

'Goodnight, then.'

'Night, Mrs Eakins. Take care.'

If he'd thought she or her son were in any danger he'd have waited in the shadows. Fred Knight thought the world of John Eakins. But John was well away, so there was no point wasting an evening. Fred walked down to the top of the woods and followed the road into town. He'd been ready for a fight. He'd done his duty. Now he felt loose and good. He boxed the cool night air a couple of times. We stick together, he thought complacently, heading for the companionship of the pubs.

'He made me jump,' Foster admitted.

'He's an odd man,' Rachel agreed, then thought she'd better

defend John: 'Your father's too soft, he'll see good in everybody. Mr Knight isn't a very nice man, and he's not typical of your father's friends – they're not all as rough as that.'

'He's a drunk, isn't he?'

'You shouldn't...' She was going to say it was rude to speak so crudely, but faltered. 'Yes,' she agreed, 'he's a drunk, and a bit of a bruiser. But he's gone now so we're all right.'

She really believed it. The house was inviolable. In some parts of the country that might not be the case, but in Hakin there was nothing to fear. And even if there had been, the fact that it was John's house, and everyone knew it was John's house, ensured absolute security. She wouldn't tell John how she appreciated him, or how she really understood that when a rough customer like Fred Knight deferred it was a compliment to John.

Rachel felt it was her due. After all, John loved her. She didn't make friends the way he did. Didn't *want* friends, not really. To get too close to women like Bev next door would be lowering. They were common, and she was above them, not in a nasty way, but unavoidably, because of a finer nature. John appreciated her, and she didn't object to his going off to London without her – she wouldn't have wanted to go all that way in any case. It shouldn't have upset her. They were an ideal couple.

Rachel frowned, thought about the walls.

EIGHTEEN

Fewer people than he'd expected around Picadilly Circus, and none of them revellers; Trafalgar Square damn near deserted. It didn't matter, though. The old feeling burgeoned – untethered in a new place, ready to plunge into oblivion... John Eakins grinned comfortably, not concerned to define the feeling too closely, simply accepting its return. Somewhere around the end of the forties, start of the fifties it had gradually slipped away, that sense of imminent excitement, and he'd hardly noticed. Must have been a contented man, he thought. You let everything slip when you think you're happy. That young woman, Bobbie – she could have talked to the young officer-type, who was nearer her own age, and probably more handsome, but no, she'd warmed to John, the mature man, the dependable man, the real man. He felt great.

He took his bearings from Nelson and headed towards St. Martin's Lane, pleased how well he remembered everything, pleased how much appeared unchanged. After demob he'd found a billet with a Mrs Champion, and was hoping to find the same house again, but if there were no rooms he wasn't bothered – he'd wander down to the river and get an overnight berth on one of the barges. Everyone had been pally after the war. You could kip down anywhere. It wasn't a hostile city.

Although John couldn't remember the name of the little street or the number of the house he trusted his feet and reached Mrs Champion's and knocked. The woman herself answered, looking no older, no different, still crumply in middle age. It did surprise him when she clapped her hands and beamed, recognising him as soon as he recognised her.

'Well Mr Eakins!' she exclaimed. 'My goodness gracious me! It must be ten, twelve years. Don't tell me, let me think – first floor, room at the front, wasn't it?'

'It was. I believe it was,' he answered, the unexpected completeness of returning to the past making him glow like a pampered baby.

'Would you like the same room?'

He grinned gormlessly and nodded, holding his duffle upright before him to get down the hallway, responding rapidly to questions about what he'd been doing with himself all these years – she didn't wait for answers, but was one of those women who took everything in because she'd already thought through every option. She went ahead of him, nodding, interrupting, getting his postwar life fixed by the time she'd shown him into his old room.

'I still can't abide fish, mind,' he was saying. 'Don't like the touch or taste of them. But life on the trawlers is good. Suits me grand. I like weather.' It was prattle, not stuff he'd tell anyone else.

'And to think, all these years I've had you in my mind running that little greengrocer's you thought you were going to have, and I've often said that's not you, that's not Mr Eakins.'

'Right all along, then, Mrs Champion.'

'And that other Welshy boy, you was thick as thieves, the pair of you – Philip Thomas. Philip. Nice boy. Did he go back to Greece and start his cafe?'

For a moment John had no idea what she was on about, but it came back to him – Phil had been in Rhodes when the British handed it back to the Greeks, and a couple of times he'd day-dreamed about heading out there to live. But he hadn't been serious, so why had she retained someone else's forgotten dream?

'Maybe he did, but he's back in town now. I'm off to see him, in fact.'

While Mrs Champion talked about other lodgers he must have known but had no recollection of, John Eakins marvelled at his old room, which was exactly as he'd left it, before Foster existed, before he met Rachel. It was bewildering, the physical persistence of what should only have been a fading memory, and made him feel unreal somehow. He half-expected Mrs Champion to turn on him demanding a dozen years' back rent.

'You unpack and settle yourself in, Mr Eakins. There's a bit of boiled ham and I'll fry you some bubble and squeak if you fancy a bit of supper.'

'Aye, that'll be tidy. And a pot of tea. Big pot.'

'Always. Come down when you're ready.'

How lovely, he thought, how absolutely perfect in every way – why's it making me queasy?

The first thing he did was write home, assuring Rachel he missed her. She wouldn't receive the letter before Tuesday, but that couldn't be helped, and they had no need of a telephone. The next thing was to unpack, using the wardrobe and chest of drawers he'd used in his previous life. It was almost disappointing not to come across forgotten articles of clothing or an old abandoned packet of Woodbines – no, he suddenly recalled, Churchman's or Park Drive: hadn't taken up Woodbines until he was on the trawlers.

Last out came the broken-handled briefcase. John emptied the contents on the yellow candlewick bedspread. One packet was unsealed, the one he'd already examined, so he chose another at random, broke it open and counted. The activity was curiously exhausting, but with remote little lightning jolts of imagined joy for the future.

Enough, he surmised, to buy a house and a car and holidays abroad and not have to work for years – all we got to do is move away from the Haven. Live like lords. But the dilemma was right there: he liked the life he was already living, didn't particularly want to buy property, had no need of a car, missed going out on a trawler. Rachel was happy. Foster too. Why be forced to give it all up on account of all this unnecessary dosh?

He was impatient to meet Phil, though he ate the supper Mrs Champion set before him, drank several large cups of tea, listened to her lonely crowded prattle as if the half-lives of all the lodgers in her head meant something. Then he headed for Soho.

According to the Christmas cards Phil sent every year the club was called *Mister Blue's*. John asked the first tout he passed, and he'd never heard of it. Another said he thought it had gone out of business two or three years ago. A couple of prostitutes gave him clear directions, but the club wasn't where they sent him. He told the next guy he was looking for Phil Thomas, and after that kept asking for Phil until he got responses. Anyone who knew Phil was given a message: I'm John Eakins, an old friend from Milford Haven. I'm staying at Mrs Champion's. Four or five promised to pass the message on if they bumped into Phil.

'You should find him at *Jack Rabbit's Live Girls*,' a man with a placard told him at last. The placard adverted to Judgment Day in an urgent, hectoring tone, but the man himself was unhurried and rather diffident.

'You know Phil?'

'Know him! He got me this job. Didn't know me from Adam. One of the best, old Phil Thomas. Anybody in trouble – go see Phil.'

That cheered John no end. He gave the fellow a half crown. When he found *Jack Rabbit's Live Girls* and stated his business, though, he learnt that Phil wasn't there very often.

'Where can I find him? Where's he live?'

'That's private information. Sorry, chum. Come back tomorrow. Why not come in now and see the show? Beautiful girls, hot music, and the drinks won't put you out of pocket.'

'Not tonight, ta.'

John Eakins pushed his hands into his pockets and wondered what to do next. It was early evening, but he didn't feel like drinking in a strange pub and wasn't tempted by the striptease dancers, or the prostitutes who hailed him every few yards. The atmosphere was vibrant enough to linger in, but he'd set his sights on a reunion.

An elderly man was coming slowly towards him. A few yards away he stopped and stared at some fruit in the gutter. A couple of bananas. The old man caught John's eye and seemed to run through a battle of dignity and abandonment, ending with scorn. It was perplexing. He took his eyes off John long enough to bend and scoop up the bananas, then stared again, angrily, as if John Eakins had personally brought him down.

'They're mine!' he hissed as he passed, clutching the prize against his chest.

John was too surprised to comment. Then he thought of the way he'd bullied the old gent on the train, leaving the window open, smoking in front of him. He was ashamed. Behaviour like that was not his. What had provoked him? Ah, yes, he remembered – Bobbie.

Whitechapel was a good walk from Soho, but obviously he wasn't going to find Phil this evening, and he was loath to return to his digs and sit with Mrs Champion for several hours. The only reason for *not* visiting Bobbie was that she was a woman. John found that infuriating. Rachel could trust him, after all. He could visit a woman and chat without endangering his marriage. Nothing furtive about it, nothing wrong with it at all. Perhaps he wouldn't even tell Rachel, because it wasn't of any consequence, and it was up to him what he did. He wasn't going to do anything *wrong*, he knew that much.

NINETEEN

After making his call from one of the mahogany framed booths in the lobby, George strode through to the hotel bar and demanded a double. His expression gave little away. The speed with which he emptied the glass hinted at anger. He continued standing at the bar for another minute, cadaverous, grim mask communicating nothing, then settled something with himself and marched to the stairs.

He and Gently shared a room, but Gently was taking a bath. George lit a cigarette and waited. Gently seemed cheerful when he came back, wrapped in an enormous bath towel and rubbing his hair with a slightly smaller one.

'You walk the corridor like that?' George accused him.

Gently stopped rubbing his hair, glanced at himself, unhitched the big towel and allowed it to drop. George grunted his disgust, but Gently was unconcerned.

'So what's the word from Bull Gravett?' Gently asked.

Bull Gravett was their boss. Neither man cared for him.

'Would you believe he wasn't there to take my call?'

'The man doesn't deserve us!' Still not perturbed, Gently shifted his great bulk to the mirror and endeavoured to admire himself. The mirror was too small; he couldn't get far enough away to see much more than his belly.

'We arrange to call at a specific time,' George went on petulantly, 'and I call, and I'm told he's out. He's either at Mable's or Dixie's or little Jackie Rabbit's.'

'Makes you spit, doesn't it?' Gently sighed. He missed the clubs.

'Put some fucking clothes on, will you? I can't talk to that bloody great arse when I'm trying to think.'

'No need to get personal. Anyway, what's the problem? It suits us, doesn't it? I mean, what could we report right now?' Gently selected a pair of underpants nearly as large as his bath towel, and smiled as he pulled them on. Then he sat on his bed and caressed his clean socks. He was a man who enjoyed simple pleasures, and whenever possible bathed and changed his clothes at least twice a day. Skin like a baby's, he thought, and so much of it.

'Inconsistency is unprofessional,' George grumbled on.

'But it still suits us, doesn't it?'

'That's not the point.'

Gently shrugged. Whenever George was irritated Gently was able to relax. He finished dressing almost with reluctance.

'So, do we go and shake John Eakins till our money drops out?'

he asked affably, deliberately negligent of his partner's temper.

George attempted to wither him with a stare, but Gently was too vast.

'Let me take you through this in easy stages,' George had to say. 'This afternoon we were ready to forget about the seed-money, right? It was gone, lost, vamoosed, vanished, glugglugglug – drowned.'

'But...'

George held up a hand: 'We saw everyone we had to see, and Mr Wary's demise hasn't put a spanner in the works. That's what Bull Gravett wants to hear, and that's what we were, unfortunately for us, going to have to tell the bugger.'

'Right. But...'

'Then we picked up a name, a civilian, a fisherman, a nobody, and it's possible he's light-fingered, so, hey, we're back in business!'

'Exactly. No clouds on the horizon so far, George.'

'So then we cut up the local talent.'

'Just a laugh.'

'Gently, if we're staying another night we need good reason, and taking our loot from a fisherman doesn't qualify, does it? Because we don't want Bull Gravett to know we've recovered it. Because he'll want it for himself. The man's a spoilsport like that – what's his is his, know what I mean? And beating up a fisherman will land in the papers, and he'll hear about it.'

'You worry too much, George.'

'Remember Larry the Staples? Big Midge Davenport? They just fudged a few receipts. Look what happened to them.'

'They disappeared.'

'Larry was a personal friend of mine, and take my word for it, as tough as you are, Larry was tougher.' He shivered at some pleasurable memory. 'I like to think we're indispensable, Gently, and I'd like to go on thinking it for a long time.'

'We could squash Bull Gravett like a crisp packet.'

'If we did he'd still make us disappear. That's what I'm saying. Larry thought that way, too, but you can't trust your instincts. Your instincts tell you Bull Gravett's a lightweight with a good legal team and some friends in high places. Your instincts tell you you're a better man than he is. You could do him any time, any place, with any choice of weapons. It doesn't work like that. I was going to let him know the money could be floating, and hope for an honest cut if we retrieve it.'

Something close to an expression emerged briefly on George's face. It might have been apprehensiveness, relief or a stifled belch. Gently's mouth sagged.

'I thought we were partners. That's stitching me up, as I read it.'

'Would I explain it if that was the idea?'

'I wouldn't put it past you. You've been tetchy since we left London.'

'I don't like sharing hotel rooms. I didn't know how bad it would be, but there's just too much of you, Gently. But that's not why I was going to tell Bull Gravett. I thought it prudent, that's all. You and me sharing maybe forty grand only makes sense if we live, especially if we outlive Bull Gravett. It occurred to me that if, say, Small Derrick Jones has any friends, and if any of his friends has a telephone and happens to have Bull Gravett's number, then you and me could be disappeared before we ever get back in the smoke.'

'I like to think you and me's invincible, George.'

'Only if we don't go off course. Christ, you've done contracts, haven't you? You know how easy it is to wallop some hard bastard when he's not expecting it and he doesn't know you from a fuck in the alley?'

Gently considered his partner's words and, regretfully, concluded that George knew what he was saying. Crestfallen, he slumped into a tight chair.

'Anyway,' George added, 'I've changed my mind. If the bastard can't even stay in to take a call at an agreed time he isn't worth the coin. So here's my idea: We have dinner here, because that wasn't a bad plate they set before us last night. Then we go back to that estate, wait till the Eakins's have gone to bed, and bust in and make John Eakins cough. I call Bull Gravett in the morning and I tell him Mr Wary made a mistake somewhere along the line, and we've been sorting it as well as we can. Someone must have talked to Small Derrick Jones and his little band – that could be that smarmy estate agent. We think the operation's been jeopardised, better go on hold for the time being... Now who can Bull Gravett trust to send? Who can say we're right or wrong? Another straight legal blimp like Mr Wary? Hardly.'

'We scupper a deal involving millions because Bull Gravett didn't take your call?' Gently began looking happy again.

'Call it professional pride,' George said modestly. Being with Gently so much of the time made him feel like an intellectual.

TWENTY

Rachel had tried on some ancient trousers of John's, but even after she'd succeeded in securing the waist with the cord from his dressing gown she couldn't get the bottoms to stay rolled. In the end she left her legs bare and just wore one of her husband's white shirts, the tail so long it tickled her calves as she moved. She tucked her hair under a peaked cap John had once brought home from Nova Scotia, glanced in the mirror and giggled at herself. Pity you can't see this, John, she thought: cute. Something about jaunty caps and shirts miles too big made men protective and eager. Rachel quite liked the effect even without reference to John. She looked lost and little and cuddly, rather unlike herself, and if there hadn't been a job to do she'd have played at dressing up a while, flirting with herself. She and John didn't fool around often enough. They must have taken marriage a bit too seriously, which was a shame in some ways. We don't laugh like we did, she acknowledged, and the blame was probably more John's – If he'd come to the pictures, dream the dreams... But John was too solid and set.

Rachel moved some of the heavier furniture into the middle of the room, not waiting for Foster, who should have been helping by now. The boy had a reluctance she couldn't be bothered to overcome. He'd saunter in when he'd made his point. She took a scraper to the section John had started stripping and after a few minutes wondered if it was such a bright idea after all. The room was empty, forlorn somehow. If she thought about it, the whole house was that way, yet they owned decent furniture and she kept everything neat. No fire in the grate, maybe that was the problem. No pictures on the walls. Was new paper going to make a difference? Rachel had chosen the pattern, but now she had doubts. She was thinking: We work all week every week, and we sit around every evening, Foss goes to school, we pay our bills promptly, and that's our lives. What on earth are we living for? For what we have? Something still to come? What else can come? Work, sitting around – this is it. Dismayed, she sat on the arm of the settee and thought of chapel and faith, and love and routine, and nothing reminded her that life could be joyful. It was Fred Knight, she decided, who'd upset her poise. And John being away, of course. But Fred Knight turning up on the back door. Every time she saw him she remembered being with Foster that time outside the docks, Fred Knight brutally slamming the door of the telephone kiosk on the poor Indian gentleman's leg. Appalling, subhuman behaviour.

She would never understand how men like Fred Knight could be tolerated in a civilised community.

Foster found his mother still slumped in reverie on the arm of that ugly green leather settee they'd bought from an ocean liner, when there was an auction of fire-damaged furniture and fittings. It was a hateful object, but his parents said it was really swish, and an incredible bargain. His mother, alarmingly, was wearing nothing but a baggy white shirt, and he could see her legs. Embarrassed for her he looked away. What did she think she was playing at, dressing so daft?

'I'll rinse out the bucket, is it?' he suggested. 'There's leaves and things have got in it. How'd you make the paste?'

Rachel broke from her wan mood and followed him into the kitchen, wondering why he was acting so nervy.

'May be a harder job than we thought,' she warned. 'Best not mix any paste till we see how long it takes getting the old stuff off.'

'I'll start on that, then,' Foster said promptly, impatient to be involved and not catch accidental glimpses of his mam looking so ridiculous. He liked her to act like a mother, or a woman who worked in a respectable office in proper clothes. He certainly didn't want to see she had two bare legs and a bare body shifting about beneath his dad's big shirt. Brigitte Bardot was different: she could be admired in his dad's shirt. So could Belinda Lee. Which was why they were on chewing gum cards. They made him want to be a hero, but weren't of the same species as his mother.

He attacked the wall with fervour. Astonishingly, huge areas of stiff paper peeled away like washing coming through the mangle, and he was so impressed with what he took to be his special male prowess that he soon forgot why he was angry and grew enthusiastic for the work. Rachel complimented her son and was inspired to try again herself, and they shrieked when she started a tear that ran from floor to ceiling.

One wall was denuded in less than two hours. They laboured on. When the next was nearly finished Rachel made cups of tea, but they set to again before emptying them. Round about midnight all the paper was on the floor and Rachel and Foster were drenched with sweat, fingers sticky, and as happy as they'd been all year.

'Put up the new paper tomorrow, is it?' Rachel said proudly. 'Will you lend a hand again?'

'Yeah.'

'It's fun once you get going, isn't it?'

'It's good, yeah.' He was sincere, but her shirt was sticking and

94

getting twisted, and he was being reminded she had a girl's body again.

'I'm going to run a nice hot bath,' Rachel said. 'How about you?'

Just for an instant Foster thought his mother had gone completely batty and expected him to hop in the bath with her. She'd been treating him like a near-grown-up all the time they'd been wetting and scraping, but mostly she didn't, mostly she had no conception of things he was sensitive to, and it was just horribly possible that she might genuinely believe he was essentially no different from the infant she'd once carried on her hip.

'No, ta,' he shuddered. 'I'm not dirty.'

'You're sweating, Foss. At least wash your top half in the basin. But don't use all the hot. And use your own flannel this time.'

Back to that – always instructions, niggles. If he was his dad she wouldn't say what he had to do, she'd let him decide on his own. What did you have to do in this place to gain respect?

'Thanks for your help, Foss,' she added as he started upstairs. 'I couldn't have done it without you.'

For some reason that touched him and he nearly ran back to kiss her goodnight. But kissing was for kids. He brushed his teeth, splashed water on his face, and decided he didn't need more washing than that since it would be cold in his room and the sweat would soon dry.

A few minutes later he heard his mother running a bath. It was good he'd agreed to help Sunday, he thought – maybe she wouldn't insist on chapel. Even if she did he had an excuse to stay in all afternoon. The two men who'd tortured Colin had scared him, but by Monday, he was pretty sure, they'd be gone for good. When Fred Knight had emerged from the shadows... Foster gulped and opened his eyes wide. The thought that they were actually there, rubbing up against the walls of his house, brought fresh cold sweat to the surface. As long as he could hear his mother in the bath, though, everything was safe. She was humming a song now. Silently her son accompanied her: 'Oh, the railroad runs through the middle of the house...'

Twenty One

Although he'd made up his mind John Eakins wandered unhurriedly, as if his limbs needed to work off other conflicts. It was out of his way to go around the top end of Covent Garden towards Holborn. He jumped a bus that took him out past St. Paul's. After that he was in streets that lacked life, were just big, heavy, dull canyons, a London he also remembered, a monotonous and wearying place. For a while he was aiming for Billingsgate, maybe to drink with men who'd been handling fish and would therefore seem familiar types, but all the time he knew he was really making for Whitechapel.

Somewhere around Aldgate he came across the beginning of the Commercial Road, and it wasn't far from there, a left and another left. The terrace, steps leading up to a front door in need of paint, lights in a couple of windows higher up; a spiked iron fence next to the porch, an iron gate, steps leading down to the basement where Bobbie lived. Her door was underneath the front steps in darkness. He thought he could smell leaves, though he hadn't walked past any trees, and the hint of nature brought nostalgia back until he guessed that was what he was doing, indulging a harmless memory, going back to London in his early twenties, not yet committed to a career, back to the strangely suspended euphoria of a time when the world was starting over, climbing out of the rubble. Not that he wanted to re-start his own life. It was the youthful feeling he wanted to savour for a while, nothing else.

He knocked gently. Bobbie's eyes widened with complete surprise. It was nice to have such a sweet impact on an unknown woman.

'Sorry if it's late,' he said. 'Don't want to bother you.'

'No bother,' she assured him. 'Didn't your...?'

'Oh aye, I've sorted my billet. I just thought...well, I don't know what I thought. I come out walking and here I am.'

'I can't leave Jenny. She's asleep.'

'No indeed – no, I only... What, parents living upstairs, is it?'

'If you'd like to pop in for a cuppa...'

'Probably shouldn't. I can go down by the market, have a drink.'

'You're welcome to come in, really, only I haven't had time to tidy up.'

He grinned and let himself be cajoled. Under the living room's centre light he could see she was not a beauty, but interesting – regular, ordinary features – could be transformed by makeup into something striking, but not to fall in love with. She was nice, that was all, and that must have been why he'd wanted to see her again. Her living room looked nice too. There wasn't going to be any temptation to sin, reassuringly. It was what had been held out on the train, an unaffected mutual liking.

Bobbie seemed slightly embarrassed, unsure of her own boundaries. She felt it necessary to indicate the door to her right and explain Jenny slept back there where, in addition to two small bedrooms, she had a small kitchen and a small bathroom.

'Look,' John said quietly, 'I'll go if you want. I'm making you uncomfortable.'

She winced: 'I wasn't expecting you. I'd have tidied up.'

His sweeping gaze took in the loose patterned covers she'd thrown over the small sofa and the non-matching armchairs – tat, no doubt, cheap off a market and disguised with covers that would need adjusting every time someone sat down. He'd been hard up, lived in rooms nowhere near this comfortable. As for not expecting him, how could she have? He hadn't expected to meet her on that train, hadn't planned for this evening, and that was what was so pleasant about coming away from home, because this was a little encounter that was happening in his life, not outside it, and it added to his life just because it was different. How could Rachel or anyone frown at him? Was it not the simplest, truest part of a man's nature to be guilelessly decent and return friendship for friendship?

'I think it's cosy here,' he said. 'I mean it.'

He followed Bobbie back towards the kitchen, wishing he could shrug away the cloud of gloomy disapproval that accompanied him. The compactness of the flat made him feel protectively affectionate towards its occupant. The mundane little details of the place, floral curtains used in place of cupboard doors, a big gas water heater next to a deep sink, the cigarette tin used for a tea caddy, were more redolent of comfort than his own home. It was a privilege, being granted access to someone else's life, and it was dreamlike, as if he had always nearly known it intimately, one of countless possible parallel lives that might have been his own.

'I could make some toast if you want.'

'No, ta, love, I've ate already. Just the tea'll do fine. Cup of tea and a few minutes' chat.' He paused and frowned, not knowing how to say that what he'd just said was all he was after, the innocence of her company if kept at this early stage. Calling her 'love' came naturally. He wanted to tell Bobbie how happy his own marriage was, how sorry he was that she, so he presumed, hadn't been so lucky. But it would sound patronising; besides, there was nothing he could do to remedy anything. Probably that was why he shouldn't have been there at all – he wanted her to know he might have been able to be good to her, because she deserved it and he was the sort of decent man she should have been able to entrust herself to, only circumstances – well, marriage – made it impossible.

John Eakins looked calm and contented, but he was muddled. He had a generous heart. If ever he saw a creature in distress he tried to help. But this was too delicate, and he'd come to her selfishly, not needing her, even. But he wished he could trust her enough to ask what he should do about a case full of money. Rachel was the one he should have asked, he realised, and suddenly missed his wife a great deal.

'Funny,' Bobbie whispered brightly, 'we don't know each other but it seems like we do. When I answered the door I'd completely forgotten you might call, but as soon as I took it in it was like, yeah, of course he's come round for a cuppa – you know what I mean?'

'I do,' he smiled. 'I expect that's why I came.' He could hear the child breathing, not quite snoring but taking those deep breaths of easy dreams and secure thoughts. He began to be conscious of Bobbie's clothing, the way her pullover hung loosely from rather small shoulders, the way she seemed more physical than before, the tiny mole on the lobe of an ear, the thinness of her hands, the way she lifted her mug. Mid to late twenties, younger than Rachel, certainly. Too young to have lost her husband in the war. Had she said he was dead? Or only away?

'Is your hand going to get better?'

'I hope so, aye. Not soon enough, though.'

'Does it need looking at?'

'It's a bit scabby – have to be careful exercising it – but no dressings, no ointments nor nothing. It's coming on. You can look if you like.' He laid the hand out flat on the table so she could squint at the scars and look away, or take hold. She did the latter, and the exploratory touch of one finger tracing the longest scar aroused him thoroughly, and unexpectedly, so that he shifted awkwardly in his chair and looked into her eyes passionately. But he couldn't go any further, or wouldn't, or shouldn't.

He felt exactly like a thief, and far more so than when he'd concealed the briefcase of money. So far he hadn't taken anything from Bobbie, yet it seemed as if he had, and it seemed as if he'd taken something at least as important from Rachel.

'I shouldn't be here,' he said, still looking at her yearningly. If only this had been happening in that earlier time, before Rachel.

And it wasn't that he was too old for this girl. Age wasn't the issue, not entirely – he appreciated her interest more than he'd have done fifteen years back, admittedly, but also knew he wasn't experiencing anything unique. Unfortunately, he couldn't be so sure of Bobbie's reactions. She understood he was married, but might be imagining he was mobile anyway. What was she supposed to think, when he turned up and acted like a single man?

Then he frowned again and wished his feelings could be shaped into words clear enough for him to understand himself. I'm not single, he was thinking, but I experience attraction for Bobbie here and now, and it could be some other woman – I'm excited by this situation. And I'm married. That's there, this is here. And I'm me, I'm the same man, here or there. So what am I doing that's wrong?

The cloud in his mind turned to thunder, because he was a seaman, not a thinker, and his questions took him out of his depth without a vessel to keep him bobbing along safely.

'I feel safe with you,' Bobbie reassured him. 'It was nice of you to come. Don't go yet. Actually I don't often have anybody to talk to.'

John Eakins was melting inside. And didn't really want to resist. Back home he was solid, and everyone relied on his strength. There was something constricting and monotonous about that. Here he had a rare chance to start from scratch and be adolescent, as silly as he wanted. He didn't want to be silly, but he liked this romantic melting towards anonymity. It was such a great relief to step aside from himself, as it were, and play the part of a tentative youth with the experience of a mature man. But he really wanted to help her, too – that must have been what had drawn him, something fragile about her, something needing comfort.

'Can I tell you something?' Bobbie asked, and as John nodded he guessed she was going to tell him about her husband, about whom he wanted to hear nothing whatever. As they were, intimate yet cautious, he was happy. Why drag anyone else into the snug little cluttered kitchen and complicate such a simple scene? 'You're probably wondering where my husband is, aren't you?' She paused and wouldn't continue until he grunted and smiled. 'I could see from the way you looked at things – you noticed there's none of his stuff to be seen.' He had to nod that this was so, though he hadn't been sufficiently curious. 'He isn't a bad man, John, but he's weak, d'you know what I mean? He's a weak man, just as obviously as you're a strong one. My parents used to say I ought to divorce him, and I've thought it, but I haven't the heart, John, he'd go to pieces.'

'You're telling me he's in prison?'

Bobbie gasped: 'I wasn't sure I should, but yes – a bank robbery. Not his idea, of course.'

'Does the child know?'

'So far she can be fobbed off. I don't like lying, but how else can I handle it?'

Her husband was a criminal. He wished she hadn't told him. It changed her. Too specific, and too far from innocence.

'I can't say nothing,' he told her gruffly, anxious to change the subject. 'If a man's weak and you already know it, that's what you've taken on board.'

'That sounds very puritanical.'

He shrugged: 'So be it.' What was it to her what he believed? His beliefs were his own. He hadn't asked her to involve him, and she had no right to take issue or imply that he was wrong. It was a ridiculous situation suddenly and John wished he'd stayed in Hakin.

'You don't want me to talk about him, do you?'

'I don't think I know you well enough.'

'No,' she corrected him playfully, 'you're jealous.'

'Eh?' He was offended at such a preposterous accusation. It alarmed him because there was truth in it – he'd wanted her vulnerability, her innocence, to let him to play a role that was partly young suitor, partly chapel elder. 'I shouldn't have come. I'm sorry. I'm not after nothing.'

'It's all right, I know that. That's why I felt I could talk to you. You're like the big brother I never had.' She seemed to half mean that, but her eyes undermined it. 'Or the big brother's big best friend.'

He marvelled that she could say these things. She wasn't a tart, and she wasn't his age, yet she was direct and unsettling and made him flounder. Mentally he was against her now, but his instincts craved indulgence. And he was loath to be back in his room, close to the money again. That stupidity that had brought him to London. He preferred not to consider that at all.

The city teemed with people, shoals and shoals, and you could wait in your room or wander the streets and be completely alone, or you could strike up a conversation and discover how simple it was to make a new beginning. All it took was that sudden introduction and a readiness to go with the impulse. After all, there was something wonderful about that, something you were deprived of once you married. It was probably the best part of life, that magical, dreamlike state you found yourself sliding into so effortlessly.

But it was short-lived. Out of it grew courtship and marriage. Once you knew enough about her, and she knew about you, the thing had shifted to a more responsible plane.

I won't see no more of Bobbie, John Eakins assured himself. I won't do nothing I'll regret. I'll sleep on the couch. After breakfast I'll thank her and be on my way, no harm done.

Because there was something else threatening, just outside the good feeling, like a storm still out of sight behind the blue sky, sensed in the slow swell of the water, a darker chance, a danger to beware of.

'So how do you manage, then, making ends meet, if he's inside?' It wasn't as if he cared to know, but he hoped it might cool him off if she carried on about financial problems – might stop her looking so winsome and so seductive.

'I don't think I should tell you,' Bobbie said rather coyly. 'I think you might disapprove of me.' But she wanted him to know, her eyelashes told him that. Flutter flutter.

Jesus H., John Eakins fumed at himself, I'd forgot it was all this nonsense to it. The great thing about a wife was she didn't tease you like a teenager.

Twenty Two

One by one the houselights around the crescent green of the St. Lawrence went out, and there was a tranquil silence long before the increments of darkness left only three lights between thirty or more houses. Bob Ryman had had a night light installed by his front door, so anyone could knock him up whatever the hour. Old Mrs Adam, a few doors along from Bob, always left a landing light through the dark hours. Rachel Eakins was still bathing.

The novelty of taking a late-night bath caused her to linger. At this hour she wasn't missing John but thinking how pleasant it was to be alone occasionally. Her back and fingers ached from the wall-paper stripping, and it was soothing to make the water soapier than usual, until the silvery smoothness formed a new slippery skin. She squeezed her breasts and squelched soapy water between them. It wasn't often that Rachel took any pleasure from the sight and touch of her own body, and she hadn't expected to this evening, but she felt she'd achieved something in the front room, and almost to her surprise her body looked and felt very supple and youthful. She lay back, closed her eyes, and thought of summer bays and picnics in the sandy coves around the headland. She drowsed lazily, knowing no one would ask her why she was taking so long. But for the water turning cold she could even sleep in the bath if she so desired.

Foster, meanwhile, had drifted into that region where memories twined through dreams and flowed smooth as a fishing line drawn by some energetic but hapless fish below the jetty, heading hopefully out into the Haven, then doubling back in the depths of indecision. Reeling in, playing out the line, reeling in.That was the worst, he remembered, when those boys broke that weak teacher's records. Nothing like that could happen in junior school, but if there were boys like them at big school Foster didn't know what he'd do. They were such big boys, and they threatened teachers. That one teacher thought he could make them his friends if he played his favourite music, and they broke his records. Glenn Ford had to teach them a lesson in the end. His mother had taken him, thinking it would be a jungle adventure with Tarzan or Stewart Granger. She'd made the same mistake more recently, another with 'jungle' in its name. *Garment Jungle* wasn't about jungles at all. *Blackboard Jungle* was about school, but at least it had 'Rock Around the Clock' to listen to. The other had been incomprehensible. Foster was beginning to be disillusioned with films, but he still believed they showed how things were in real life. So the school in that film showed what it was going to be like in a proper school. That meant the school he was at wasn't authentic. They'd have tough, nearly adult kids like Vic Morrow when he reached big school, and Foster would want to protect that poor sensitive teacher and he was afraid he'd be too timid when it came to it. His dad wouldn't, his dad was closer to Glenn Ford. Except he wouldn't be a teacher.

Foster rolled towards sleep. He couldn't have been in bed long, because he heard his mother shifting in the bath. It was unusual, her taking a bath late at night. Next door must have heard the water through the pipes. It sounded like an engine room, his dad said. Mam often made him turn his records down in case next door were disturbed. He never heard *them*, but they didn't own a gramophone and went upstairs at nine every night. If he got very cross he sometimes cupped his hands to the connecting wall and yelled, but he never found out if that made them jump out of their skins.

Foster was tired and comfortable, enjoying the flickering way some of his thoughts were sensible and others weren't quite but it didn't matter. He wished he had a dog who'd curl up on the bed and be his best pal. That little dog he'd found in the rocks and carried to the RSPCA – what he'd expected was the man would grin kindly and say It's yours, son, and he'd have carried it all the way home and mam and dad would have given in and allowed him to keep it. The book he was reading in school was about a man called Romany who travelled around the country lanes with Raq, his dog. That was what Foster would do when he was big enough. It was better than going on the trawlers because you made friends with people wherever you built your fire, and you got to understand lots of animals and birds until you knew more than anybody else about nature. He'd still do the skiffle group sometimes, on visits back home, when he'd camp out on the green where his horse could graze, but most of the time he'd just loiter around the country, living off the land, just him and Raq. If he met Brigitte Bardot he'd let her sit next to Raq on the seat beside him, and anyone trying to smash the poor teacher's records would be in for it.

Foster was hearing voices. At first he assumed they were coming from some part of his stories he hadn't got to yet, but gradually he came to think they were real and in the house. Soft, men's voices, in ordinary conversation, not voices he knew, not his dad. They were quiet enough that he might have drifted away from them, because they didn't sound alarming, but gradually he became curious. His mother hadn't emerged from her bath yet.

She was singing the Calamity Jane song about the Deadwood stage. That was Doris Day in brown leather with lots of fronds. Whip crack away. Rachel didn't remember all the words, so the Deadwood stage kept coming on over the hill and the whip kept cracking away even after she'd digressed to some lines about the secret love she once had within the heart of her.

Foster checked that his pyjamas were presentable, then made his sleepy way downstairs. The men's voices were subdued even when he stood just outside the kitchen and wondered if it was rude to push in. His mother had abandoned Calamity for Johnnie Ray, and although she was far too restrained to capture the poignant heights her slurred syllables were at least full of the right kind of revelling in pity: Iffa your sweetheart... Even so, Foster hoped the nocturnal visitors weren't listening too closely...so goooo on and ker-rye-yuh! He couldn't believe other people would want to applaud.

The voices continued and Foster was too dopey to construct anything sensible from his bewildered, somewhat retarded realisation that their accents were English and that strangers shouldn't have entered his father's house so late without knocking. But Mary, the teenager who lived next door to Colin and sometimes wore white heels on the walk to chapel Sunday morning, she played Johnnie Ray's records and sometimes you could hear them when you were right down the other end of the green. She was courting a man off the same trawler as his dad who wore his hair like a ted. She had red knickers.

So when Foster walked in and recognised the bullying reporters he was taken completely by surprise. The tall thin one was holding a packet of digestives, his dad's favourite, and dipping into them casually. The tall fat one was drinking from his dad's big mug. Both were standing, both wearing long coats and gangster hats.

'Well here's the first one,' Gently said, taking another swig of tea.

'We were expecting your father to come first,' George explained, snapping a digestive and nibbling the edges like a hamster.

'We've been given the runaround today,' Gently went on, 'so now we're here we want everything to go well for us.'

Foster stammered, 'You can't come in,' which made George spit crumbs through a fractured cough.

'We met you this afternoon,' Gently leered. 'Which one of the Three Stooges are you?'

George cancelled the remark he'd been about to make and stared sceptically at his oafish partner: 'There were four of them,' he said quietly.

'Not on your life,' Gently countered. 'Three. Always. There's Mo... There's Mo for one...and two others. You're getting confused with Abbott and Costello.'

George glared into a dimension beyond the pantry door. How can you respond to someone who's barking mad? And very large? He settled on the pretence that Gently hadn't uttered a word.

'What's your father up to?' he asked the inhospitable boy. 'In the bathroom tickling your mum, is he?'

Gently guffawed: 'That's a good one, George.'

Foster could tell they were being dirty, and it was outrageous for anyone to be dirty about his mam and dad. Worse than blaspheming, which you could go to hell for. His pyjama trousers were held up with a cord tied in a bow – no buttons for them to cut off, except on the jacket. He still felt horribly exposed, though – under dressed, with them in coats and hats, even though he was properly dressed for being in his own home so late at night.

'Our dad's not home anyhow,' Foster boasted conclusively. 'He went off before I got up this morning, so you're not allowed to stay.'

'Bugger's skipped!' George groaned.

Gently was slower to react. He placed the mug on the draining board and began to shake his head. That seemed to be it, until suddenly he twisted and whacked the mug with the flat of his hand. Tea spurted as the mug skidded from the draining board, hit the wall and exploded.

The next sound was more distant and less distinct, but they all knew what it was immediately: Rachel abruptly sitting up, straining her ears, then clambering out of the bath. A few seconds later the bathroom door clicked open. Then there was a brief pause, as she listened for a follow-up to the sound of a mug breaking and three pairs of ears listened to her listening. Foster was frightened she might come downstairs wet and naked, and was about to call up It's all right, Mam, I dropped a cup, when a hand clamped his mouth and wrenched him into a tight repulsive hug.

'What was that?' she called anxiously and without a great deal of authority. 'Was that you, Foss?'

He wanted to yell that he was being kidnapped by gangster reporters or something. He wanted to warn his mother to put her clothes on. He wanted his dad and Bob Ryman to come through the back door and make everything all right. He couldn't get anything out of his mouth. All he did was make his eyes bulge and burn. Rachel had gone into his room to check that he was sleeping peacefully. Now she was coming down.

Thank God, Foster thought the moment she joined them, she's wearing a dressing gown, all properly tied and decent!

She was also wearing a pink rubber bathing cap, to keep her hair dry, and the effect was to make her ears too prominent, but Foster didn't care if the look was unflattering. Before Rachel could grasp the situation Gently pinched her face into his huge hand, dragging her in by the cheekbones.

'You were very cool when we came this morning,' he reminded her accusingly. He shook her face. 'Kid says he's skipped. Where to?' He gave her face another painful shake before releasing it so she could speak.

Foster saw tears in his mother's eyes. But she wasn't going to cry. It was just the pain. She rubbed her cheeks and chewed a few times.

'What d'you mean, bursting in here? Who are you?' she demanded.

Foster was surprised, proud, and made anxious by her reckless aggressiveness. Her tone intimidated him, but these were very big men, unlikely to shrivel before a woman half their size. George gave Foster a bit of a shove, to bring his captured state clearly before his mother's eyes.

'We ask the questions, sweetie.'

'Don't threaten me! I'll call the police if you don't get out of my house this instant!'

'Shit, she's stupid!' Gently complained to George. 'Got a stupid cap on, and she's even stupider than that.'

Rachel's hand automatically fled to the bathing cap, which she'd forgotten about. She pulled it off, then wished she hadn't, because it was like insisting on being vain no matter what was happening. Her hair fell over her ears coyly, at the same time as Gently swept his shiny great head close to hers to address her very loudly:

'*You're a stupid stupid woman*! I think I'm going to lose my temper in a bit, and that's going to make you *sorry*!'

Even though she couldn't pull away from him his last bark shocked her head back.

George then said, calmly, 'You'd better calm down, Mrs Eakins, if you don't want anyone permanently injured. Think before you speak. You're not going to call the police while we're here to stop you, obviously, so the thing to do is cooperate.'

'Who are you?' Rachel asked, drained of fight suddenly. 'What do you want? We don't have anything.'

'Your husband knows what we want, and it's hard to believe he didn't confide in you. But just tell us where he is and my friend may decide to control himself. We...' He paused and chuckled without looking merry. 'I was about to say we're reasonable men, but that wouldn't be quite true.' His hand flashed across Foster's face and a moment later blood dribbled from the boy's nose. 'That didn't even hurt him,' George said calmly, though Foster wriggled and his eyes smarted.

'Why pussyfoot around?' Gently asked. 'I'll take her upstairs and she can help me look.' He leered at Rachel: 'You'd like that, wouldn't you? Smell nice and clean, you do, all soapy.'

George had taken his hand away from Foster's face, and Foster was thinking fast through the dull ache in his nose.

'I dow wod dey wad, Mab,' he panted. 'I dow where ith hid.'

Rachel stared at her son, partly because she didn't have the remotest idea what these men thought her husband was in possession of, so therefore Foster couldn't possibly know either; partly because his bravery astonished her. There'd been too little time for her to react to the sight of her own flesh and blood being smacked in the nose, and she was unable to rush to his aid anyway, but she did register his self-possession. And then she wanted to shut him up, because he was bluffing, the little fool, imagining he was the hero in some film, and what she took to be his idiotic ignorance of the seriousness of their situation made her hate him.

'He doesn't know any more than I do,' she pleaded.

Foster had seen the top of her dressing gown beginning to bag open, and if the men saw her breasts they'd be lewd, and if *he* had to see them too it would be the most appalling embarrassment imaginable. Why couldn't she keep her proper clothes on? Why hadn't she locked the house before taking a bath? But that was unfair, because it was rude to lock the back door and no one did. Further anxiety was forestalled when George dragged him to the sink and forced his head back and poured cold water over his neck for about a minute. Then George scrubbed under his nose with a damp flannel that smelled musty.

'Keep your head back and it'll stop soon enough,' he said. 'Haven't broken your nose, you're all right. Now, show us where it's hidden.'

Foster pointed, and Gently hooted derisively. Foster had one hand up to his nose, and with his other pointing he'd reminded Gently of Hitler. Nobody else saw it, though, so Gently had to mimic it himself, laboriously. It wasn't even humorous.

George accompanied Foster to the shed. The moon was higher than before, when Fred Knight had surprised him, hiding there to help John ward off these enemies. There was a long blade of cloud that looked as though it was edged in silver. All the gardens were still, white fence-post sentries on guard. To be at sea now!

George pushed Foster towards his mother and tossed the wallet to Gently.

'Still damp from a drowned man's pocket,' he said sternly. 'We're dealing with a pretty callous individual, this Eakins. But I'll bet he's done this off his own bat.'

'You've got what you wanted,' Rachel said, clutching Foster to her side and not yet comprehending entirely, 'so why don't you leave?'

She was beginning to be frightened, less of these men than of what her husband might have done. It irked her that she hadn't pressed John harder, and that she hadn't been able to guess he'd broken the law – she'd known all along something was wrong, for him to be so eager to go to London all of a sudden. She needed to see and confront him at once, to get to the bottom of it, to help him.

'Last go,' George sighed, as if he were tired of being so bloody reasonable. 'Where are we going to find him?' He studied her face coldly. 'We've made lots of enquiries today. We know where you work, what you do, where the lad goes to school. We know you have relatives near Cardiff, some up in Bangor – which would he go to? Or is there somewhere else he'd want to hide? You only have to say, Mrs Eakins. That shouldn't be hard, not if you consider the alternative.'

He didn't specify the alternative, but Gently's hand tightened on her arm and caused her to see a vivid X-ray picture of the bone, quite thin and snappable. What muscle there was on her arm reminded her of the meat on the turkey's legs at Christmas, that parted company from the grey bone so easily.

'I would tell you,' she said earnestly, 'but he didn't *say* where he was going. He's a man, he goes off sometimes.' While she articulated what she prayed was a convincing lie she pressed her fingers into Foster's hip, hoping he wouldn't be so naively honest as to remind her of the truth.

'The man you love takes off with a briefcase full of money that doesn't belong to him, and you don't think to ask where he's taking it?'

'What briefcase? What money?'

'Pardon me if I don't swallow it, darling.' George looked at her balefully for a few moments, then nodded to Gently: 'Off you pop, then, chum. Don't be too long with her.'

Rachel protested and struggled to kick free, exposing her legs and hurting a big toe against the jamb as Gently yanked her into the hall. Foster felt like a craven coward – men were meant to save the womenfolk and he'd just let her go as if he was no man at all. They probably had torture weapons set up already somehow amidst the torn wallpaper in the lounge: chains, red hot pokers, branding irons, pliers, whips. She'd talk.

George boiled the kettle and asked Foster if he wanted a drink while they waited. Foster couldn't speak, hearing thumps, bumps of furniture getting moved. No voices, no screams, no sobs. Mainly what he heard was a hum in his ears from straining against the dull and scary silence. He heard the silty shushing of his pulse. His mam would tell his dad how he'd done nothing to help, and his dad would look solemnly at him, be disappointed, and he'd have to endure that look for ever.

'You have any imagination?' George asked him.

Foster was almost glad of the distraction. He nodded, watching George take out a knife and extend the long blade. George glanced to make sure the boy's horrified attention was fixed, then he casually applied the point to his fingernails, cleaning each one with a neat movement, as if he were twisting out a bad bit from an apple.

'Some people imagine pain comes from having your leg ripped off, something like that,' he mused, scraping away meticulously. 'But just think what I'm doing now – if this was your hand I was holding, and you were squirming on the other end of it, unable to predict what I might do next – then just a little prick could give you agonies. And then, think what a good point could do – how would it feel if it went right in behind the nail, all the way down? Mmm? Nasty to think of. And a sharp blade like this could skim off the skin off the pads of your fingers, one at a time, just taking tiny little pieces of you. It's amazing how much pain you can put the average body through before you start doing serious damage. I'd think about that if I was you, son, and tell your mother.'

He stopped talking when Gently shambled back looking flushed and amused.

'Any joy?' George asked.

'Not a dicky-bird. Said we could turn the house upside-down if we want, so I don't suppose it's here. He's taken it, the bugger. And she still won't say where he's scarpered to. I told her she'd better reconsider before we come back. Let her sleep on it.'

'Yeah, but she won't sleep,' George predicted. He slapped Foster's face again, but not hard, more as if they had an understanding. 'Remind her not to go blabbing to your neighbours. And especially not the police, not if she wants your old man to stay out of jail – this is a private matter. We'll be back again before mid-day, son. Ever seen a house destroyed throughout? It's fun, less so when it's yours.'

With that threat he and his partner coolly took their leave, confident they could return after a night's sleep to find Foster and his mother waiting in dread – there was nowhere they could go, after all. And the wait would give Rachel ample time to relive the relatively mild but potentially so much more hideous ordeal: she'd know she couldn't prevail against confident professionals. And she'd know there'd be the devil to pay if she attempted to mislead them. She'd have to betray her husband. In their experience, that was what everyone did, if you gave them a few hours to come to their senses. Because she could get herself to believe they might not destroy him – at worst he'd get a beating and lose the money. By midday she'd believe that was the only way to survive. Women, George believed, were pragmatists by nature. Force them to talk while they were scared stiff and you couldn't be sure of anything – they were emotionally unreliable – but give them time, coupled with a plausible threat, and you were guaranteed the truth. Men, by contrast, had this competitive thing to cope with, and would probably top themselves if you went away. It was a nuisance Eakins had slipped away, though. George wasn't complacent about deceiving Bull Gravett, and any delay made his stomach play up. He was in no mood to tell Gently, but he was thinking that as soon as they found out where Eakins had gone they ought to call London and settle, despite all the work they'd put in, for a percentage.

Foster remained in the kitchen in case the men came back. His nose had stopped bleeding and he had dry blood over his lip. His feet were so cold they hurt more than his nose anyway. He didn't know what he was supposed to do next. It seemed to be out of his hands, which was strange, because in the pictures the main characters acted as if the next move was always up to them. Nothing had prepared him for a world where you had to wait around helplessly until someone else decided to come and attack you again. Probably, he decided, it was up to his mother, as the only grown up available, but she wasn't going to know what to do because she was a woman. Besides, she'd decided to stay in the front room, even though she didn't know the men had gone – for all she knew they might be sticking knives down his nails or slicing off bits of his skin, peeling him like an apple, but she didn't care enough to come and make them stop. His dad would have.

Foster blamed her, but it was partly an excuse: he was apprehensive about going to see how she was. If the fat man had beaten her up she might be bleeding and ungainly and he wasn't confident he could do the necessary things to help. Eventually, reluctantly, he had to, because he was still afraid they might sneak back to see what he was doing, and they'd mock him if he hadn't even moved.

Rachel was only beginning to stand up when Foster began opening the door. He couldn't see anything the matter, except there was something not right about her eyes. She had a dazed, vacant look, and was trembling all over. When she took a step she tottered and nearly collapsed on the settee. Foster instinctively backed away, as from something intimate, then overcame his confusion and stepped close enough to support her regardless of the awkwardness of offering to embrace his own mother. He caught an odd, not very nice whiff of something, hard to be sure amongst the stronger smells of water and old damp wallpaper, but it was an unpleasant odour.

'I've got to get upstairs,' his mother said determinedly. 'The bath.'

'You don't want another bath, Mam,' he muttered miserably, thinking she'd lost her senses.

'Go to your room and get dressed,' she said obstinately, as if she'd already told him three times. 'Put out a set of clean socks, pants, a vest, a shirt. Now, Foster.'

'What for, Mam? They've gone now. They won't be back for hours. There won't be enough hot for you to have another bath, neither. Is Dad in trouble, Mam? Can we get Constable Ryman round?'

He had helped her to the stairs. She was gripping the banister as well as leaning on him, and it felt too crowded to go up side by side. He thought she was making a big scene of it, when he was the one who'd been hit in the face. It didn't look as though anything had happened to her, and she wasn't some ancient old crippled lady. She should have been fussing over him, to give him a chance to insist he was okay and didn't *need* any fuss. It was frustrating how she always got it wrong.

'Those men are criminals, Foss,' she explained, labouring her breaths. 'Dangerous. And we can't go to Mr Ryman because I don't know if your father's got himself mixed up with them somehow. Something's badly wrong, that's all I know. Now do what I tell you, quickly. We're getting away from here tonight.'

'But we can't, Mam. Where can we go? There's no buses or nothing.'

'I'll handle it, Foster,' she insisted, and sounded so firm he did-n't doubt her belief in herself. But he did wonder what that big fat man had said to make her so certain all of a sudden. 'We're going to get to your dad in London. We'll find him.'

Foster didn't know if he wanted to weep or cheer. His dad! His dad would sort everything out in a jiffy. When he was with them they had nothing to fear in the whole world.

The water was only lukewarm. Rachel didn't seem to notice. She let it rise around her until she was numb. It didn't stop her shud-dering, and her disgust and shame weren't sucked away when the water went. She dried her body and used a lot of talcum powder, but the entire house was fouled and she had to get out into the night air, away from the estate, from Hakin and Milford and the Haven, away somewhere, anywhere away.

TWENTY THREE

Foster wanted to believe his mother was capable of finishing what she'd started because he had to go along in any event, but sneaking away from home in the dead of night needed a frontiersman's skills. It just wasn't the type of thing she had any training for. Any minute he was sure she'd change her mind, say his hair could do with a bit of a trim, or turn back to make sure he had a spare pullover; then she'd do something sensible like wake Petey's dad next door, or P.C. Ryman across the green, and he'd be packed off to bed while the men went off and caught George and Gently and put them behind bars where they belonged. On the other hand, he was secretly relieved that she didn't call on his own expertise and tell him to lead the way – he knew about tracking and hiding, but this didn't seem like the time or place to test out his skills. George and Gently would probably cheat, for one thing. When he told his friends about this adventure, he decided, he wouldn't say his mam took charge and made him follow her, he'd describe it as a team effort: We did this, then we did that... Foster traipsed behind a little easier in his mind once he'd got that straight. Even if she thought he was just an encumbrance he could quietly keep an eye on everything, not interfering unless she really messed up.

He'd never seen her take the short cut over the fence and next door's stile – he was surprised she even knew it was possible. He'd never seen any of the women on the estate do that. It belonged to the men. Still, she did it without making an excuse and he had to admit she was determined.

Rachel carried the bag that held his clean set of clothes and, presumably, hers. She'd infuriated him, while locking the back door, by warning him not to make a sound, but he was too conscious of all the dark places where George and Gently might be lurking to grumble aloud. Being with his mother was making Foster more nervous than he'd have been with Colin and the others, that was the only explanation for why he felt so sick-scared and couldn't enjoy it. This time it was real, of course, not playing, he understood that, but in Hakin under a bright moon no real harm could come.

All the way down the hill there were possible hiding places, and he kept remembering George cleaning his fingernails. Foster wanted to hide his hands under his armpits. The worst part was crossing the bridge which separated Hakin from Milford itself. It was only a short bridge, but they had to be completely exposed while going over, and if George and Gently were waiting on the far side that would be terrible – you couldn't say you were only out for a walk. It was obvious you were making a break for it, so they'd know you were a coward trying to trick them. A break for what, though? That was the other nagging concern. She'd said they were going to London to find his dad, but how could they, at this time of night? And there was nowhere to hide in Milford. He wished his breathing wasn't so loud. He couldn't hear his mother's breath but his own was loud enough to be identified miles away. Nothing else was breathing. The water was silent and so were the trees, and no birds sang. It had never been this quiet before. He was breathing like a locomotive. And the moon made his hands stand out clear as day.

In the shadow of the big dock gates Rachel paused to listen and look.

'So far so good,' she murmured. 'Okay, Foss, we're going across to the doorway opposite. Quick and silent. Once we're there get as far inside it as you can, because there's light on the step.'

'There's nobody about, Mam.'

'Let's hope it stays that way.'

He couldn't see any particular advantage in gaining that doorway. It wasn't significantly nearer London. If he'd been doing this with his father he'd have been uncritical, but then his dad was often out late, his mam never was, and if any strangers happened along now they'd know instantly she shouldn't be out like this, just because she was a woman. The same went for him – boys were never out now, only men. In fact Foster was perplexed to discover a time of night when there weren't men about either. It was Saturday, well, Sunday now, but he'd always imagined that when he grew up he'd go out at all hours and join the matey nightworld of the good drinking men of Milford. What had happened to them? Was it another lie? Did they all have to go to bed after midnight?

Rachel pulled some keys from her pocket and unlocked the door. On the other side was a musty cold hall with a funny kind of light that wasn't a switch but a fat round button you pushed in. That was new. Rachel hurried him upstairs, saying the light would go off again in under a minute. She unlocked another door and the hall light obediently went off as she and Foster slipped through into what he belatedly realised was the office where she went to work every day.

'Are we breaking and entering, Mam?' he asked timidly.

'Just entering,' she assured him. 'Don't fret, love, I don't need permission.' Although she took the time to say that she was already concentrating on whatever she had in mind, and Foster felt he was only there by chance and might be left behind if he wasn't careful. 'Take a seat and be quiet a few minutes, there's a good boy,' she said, without glancing his way or indicating which of the chairs he should go to.

She hadn't turned the main lights on, only the shaded desk-lamp, so *he* thought they were breaking and entering, no matter what she told him. The window overlooked the docks and he could see the gates across the street directly below, and the buildings behind the high dock walls, and the long roof of the trawl market running practically to the end of the harbour. It felt funny being in his mother's office, realising this was a world she could claim her own, these desks, typewriters, wooden filing cabinets, all these pencils and paper clips and inkwells and rulers – it was more imposing than he'd have thought. His headmaster's office was the grandest he'd stood in until now. His mam's desk was bigger than the head's, and the wall charts looked more complicated than the ones they had in school. Foster felt estranged from his mother, couldn't possibly claim familiarity with the woman for whom all this was familiar.

'I've written my boss a note,' Rachel explained as she got up and moved towards the big green safe. 'We've got a savings account here and I'm withdrawing most of it.' She spun the knob expertly, left so many clicks, right so many, left again so many, presumably wanting Foster to know she had a right to take out some money, no matter what his father had done. It wouldn't do for him to fear that both his parents had suddenly turned into thieves.

When she'd finished with the safe Rachel crossed to another desk and unlocked its main drawer. It took her a few seconds to sort through the sets of keys in there and pluck out the ones she wanted.

'Let's go,' she said briskly at last. 'Wake up, Foss. This is no time to get petrified.'

He didn't know what it meant but scowled anyway. What he was was baffled – breaking into a strange office, writing notes, taking money out of an enormously serious-looking safe, grabbing keys from a locked drawer – and he worried that his mam was only pretending to know what she was doing. If she'd had any real idea she'd have told him by now.

Back down the stairs, out into the street, check both ways, hardly daring to breathe, flit across the road. Even if she didn't know what she was doing she knew where she was going for the moment, and Foster resigned himself to following, more because he was disorientated than because of newfound admiration or trust.

'Mrs Eakins!' the guard beyond the gate exclaimed, nearly giving Foster a heart attack. Where had he sprung from? 'Nothing wrong, is it?'

'We've got a pick-up in Newport first thing Monday morning,' Rachel explained breezily, and it didn't even occur to her son that she might have made up the story, she was so matter of fact about it. 'The boy's never been out on the road by night. Thought I could give him an early birthday treat – take him up the valleys – Risca, Newbridge – see a few relatives tomorrow – well, tonight it'll be.'

'I'm supposed to turn a blind eye, is it?'

'I'm counting on you, Billy,' she laughed, as if she was flirting.

'No chitty to sign? No manifest? Bill of lading? Nothing official?'

'Who signs from the office, Billy?' she scolded him, then relented and handed him a piece of paper.

'I'm sorry, Mrs Eakins, I know you signs everything, like, but...' he gave the paper a cursory glance, then stuck it on a nail.

'If anybody calls the office from Newport on Monday - well, they won't, but you've got the paperwork and if I get lost it's my lookout, all right?'

'Right you are,' he beamed. 'Sorry I had to give you such a hard time, but it's my job, you know.'

'That's perfectly all right, Billy.'

'It *is* unusual, at this hour of a Sunday morning.'

'You're right to check, Billy. You're good at your job, and I'll tell Mr Fisk he's nothing to fear with you on the gate.'

'Mr Fisk be blowed!' Billy said with a kind of abashed rebellious flourish. 'He may own it, but we all knows who do keep this company's books filled. You ought to be a partner at the very least, that's what the lads say.'

'Billy, you're a cherub.'

Foster had little idea what was going on. His mother climbed up and unlocked the door of a lorry and told him to get on board. She went around the driver's side and let herself in. The seats were made of soft leather strips, cold but comfortable. A huge gear stick came up out of the floor between them. He sank back into his seat and worried about getting caught.

'Poor Billy's thrown,' Rachel said. 'He has to do what I say, and he must think it's a bit fishy – poor dab, no more brains than a piece of plywood. But we've got no choice.'

Foster stared at her in disbelief. As far as he was aware she'd never even ridden a bike. The motor started and the cab shook

116

noisily. The headlights came on next. Rachel shifted the gear stick and the juddering lorry bounced ahead and stalled.

'I'm rusty,' she apologised, and started up again. She wound down her window as they reached the guard. 'You don't need to worry, Billy,' she lied smoothly, 'I've cleared it with Mr Fisk – left him a note on his desk. I'm going to be looking into how efficiently we run the fleet of lorries in a couple of weeks – seemed to me the best way of approaching that was to get in a little practice person-ally and time a couple of runs.'

'Ah,' Billy sighed, 'I got you, Mrs Eakins, I got you now.' And he saluted as she pulled on to the road and turned right to head up the hill through town.

She can do it, Foster thought, she can actually drive! My mam knows how you drive lorries!

'Why haven't we got a car, then?' he asked petulantly.

'We don't need one. Couldn't afford one if we did.'

'But how...?'

'The war, Foss. We all learnt a lot of skills in the war. Ambulances, mainly, though once I got to drive a tank, only a few yards, mind, on an aerodrome.'

'Cor, Mam! Blimey!'

'Don't be uncouth. I've told you about that before. You don't want God to blind you, so don't tempt him.'

'No, I said Cor, not Gor...Sorry, Mam.'

He wasn't going to argue the point. He was glowing in the dark. It was little short of miraculous to have a mother who'd been in a tank.

In a few minutes they passed out of the town and headed through open countryside beneath the moon and stars. The buck-et seat was springy and the motor was loud, the warming interior air already getting to his feet and filling the cab with a faint smell of leather and oil and metal parts. It wasn't a film and it wasn't a dream: he was going to stay up all night, driving along in a lorry, escaping the bad men and driving to his dad. Magic.

'How're you feeling?' his mother asked in a while.

'Fine. I'm enjoying it.'

'You must be scared stiff, and confused as well. But it's as much a mystery to me, Foster. The main thing is to put some distance between us and those louts. Your father...well, if he's got into some sort of financial difficulty with men like them... That dead man you found, did he have a briefcase, anything like that, when you saw him?'

'I don't think so, no. Was he important?'

'I don't know. There's been a lot of talk about opening up the Haven. My employer, Mr Fisk, has been seeing people about new roads, expanding the business...a couple of months ago somebody in the office said they'd heard Milford could be like Las Vegas if we're not careful. But your father would have said if he was getting in on any schemes to invest in the town.'

'Are we going to be rich, then? Is it something good?'

'See if you can get some sleep now, Foss. You should have been asleep hours ago. Let me concentrate. We've got a long haul just to get across Wales.'

She hadn't let him sense her fears, and fortunately there was no traffic to test her. Driving at night was easier, in some ways. You only had to look at the stretch of road in your lights, and as long as you kept a steady speed it seemed unchanging, coming towards you without surprises. She wished she could get the front room out of her thoughts. Every time she remembered she wanted to shift in her seat. She held the wheel tightly, but it kept shuddering against her hands and they felt bruised already, and her legs ached from stretching so far to the pedals. She began to hum the tune about the Deadwood stage. Faintly, Foster joined in, drowsy at last. She tried to wind up her window, because the cutting breeze seemed to be catching her eye, causing the wetness and the tear on her cheek. Rachel sniffed. It was Sunday, but there was no sign anywhere around of the sky lightening towards dawn. Hours to go before daylight. She tried humming hymns. A buzzard swooped heavily across the road, startling her, but she didn't brake or swerve. It was all right, she was handling it, more scared than her son, perhaps, but also more capable. She risked a glance across. He looked asleep. She envied him his ability to let something frightening slip away so easily. In his life one incident was succeeded by the next, and he could always look forward fancifully. Gradually he'd lose that, as he realised that the things he expected with such wide-open and unrealistic eagerness very rarely came to him. Living was about settling for less, and when you did that you dwelt more on the things that had gone before. There were no rainbows. There ought to be loyalty, though, and trust. Love, was that?

Twenty Four

John Eakins was tense and irritable, and Bobbie, hurt by his reaction, becoming indignant. All she had to do was tell him to go and he'd have left the table, but she didn't, she felt compelled to goad him, and he felt helpless and caught, bound to listen.

'You've gone all dark,' she observed gloomily, without surprise.

'Well,' he said, 'it just seems...well, I don't know, a bit of a shame.'

'Next you'll be saying you're disappointed in me.'

'You're right, I don't know you well enough – don't know you at all, do I? But to my way of thinking, pictures like that... I didn't see you as the type, Bobbie, that's all.'

Bobbie had confessed to modelling, then she'd slipped into her bedroom and returned with some evidence – black and white pin-up shots. Photos of that type, John believed, could only be brandished by a woman who meant to seduce him. They were intended to make him forget himself, but he didn't need to forget who he was, only bring back who he'd once been. The sight of this pleasant young woman reduced to small monochrome studio nudes struck him as either pathetic or offensive. The atmosphere now was decidedly unpleasant, whereas before she'd started getting coy and insisting on showing him the things it had been innocent and dreamlike.

'There's nothing dirty about modelling,' she pouted. 'It's artistic. These are artistic studies.'

'I don't think so,' he chuckled hollowly.

'Could you take pictures as good? Look at the lighting? See how sharp the details are? Why do you have to sniff and say "pictures like that", as if it's so obvious?'

'Well you haven't got no clothes on, for a start.' It wasn't a discussion he wanted to have, despite her insistence.

'So you think the unadorned human body is dirty, do you?'

'I never said that, did I?' Maybe I did, he thought, I just don't care.

'At one time I posed for Life Classes, in a proper art school, but you have to hold a pose so long it's like being something else, made of stone or something. You can't really put yourself into it.'

'I suppose that's all right,' John conceded, hoping to get clear of the subject. 'Art school, painters – that's not so bad.'

'You're not listening – that wasn't art, not for me. Some of the drawings may have been good, though I doubt it, but I'm talking about my contribution. In photographs it's *me* as much as the photographer.'

'So what about the couple you showed me in stockings and corsets and stuff?'

'Glamour. What's wrong with glamour?'

'I've no idea,' he retreated wanly. 'Not my cup of tea, I suppose.'

He could understand why she was getting aggressive – she was really ashamed of what she did, he imagined, and needed to justify it. If she'd only said it was impossible to make ends meet so she'd been forced to do something demeaning he could have accommodated that. But to show him her portfolio as if it were a wedding album, then to claim artistic expression was involved, that just took the biscuit.

'I thought you'd be more broad-minded,' Bobbie complained, and appeared to be genuinely disappointed. 'You don't come over like a man who's had such a sheltered life.'

'Depends what you mean "sheltered" – I haven't had to give much thought to why some girls let themselves be seen like that. Haven't been with a prostitute, either – not in the war or afterwards – never wanted to, nor needed to. Is that a sheltered life? I don't feel like I've missed nothing important.'

'You're a bit high and mighty, aren't you?'

'Not so I'm aware of. I just do what I want, and some things have never crossed my path.'

He wondered if she was right. Mostly he'd had a good opinion of himself, until quite recently. Did that mean his life had been off course, or narrow? Bobbie's earnestness was bewildering. The only reason he'd been drawn to her was that she was a young mother who'd seemed to welcome his friendliness. Not a sexual thing at all. But somehow she must have decided he wanted to sleep with her, must have fancied him, and he couldn't deny he was pleased, flattered and even attracted. It was the method, the cold black and whites, that repelled him. Somehow that cheapened *him*, as if he and every man could be relied on to react predictably.

What it came down to was his lack of real certainty – big, mature and confident as he was, he didn't actually know much about women. Rachel was the only woman he'd spent a long time with, and he wasn't sure if he really knew very much about her. Whether or not Bobbie realised it she had turned the tables, making him the gauche novice who worried that if he resisted he'd be a chump. The innocent, rather romantic feeling of friendship he'd experienced on the train was clearly fragile, and possibly had only existed in his own mind and because of his own naivete.

What was it in him that wanted so inflexibly to resist her charms anyway? Because surely it didn't matter, objectively, if he slept with her or didn't. To whom should it matter? No one need know, and plenty of men had plenty of affairs. Just because he'd been untempted didn't mean he had any fundamental objection. And if the girl was willing, or even eager, assuming it was going to happen, then why shouldn't it? Experience was experience, good or bad. Yet he seemed to be governed by a moral conscience that dropped a boulder in front of his free roaming spirit without consulting him. He prided himself on being basically decent, a righteous man, but wanted to believe the credit was won consciously from an ocean of choice. If it was nothing better than some damned mechanism turning him into a blessed robot, that was on the same level as expecting the pin-ups to arouse him.

Bobbie shuffled the photographs together unhappily, then returned them to her bedroom. She didn't come back immediately. He began to wonder if he should leave, having offended her. There was something guileless about her, regardless of her occupation. The woman had a right to her own existence, of course, and it was only to be expected that the details of her private life would be novel. His condescending disapproval said more about him than her: why did he feel so strongly she had no right to be who she evidently was? He didn't know her, and didn't really want to know her. All he'd wanted was for her to conform to an unlikely picture of innocence, to indulge him.

I haven't been myself since I picked up that bloody briefcase! John thought harshly. What made me do such a thing?

He looked up. Bobbie came past and started filling the kettle. He couldn't be sure, but he sensed she'd been crying. It was all too involved.

'Look,' he said uncomfortably, 'I'm sorry we've got off on the wrong foot. I'm just a trawlerman, I don't know about much else. I been up since before dawn and I'm tired.'

'I'm tired as well.'

'I'm just...my heart's not in it, do you know what I mean?'

'Not in what?'

'I don't know. I came here because I didn't want to spend the evening in my digs. I just felt like chatting, I liked you on the train.'

'I liked you, too.'

'Back home, I did something I shouldn't have. And I ought to be putting it right. But I don't know whether to steam ahead or what. Like I say, with that on my mind... I'm sorry, my heart's not in anything at the moment.'

The young woman looked down at him and seemed to understand, or be prepared to go along with his indifference.

'I'll bring you a couple of blankets,' she said.

'It's funny being back in London,' he said. 'Almost like I thought it would be, but... I don't know, maybe it's me that's changed.'

Bobbie didn't respond. She didn't know him. She was willing to let him sleep on her sofa, that was all. As if he were a harmless stray she'd found on the doorstep, not a man with a fortune. For the first time in his life he felt he wanted to explain himself in considerable detail, but at the same time the uselessness of such an undertaking washed over him in wave after wave of insurmountable strangeness: We're all strangers here – the words came into his head as fully-formed and heavy as some dire biblical judgment.

Bobbie had given him a couple of rough grey blankets which smelled of damp. She'd gone to her room. John lay on the sofa wondering if he'd succeed in sleeping, and suddenly he attempted to see Bobbie's face and failed. They'd been in the kitchen for hours, and her features eluded him already. For comfort he then thought of Rachel but, to his dismay, the same thing happened. He had a general sense of her but couldn't actually call her exact features to mind. And he was so far from her, in this strange basement on the rim of a relationship he didn't want to fall into.

If he'd had a picture of Rachel he'd have studied it, but he didn't carry any pictures. In all his time at sea he'd never experienced such a yearning. Some of the men carried family snaps in their wallets. He could do that – he had a wallet.

John Eakins groaned – he'd remembered the other wallet, the dead man's wallet. Normally it should have been secure enough where he'd dropped it, but because he was away from home Rachel would enlist Foster's help in keeping the place tidy, and the lawn needed mowing. As soon as the boy pulled out the mower... It was cruelly clear: Foster would show Rachel the wallet and Rachel, with her efficient careless honesty, would take it round to Bob. That was it, then, he was as good as behind bars already!

John Eakins writhed and groaned on the sofa. His bad hand was itching so much he wanted to scrape the skin and flesh away. There was no possibility of contacting Rachel, who would betray him so innocently because it wouldn't occur that he was capable of going wrong: We're strangers, he cried in silence.

Twenty Five

'Wish we were back in the smoke,' George said wistfully.

'That's the truth,' said Gently.

Their car had come to a halt part-way up a long hill. On either side fields stretched off to the horizon, and it was hard to avoid the sensation that just beyond lay a fall to total emptiness. Definitely there were no cities, and for George and Gently what lay outside London was barren land, except perhaps for Manchester and Birmingham. They might as well have been stranded in the Sahara. Ahead was nothing more interesting than a black sky pricked with far too many stars. The stars were a mockery of the city at night, just twinkling rubbish.

George and Gently had passed a bottle of whisky back and forth a few times, to keep the boredom at bay, but they'd travelled a long way for Mr Wary's briefcase and seemed little closer to securing it. Shortly they'd have to decide what to do next. Running out of petrol was a difficult thing for two tough guys to deal with. George had said he reckoned that little spiv he'd cut in the afternoon must have siphoned the tank before they got there, and Gently hadn't contradicted him. The truth was, George had last filled up when they drove through Cardiff Friday evening. It was George's oversight. Gently had no plans to make any mileage out of it. There was a nasty, petty side to George's character.

'You didn't actually beat her up, did you?' George came around to asking. He might have asked sooner, only it wasn't an important consideration.

'Nah!' Gently scoffed, hoping to go into details.

'But she'll tell us where to find him?'

'If she knows where he is she'll tell us as soon as I smile at her again. But I reckon a good pounding would have got it out of her tonight – or you could have made the kid bleed a bit more.'

'Sure, then in a day or two somebody notices, asks the obvious.'

'So what? We'd be well away.'

'But Bull Gravett's still got transactions to make, hasn't he? So far nobody's panicked.'

Gently muttered something deliberately incomprehensible. He hated the fact that in working for a jerk like Bull Gravett he was having to curb his natural desire for quick results. Then he remembered what he'd done as an alternative to beating up Rachel Eakins, and he was proud of that anyway.

'I made her squat down with her back to me,' he started.

'You must have had a twisted adolescence,' George interrupted. 'I don't want to know, you sound too smug by half.'

Gently's smile broadened: 'So all I do is crouch down there behind her and do a good big one on the floor – there's wallpaper all over the floor, a piece is tickling my bum.'

'I don't know how you can.'

'It's a special gift.'

'I wouldn't even want to.'

'You have to get 'em off guard, George. A sock in the mouth, even a shagging, they're more or less expecting, so it won't necessarily make 'em cough, but have a poop, be a bit nonchalant, and you've messed up their sense of proportion. So then all I have to do is lift up her dressing gown at the back, see, and plonk her down on my pile. You should have seen her expression, George! Poor cow's probably still glued to the spot! Must think she's been dipped in hellfire!'

'Christ!' George exclaimed, and took another swig of whisky. 'You're seriously damaged, mate.'

'Yeah,' Gently chuckled, 'and that's what she thinks, too. Suddenly she's been dumped into a world she won't have seen in the pictures or read about in the magazines, and it's too personal for her ever to talk about it – that's what you wanted, right? A terrified woman who'll only talk to us.'

George nodded reluctantly. He favoured straightforward lethal violence himself, at least it was manly. Gently usually preferred it as well, but also had this peculiar side to him, and the fact that they made a very effective team worried George a little. He'd read the occasional article about violent men and their hang-ups, but regarded himself as perfectly normal, just more realistic than most.

'I think it was a nasty thing to do, even so.'

'What would you have done?'

'Dunno. Cut off her navel or something – no, you're probably right, I couldn't have cut her. But I wouldn't have done my business with her in the same room.'

'Maybe I lack imagination.'

'You can say that again, pal!' He passed the bottle and Gently took a swig as soon as he'd stopped chuckling.

George sighed. They seemed to have come to the edge of the world in search of this money and he'd felt, even in that kitchen, the fragility of the things people accumulated to make themselves feel at home. It was depressing, and threatened to make him question the richness of his own life. Maybe he lacked imagination too – possibly the area would be worth coming back to in ten years, but he just couldn't see how any amount of investment was going to rescue it from teetering over the brink into nothingness. And everywhere outside London there were the same useless lives going on, people who'd never matter pursuing futile lives in dismal houses and getting nowhere, and not even noticing. Deep down, George thought, the gulls and the aimlessness of life upset him more than they upset Gently. He wasn't sure why, except that he was more intelligent than his huge partner. He supposed it grated on him that he hadn't yet made a fortune even though the world was packed full of suckers. He deserved to be better off.

'We may as well start walking,' George said. 'Nothing's on the road, and we aren't going to find a garage this time of night. I'll carry the guns, you get the rest.'

'Not been a bad day, though, apart from this.'

George didn't bother to respond. Even sarcasm was a waste of breath. All in all, he thought, it's been a bloody dismal day. Working in London you dealt with gangs, fellow professionals, and there was a purpose to it, but out here all you got was the sense that nothing was worth the effort, that you might as well be dead already. He had to have his range of suits to choose from, his jewellery, his scale models of vintage cars; he had to have respect from head waiters when he entered one of his clubs; he wanted to be back amongst his own kind. Aside from that his legs were tired and the prospect of walking back to the hotel was daunting. And then, if the Eakins woman didn't know where they could find her husband the chances were they'd lose most of the money to a competitor, rendering the entire outing redundant.

He was unlocking the boot when a shine appeared on the paintwork. He turned and saw the lights of an oncoming vehicle. It almost brought a smile to his cadaverous face, the possibility of a lift into Haverfordwest. As the lights neared he saw it was a lorry labouring up the long hill, and he was glad because a lorry was more likely to stop than a car. He stepped out into the road and held up a hand. Gently did the same. The lorry was climbing slowly anyway, but the driver shifted down a gear and George had a moment to relax before he saw inside the cab and recognised Rachel Eakins behind the wheel and leapt out of her way.

Although less confident about driving than she appeared to her son, Rachel had convinced herself she should be able to keep going for hours. The shock of heading slowly up the hill and seeing her tormentors filling the road as if they'd been lying in wait caused her to lose control – actually swerving right at them was not intentional. Then she was horrified in case she couldn't regain enough momentum to leave them behind. If they sprinted they might just leap on to the tailgate. But, mercifully, she saw them shrinking in the mirror. What of their car, though? They'd catch her in minutes.

She wouldn't have the stamina to reach London anyway, wouldn't even make it across Wales. She needed to find a fork in the road, some alternative routes to give her a bare chance of staying ahead long enough to think how to hide. If she could put a few miles between them, then choose any track away from the main road, maybe she could pull in out of sight, maybe they'd go by, maybe she could rest.

A headlight jiggled somewhere ahead. Rachel had to check to make sure she was keeping to the correct lane. Her arms were sore from the tension of holding the hard wheel steady. Approaching was a motorbike, a motorbike and sidecar. Her first thought was it could be the AA, but even if it was this was one situation the AA couldn't resolve, and she wasn't a member anyway, so the slight lift in her spirits associated with uniformed officers of any kind sank again. As he went by she took in the black torpedo-shaped sidecar, the rider's goggles and gear, and realised it had been Mal Mabey, who might conceivably have helped after all... But no, she realised, although Mal would have wanted to assist she couldn't have risked involving him, not until she knew exactly what John had done to have London gangsters after him.

There's odd, thought Mal Mabey, I'm sure that was Rachel Eakins. What in the world's she doing driving one of Mr Fisk's lorries this time of night? Or at any time? He was puzzled, but also mildly inebriated, so the curiosity made him smile inanely, wind whistling through his teeth. There was an outside chance of a story in it, but so remote he knew it would be a waste of time to turn and follow her. The wind blew up his bare legs, making him grin even more. Girls must have all sorts of interesting sensations we don't, he reflected boozily.

Mal Mabey was on his journey home from a fancy dress ball. He'd gone as a bobby soxer, in daps and white ankle socks, a wide-bottomed polka dot skirt of soft felt, and lots of flouncy tulle petticoats. The outfit, which he'd enjoyed putting together, hadn't been the surprise hit of the evening. Several men had dressed as girls, and Mal turned out to be the only rather flat-chested one. He'd wanted to look plausible rather than hilarious, and even his make-up was underdone. Under his leather frock-coat he still wore the blue mohair cardigan, the billowy skirt and petticoats, though his riding boots had replaced the daps. He wasn't thinking how strange

126

he might look to a stranger. He wasn't expecting to meet anybody.

'So she was going to stay put, was she?' George was griping.

'I don't believe it,' Gently was admitting. 'How'd she get hold of a lorry?'

The two slow-moving big men must, Mal guessed, have run out of petrol. There was no likelier explanation for two men on an isolated road next to a car. He put it down to his journalistic perspicacity. Mal always carried two full cans in case he had to do some unexpected trip after an elusive story. Being courteous as well as nosy he was bound to offer assistance. A hundred yards past them he executed a perfectly sober one-point turn and, feeling uncommonly heroic – Is it a bird? Is it a plane? No, it's Supermabey! – he puttered up to George and Gently.

'I think I've got just what you want, boys,' he made the friendly mistake of saying.

The Welsh accent, George thought, grated on civilised ears. The Welsh accent, Gently thought, needed the living daylights kicked out of it.

Gently took one look at this grotesque figure, remnants of scarlet lipstick below the ludicrous goggles, petticoats fluttering up between the parted wings of the long coat, white knees bare and repulsive, and that look, which had just processed the reckless proposition, provoked the man to action.

George made no attempt to stop him. It was Gently who pulled Mal Mabey off his bike and threw him against the thorny hedge, Gently who landed the first angry punches, but it was George whose shoes caused the broken ribs and ruptured spleen.

Afterwards they came across the cans of petrol.

'Well look at that!' George said. 'Make us a funnel, Gently, and we'll be on our way.'

Gently glanced about, then with great ingenuity smashed the bike's headlight, ripped it off, demolished it and held out the reflector. It worked admirably. George tipped the can while Gently held his improvised funnel in place.

'Can we spare some to douse that pervert?' Gently asked.

George threw an empty can at Mal, who was making ugly phlegmy noises.

'I think he's learnt his lesson,' George said. 'We need to catch that bitch you should've nailed to the fucking floor.'

'I'm sorry, George,' Gently said. He felt conciliatory because he'd enjoyed working on Mal Mabey.

'It's not your fault, mate,' George said, equally revived in spirits.

Why? Mal Mabey wondered from the ditch. Are they business-
men? Can't be local. It's a story. It's a scoop. It... He passed out.

TWENTY SIX

The money had been reclaimed, more or less, from the sea, so it was no different from a haul of fish and belonged to whoever netted it. It belonged to John Eakins. And nobody was ever going to know anyway.

He eased himself over, making sure his right hand wasn't trapped because if he slept on it there'd be an agony in waking. The money wasn't the problem, he realised. His fitful sleep was due to Bobbie, his regret that he hadn't made a pass at her. He'd been wooden and naive, it now seemed. The more he examined it the less credible seemed his whole attitude. The woman had expected sex. With her weak husband in prison she probably longed for a stable man's arms to comfort her. He'd denied the poor dab a little harmless tenderness, out of some prim resistance he couldn't comprehend. He'd never behaved that awkwardly around girls in his youth, always steaming ahead confidently, sure of what was wanted, certain of his right to provide it. Life had been a lot simpler back then.

He tiptoed back through the dark little corridor to the kitchen, then sat at the table and perused the label of the Camp coffee bottle while a kettle boiled. Chicory, whatever that was – hadn't drunk the stuff in years. Thought they'd stopped making it. It occurred to him he wouldn't have minded another look at those pin-ups now, but he heard Bobbie's mattress and his vague desire was cut off instantly. He allowed it would be nice to *have* slept with her and be safely on the far side of the experience, relaxing over a drink of poor man's coffee. But to be *about* to undergo all the tensions of fitting together and trying to sound sincere when you only felt awkward, to have guilty recollections of how much easier the whole thing was with Rachel, that was just too dreadful. And what sort of woman could expect a man to disregard his own wife so readily? He grew indignant again, as if he'd been branded a liar by someone despicable.

A door opened. Not Bobbie, though. Her little girl, stumbling to the lavatory, eyes half-closed. She glanced his way but gave no indication that she'd seen him. He could hear her peeing for a few seconds. Foster'd been tiny and cute like her not so long ago, but was practically grown up now. It went so soon, the lostness, the sweetness. Water flushed the bowl.

'Do you live here?' the girl wandered in to ask.

'I'm a friend of your mam's,' John answered uncomfortably. 'We met on the train.'

'What train?' It had been a long day for her. She wasn't entirely sure about where she was at the moment, and frowned hard. 'You're not my daddy, are you?'

'Sorry, I'm not, no.'

I've got my own family, he wanted to insist, and I don't need nobody else's, thanks very much. As soon as he was alone he realised he'd been wrong to take the hospitality of this trusting, rather dismal house. What right had he to involve a stranger in the playing out of some nostalgic daydream, when there was no intention of ever involving himself with her?

He slipped out and up to the street like some kind of burglar. The air was cool with Sunday morning's breeze, and John Eakins walked alone through dreary empty streets and had no song to whistle and no lightness to his step.

He felt strongly opposed to himself, bewildered by his loss of direction in recent days. He thought he'd come to London to see old Phil, get drunk on old times, freshen up his soul with a few nights on the town, and then dump the money somehow and go home clean and noble. Instead he'd slipped through the net to let himself flounder in dark cold waters. I'm not myself, he muttered, all this time off work has made me lose something.

He really needed sleep. A few hours. A whole day. Sleep.

The streets weren't familiar and easy any more. He got lost. And it had been just as boring and overbearing in the old days, he now remembered. The good moments hadn't been unbroken. He'd moved away from London as soon as he could, precisely because it was such a limiting hole to be stuck in. It went on and on, and sometimes offered distractions, but still went nowhere. He nearly let himself cry, like an infant a few miles from home with no idea which way to turn.

Dawn. Sunday in the shut-down city. John Eakins longing for the open expanse of the sea, and the securing dream of wife and son sleeping peacefully on the St. Lawrence estate. Although he couldn't have lost it forever he felt as if his simple life had been flung away on a whim.

I should never have took a train this way, he berated himself. It's backtracking. West is the only way – always out to sea, where you know your way home. In London it's all stone and confusion – can't even *smell* no sea from here! London's just a deep stone hole, and you can't got nothing from no hole.

TWENTY SEVEN

Something was thumping the door – a cracked church bell, it sounded like. Rachel's head bounced off the window and her cheek hurt. Disorientated, she sat up and stared out wildly, seeing nobody and struggling to recall where she was.

'You up in the cab!' an angry voice shouted, and there came another clang against the door. 'Shift it now – you can't park up down by here. I'll shoot you radiator off if you gives trouble, I'm warning you now!'

An irate farmer, a Welshman. Rachel was relieved. She unlocked the door, ready to start apologising. A shotgun wavered near her feet. On the far end of it, lower down the bank, stood a wiry little ancient in a yellowy-brown jacket. He looked at her face and lowered his weapon.

'Blow me down!' he exclaimed. 'I know you, don't I, from Sundays?'

'Rachel Eakins,' she said, wondering how a member of her congregation could be so far from chapel. Then she realised she hadn't travelled far. She recognised him as one of those humourless farmers who came from the outlying farms and didn't mix with the families of fishermen. Some of them only spoke Welsh, though the services were in English, and they shared nothing in common beyond the fact that all were Baptists. 'I had to pull off the road,' she explained humbly, a bit scared.

'Don't you fret, Mrs Eakins,' the old man said in a completely altered tone, protective now. 'I thought you was one of them sheep rustlers, but you lorry's in the way anyhow – has to get the herd past by here, see, and over the road to my son Evan's land, and the boys could hardly drive past with the churns earlier on. If you can just come a few yards forward where it's wider we'll be right as ninepence.'

'I'm sorry to be a nuisance. I'll reverse up to the road and be out of your way.'

'Nonsense, nonsense! Won't hear of it, Mrs Eakins. You haven't took you breakfast. That you boy beside you there? I seen him at chapel too – both of you, now, come down and come along and get some food in you bellies.'

He was determined to be a good samaritan after his uncharitable start, and in truth Rachel was not ready to resume her flight out of Wales just yet. She shook Foster and informed him the neighbourly farmer had invited them to breakfast. She'd heard farmers were a tight-fisted lot, and wondered if he'd charge – that was okay, she had cash.

'Have they got a lavvy, Mam?' Foster whispered.

She didn't answer because she was being polite to the farmer. Foster descended and caught them up, looking about with interest. They were in a wide, sheltered valley, but he noticed a car slipping across the opposite hill, so they weren't too far from the road, even though it felt as if they were miles from everywhere. There were puddles of sluggish mist hanging over the grass, but the sky looked as if it was going to be blue once the day got properly started.

Rachel didn't see the car. She had turned down the lane in darkness, then driven far enough to be certain the lorry was hidden from behind. As far as she was concerned they were as safe as if they'd flown off the world on to a planet where no roads existed, so there was no haste to leave. The valley, the old man proudly boasted, was called Paradise Valley on the map, and the farm had been in his family nearly two hundred years – he'd lived through nearly seventy of them. His sons, men in their forties now, had sons and daughters of their own, and although they didn't all live in the main house they were all within a few fields, like a tribe of Israelites.

'That's nice,' Rachel said vaguely. It sounded biblical and proper, and rather archaic, and she was not sure she'd have wanted such a big close family forever walking in and out of the kitchen – the estate was bad enough for that type of thing, but if everyone you bumped into was a relative you'd surely lose any hope of thinking for yourself. Not that Rachel pretended she had significant thoughts, she just liked to be undisturbed.

'It's good this early, isn't it?' Foster commented, his enthusiasm surprising his mother.

'Yes. So calm,' she agreed. And it was beautiful to see the muted colours of the meadows and the trees and feel the freshness of the air against your skin; it was possible to push last night away, not entirely, but at least for a while the uneasy feeling in her stomach seemed more like a fading reaction than a growing fear.

And yet there was something about Paradise Valley that troubled Rachel even as she sensed its tranquil, remote beauty. She couldn't identify it at once, and imagined her own relative worldliness was the problem – even in chapel she sometimes felt intimidated by the clenched piety of elders like this farmer. Her own faith was sunny, sentimental and probably simple-minded, based as much on pictures of gentle Jesus as on actual scripture. Her heart was moved by names like Canaan, Hebron, Galilee and Bethlehem, which evoked pleasant memories of her own infancy and an imagination then unfettered by understanding – the words were magical poems to her, not real places.

Suddenly the connection came back, and had nothing to do with childhood or Paradise Valley, just this general feeling of inviolable natural beauty: she had gone to the south of England once, oh, long ago, before John, but in the war – must have been forty or forty one – after the Battle of Britain – yes, and to visit a young man, courting him, not sure how seriously, not entirely convinced, but happy to pretend at any rate – he was something in the navy, David Barrington, and had blue eyes, sandy hair, a slight stutter – parents in a house made of flint – she'd never seen anything like that before - but she was scarcely more than a girl then, and they were walking on the downs that day, early morning, just like this, and climbing a steep hill where instead of normal earth beneath the grass, or coal dust, there was chalk – it was all chalk, and the film of dust on your shoes was chalky – sheep were grazing on the hill-side – David explained – what was it called? – the copse or wood they had to go around – it was called a hanger, David said – and she was ever so impressed, and there were more finches and larks than she'd ever seen in her life, and the sky as they neared the top of the hill was immense and packed with such white cumulus stacks of cloud that she felt she was in heaven – and his blue eyes the same – only his hand, when he held her hand, his hand felt weak in hers and that nagged at her and seemed to disprove the loveliness everywhere else – but despite that she was happy to be in England and suddenly felt proudly patriotic, as if she'd needed this vista to get the old this-is-what-we're-fighting-for feeling – at the same time the war was impossible – couldn't be happening anywhere remotely near that part of the downs that morning with that young officer. And then she saw the wreckage of a bomber with about a dozen cows in front of it, and it was silly, really, to be at all surprised, but Rachel's brief suspension in paradise was over, because obviously no place was immune, no matter how serene it felt.

And they rounded a bend in the lane now and she saw several children playing soccer in the yard, horses watching from their stalls, chickens and geese wandering unchecked, and a solid ancient set of buildings that had never been attacked by anything worse than winter weather, and she thought: it's foolish to fear anything here, but even here evil could come at any second. She looked back quickly, but the lane was clear. Foster took her hand and then let go again. She smiled at her son. We've intruded on a little world that isn't used to strangers, she thought. Sinai, Lebanon, Jericho, Beersheba – we are welcomed, but we shouldn't linger here, there've been Sputniks, and a husky has been in orbit: timelessness isn't an option.

She couldn't have shared her discomfort with Foster even if she'd needed to, because it didn't make sense. Rachel knew she was right, even so. Paradise Valley was not their destination, and they'd only come in by chance. The important thing was to regain the road, get to London and find John. The important thing was to have the family together again and not be in the dark. The important thing was to resume continuity, because the inexplicable couldn't be as powerful as it appeared.

The old man ushered his guests indoors, deferring almost as if he thought of them as big-city sophisticates. Immediately they found themselves in a dark cluttered kitchen, nothing like the one at home, split carcasses hanging from a rail, pots boiling on the range, the farmer's wife taking a break in a rocking chair by the big oak table, cats slowly writhing in her ample arms. Rachel nearly clapped her hands, it was such a clever reconstruction of golden olden times, but they weren't acting in the pictures, they meant it, knowing no better. In their fertile by-passed valley the fifties had also passed them by. She wondered if they'd even been aware of the war.

'This is Rachel Eakins and her boy,' the old man told his wife. 'She's from chapel and haven't had a bite to eat all day.'

The way he said that, Rachel imagined his day began while the rest of the world was sleeping. The sun hadn't come over the hill yet and she was suppressing sleepy yawns. The old woman beamed at her, a look aglow with such motherly understanding Rachel was forced to avert her eyes in embarrassment. Defensively, too, because people who threatened to understand everything when they couldn't possibly know the first thing were generally hard to get along with unless you wanted to behave like a child. When she looked up again the woman was moving towards the range, one remaining cat attached to her skirts by its claws, swinging placidly to her rhythm.

Breakfast was lavish with eggs from their own chickens, bacon from their own pigs, sausages one of their sons made – not Evan, Samuel, on his smallholding over the rise – black pudding, tomatoes, thick hunks of bread – shop bought, from Haverfordwest, apologetically, though mother made it when she had time – and a choice of preserves.

'My name is Ezekiel,' the farmer said, 'but Mother calls me

Father, and my boys call me Gramps now, because that's what theirs call me. I'll be on my way in a bit, but Mother'll look after you needs. Don't attend herself, being high church and having fell out with her vicar. Has her own service by herself here, isn't it, Mother?'

'The good Lord hears my prayers here as clearly as he could in that nincompoop's palace of new ideas.'

'That's her church she's on about,' Ezekiel smirked. 'Now before I go, Mrs Eakins, is there aught I can do?'

Rachel smiled and shook her head: 'That breakfast was wonderful. We'll be fine now, thank you.' It was clear they weren't going to be given a bill.

'There's a problem, child,' Ezekiel's wife observed. 'You can share your trouble with us. Fight with you husband, is it? No, no, don't pull the blinds down, Father and I have brought up a batch of men, and we've had our share of grief and come out strengthened.'

'Only if you do want to get it off of you chest, so to speak,' Ezekiel added. He glanced thoughtfully at Foster: 'You can get down from the table and play outside with the nippers, if you want.'

Foster had been praying no one would make that suggestion, which was invariably made when you visited relatives you didn't want to visit in the first place. Grown ups always imagined you wanted to mix in with kids you didn't know from Adam, as if kids were just one undifferentiated ingredient.

'Mam,' he whinged desperately.

'Oh... Is there a lavatory he could use... And then we really have to be making tracks.' Rachel didn't know how to begin to explain what had caused their flight from Hakin. If Ezekiel and his wife kept pressing she'd start crying, but there wasn't a thing they could do to help. Even if she never saw them again, though, she didn't want them believing she and John had argued.

Foster squeezed between the split carcasses of two pigs, took a breath and stepped out. The other children were running down the track, disappearing around the bend as if an ice cream van had piped them away. Weird place, was all he thought – who'd want dead animals in the kitchen? The whole place stank, too, inside and out.

'Long journey ahead of you, is it?' Ezekiel's wife was inquiring. 'I'll put a few sandwiches together now just – look like you've been starving youself, isn't it, Father?'

'She do, aye. They all do, these days, the young ones.'

Rachel forced another insipid smile. Obviously they were a nice old couple, but she had no use for their way of living. She'd adjusted to the times, had a steady job and a good wage, the right sort of house, a wireless, a television – couldn't expect Mother and Father here to appreciate the new privacy of more compact family units. She wondered how their presumably middle aged offspring coped with being so close.

'They're not kicking a ball no more,' Foster excused himself for coming back in. 'I think they heard a car or something.'

Before he'd reached his mother he saw her stiffen at what he'd said, and he guessed what she was thinking and had a moment to consider himself much better adjusted than her – what had happened Saturday night was behind them now – before the doorway darkened.

The two big men didn't bother knocking the open door or removing their hats. They strode right in and Gently, inspired, strode on up to one of the hanging pigs and gave it a real boxer's punch which made the S hook squeal on the rail. The carcass swayed leadenly and the one near it shivered. Gently looked at his fist, disappointed he hadn't made a greater impact.

'We've been up and down these roads for hours,' George complained. 'You damn near gave us the slip.' He kept staring at Rachel, waiting for her to say sorry. She didn't, so he studied Ezekiel instead: 'John Eakins a pal of yours, Grandad? A relative? Go and tell him we're here and we're pissed off, there's a good chap. He can't hide. We'll tear this place apart if we must.'

'John's not here,' Rachel said anxiously.

The old man didn't look in the direction of his gun, which was propped beside the coat stand. He didn't move a muscle. All he did was think about it, and somehow George read his mind, smiled, turned and went to pick it up.

Rachel kept her eyes on George because she couldn't bear to look at Gently. If she saw Gently she might shriek. George's leanness lent him, she thought, a moral demeanour, quite inappropriately. But he looked like an elongated version of old Ezekiel, a man who wouldn't indulge his body, an Old Testament man, rigid as a flagpole, sick with the power of certainty, which resembled rectitude. Possibly he possessed a noble side; possibly he disapproved of his partner's perverse manners. What was the opposite of gross? Gently was gross, George merely frightening. He cracked open the shotgun and tut-tutted because Ezekiel had unwisely left it loaded. Then he stepped outside, out of sight, and emptied one barrel. Chickens squawked madly.

'Crude weapon, this,' he said, coming back and placing it where he'd found it. 'Effective enough, though.'

'You've never shot at one of our birds!' Ezekiel cried in disbelief.

George simply stared at him. A few feathers drifted in the doorway.

'Oh, my good Lord – Father!' the helpless old lady gasped: 'The children! He's shot one of the little ones!'

It was a chilling thought, even though Foster had told them just a few seconds earlier that the children had left the yard. Rachel, against her better judgment, glanced at Gently as he turned. He'd been closely examining a side of a cow, and the pair of early morning flies that were crawling on its pale skin. He could have been planning to set up a rail with punchable carcasses in his own place – that sort of novelty appealed to him – or he could have been thinking about how hygienic these old-time farmhouse kitchens were, and how it never occurred to you when you tucked into your steak in a good restaurant that flies might have pissed and shat and lain eggs in it. The poor old woman's fears for her grandchildren interrupted whatever thoughts were passing through, anyway, and he turned to see how George would respond.

Rachel noticed, and her heart sank below the depth it had dropped to when the madmen arrived. The fact that the repulsive Gently glanced at his friend curiously was sufficient; it meant George was capable of killing an innocent child to frighten John from hiding.

'The kids ran off when we walked up,' George laughed. He drew a handgun from his coat. 'I flashed this at them.' He chuckled. 'Took off like wild animals.'

'Like we were tax collectors,' Gently chimed in, remembering a previous subterfuge, perhaps.

Rachel didn't feel any easier. Either man could murder anyone and not care. They killed human beings with as little compunction as these Paradise Valley folk showed when slaughtering beasts for the table. She wanted to lie down in a dark room with a bowl beside her. Killing animals for food was necessary, she supposed, but she didn't like to think about it. Farms were only idyllic if you weren't squeamish. She was, really. She'd been hopeless with the lobsters. But farmers weren't wicked. They reared livestock in order to feed everyone. People had to eat, so obviously a degree of suffering was natural, and God should have made everyone a bit more callous accordingly. But George and Gently surely went too far.

'Tax man always has his brolly and his briefcase,' Ezekiel said. His manner was odd, and what he said sounded inane. He was behaving as if he'd heard good news and was concealing it badly by prattling. 'They don't run off from him. They wait and listen.'

'Why's that?' Gently had to ask.

'Because every year he drives out here in his old Ford, and Mother or me starts talking, and he can't understand a single word we say. Every year. So then he has to drive off back to his office and find someone to interpret. Then he comes back with his Welsh speaker, and then we talks to him in English, like we're doing with you.'

'What's the point of that?' Gently asked.

'It's just what happens, it's no point to it.'

'We have a right to talk in our language,' the old woman said, mildly vexed that her husband had missed the crucial principle.

George had moved to a half-table under a window. He'd opened a big book. 'What's this, then?' he asked coldly. 'Is this supposed to be a Bible?'

'Not exactly,' Ezekiel said.

'Not at all,' George sneered. 'The Bible's in English. This is all foreign words.'

'Welsh,' Ezekial smiled. 'But it's *Pilgrim's Progress*. There's old coloured prints in it. My father passed that to me, and it was his father's before him.'

George nodded, glad to get the family history, then he ripped a bunch of pages from the book and tore several times before scattering the fragments. The old woman clutched her husband's arm, afraid he'd go berserk. He trembled.

'I don't like foreign rubbish,' George said.

'But you're in Wales,' Rachel tried to explain without being antagonistic. 'Welsh isn't foreign to these people. It's their language.'

'Well it's a fucking useless one, and if they don't want to speak English they should go live in a tent.'

'We had a war to keep fucking foreigners out,' Gently came in.

Rachel bit her lip. These men were not stable, and she hoped Ezekiel wouldn't provoke them further by some innocuous word or deed.

'I'll pray for you,' he said emotionally. 'You're both a long way from home, and you have lost your way in the world.'

'Are you talking about us?' George said, stepping away from Bunyan.

'Mother and me have had all the riches God can bestow, and

sometimes we forget how pitiful is the spectacle of a soul in torment.'

'He is talking about us,' Gently mocked. 'Fuck me with a feather! This feeble old fart thinks he's God Almighty!'

'You have no centre in your life,' Ezekiel droned on recklessly. 'Your cruel eyes have greed in them, and you can't see nothing beyond that.'

'Well, you're spot on there, Grandad, so where's John Eakins hiding with our money?'

'I told you last night I don't know where he's gone,' Rachel said. 'It's no good trying to frighten these people. I pulled off the road after I passed you on the hill. Slept in the cab. They invited us to breakfast, that's all.'

'Is that all?' George asked knowingly. 'Excuse me if I don't believe you. How did you get the lorry? Why were you on the road, if not to run to him? Now I'll tell you what we'll have to do – we'll have to turn this place upside down, and if we don't come up with your husband we'll have to hurt somebody. Perhaps we should *start* by hurting somebody. Think quickly, Mrs Eakins – do you want to be responsible for what we do next?'

Rachel was trapped. The kindly old couple had done nothing wrong, and she couldn't allow these monsters to go to work on them or their property.

'I think he's in Cardiff,' she said.

'No you don't,' George said evenly. 'But you realise we'll take the boy with us, don't you?'

'All right,' she said, 'all right. Let me think.' She was desperate for time, but however much they granted it wouldn't improve anything. 'He's gone to London. I don't know where exactly. All I know is he's gone to meet a pal he was in the war with.'

'Somewhere in London,' George mused. 'And you were off to find him. How did you hope to do that? It's a bit bigger than Milford Haven, isn't it?'

Rachel was thinking quickly, but not clearly. London was true, and shouldn't have endangered John. What were the chances they'd have heard of his friend, Phil Thomas? Remote, surely. She could risk it. She had to risk it, otherwise...

'I wasn't off to find him,' she tried forlornly. 'I told you. We wanted to get away from the house, so you wouldn't find us when you came back.'

'No,' George said. 'Not good enough.' He turned to Ezekiel. 'You're the man of the house, chum. What are you going to do when I break your nose?'

'Bleed all over you if I can,' Ezekiel said gamely. 'It've been broke before. Makes no odds to me.'

Foster's skin shivered as he listened and watched. No one was paying him any heed, and he stayed still. But he could see the light outside getting brighter by the minute, and he reckoned that he could duck, swerve and reach the door without being collared. Gently was in his way, but it was possible. Survival urged him to make his break. But something else restrained him. He couldn't abandon his mother. He couldn't even abandon the old people, he realised. It was a rule. No hero ran away and saved his own skin when others were in danger.

'What if I bust your old lady's nose first?' George asked. He was playing with them.

'I doubt you're as cowardly as that,' Ezekiel said, 'but if you are, Mother can't hit you back. You're younger than us, and stronger, so you can do whatever you want in that line – that's up to you. I'll try to resist you, though it won't do much good.'

'Break his bloody nose, George,' Gently complained. 'It might at least shut him up for a minute.'

'All right,' Rachel interrupted. 'John's friend works in a club in Soho. He's called Phil. That's all I know. Honestly. I thought if we could get to London we could ask around the clubs. But I still don't know what this is about. My husband isn't a criminal. If he's done something wrong it must be by accident. You can talk to him, if you find him, and he'll explain, I'm sure – there's no need for threats or anything.'

'Know any Phils in the clubs?' George asked Gently.

'One or two,' Gently said.

'You and the boy will come with us, then,' George said, and to Ezekiel: 'These are shifty customers you've been feeding. Me and my friend here are on the side of the angels, trying to get back something that belongs to our employer. We won't harm you. This woman's old man picked a dead man's pocket – ask her. It's true. He took something more. We're doing our jobs. All right?'

'You may be telling me true,' Ezekiel said, 'but Mrs Eakins is a good woman and you should be ashamed, if it's your job to frighten people.'

'Bollocks,' Gently said on George's behalf.

'In any event,' Ezekiel continued, giving a complacent grin, 'Mother and I won't help you in your work.' Before George or Gently had had time to scoff Ezekiel had looked beyond them to the door, and waved in his sons. 'Don't shoot yet, boys,' he called proudly, 'not unless these buggers try any more bully business.'

The sons, in striking contrast to their parents, were powerful and in their prime. The children had raced off to collect them as soon as they saw George's pistol. There were three of them, another, Evan, was on his way. All three carried rifles. They'd heard the shotgun blast. They now saw the torn pages of the Bunyan family treasure on the floor. They were ready to murder if their father told them to.

George and Gently were imperturbable, but realised things had changed. Being professionals, they didn't go to pieces. Indeed, they seemed quite good-humoured, if unruffled expressions and an apparent acceptance of defeat could be called good-humoured.

Evan came in: 'Look what I found in their car,' he said, emptying the weapons on to the oak table. 'Proper little arsenal, isn't it?'

'Mrs Eakins,' Ezekiel said gravely, 'I don't know what you've fallen into, but if you want my boys to hold these characters a few hours while you gets on you way, we'll be happy to oblige. After that we'll have to turn them over to the police, mind, even if that's awkward for Mr Eakins. I'm sorry.'

'Be careful,' Rachel urged gratefully. 'I think they're professionals.'

'Hear that, boys?' he grinned to his sons. 'Isaac there, he was with Monty at Alamein. David and Jonathan went through the Rhine. Evan was decorated. My boys can make mincemeat of professionals like these, don't you worry about that.'

'You're making a mistake, mister,' Gently told him. 'We have a right to get our property back. It's her old man who's the bad apple here. Why was she on the run if there was nothing to run from?'

'Maybe it is a mistake I'm making,' Ezekiel agreed. 'Life's full of 'em. Come on now, Mrs Eakins, you and your boy make tracks now. We shall entertain these law-abiding buggers who have made us miss chapel.'

'Mam,' one of the middle aged boys said respectfully, 'best you do go outside with Grandad now, is it? Walk you down to this lady's lorry.'

He didn't explain why, but from the disposition of his brothers, all of them crowding George and Gently, it was possible they wanted a few words in private. Rachel hoped the beatings would be severe, but not fatal.

'I need to get to a telephone,' George muttered to Gently.

'You'll have you chance to make a call when you get into custody,' Isaac told him. 'You'll still be able to talk out the side of your mouth.'

'Probably,' David murmured darkly.

Back on the road Foster didn't speak for the first few miles. He was sulking. Rachel had to concentrate just to keep going.

'I'm upset too, Foss,' she said at last. 'This is a horrible thing that's happening, and we're both in the dark. But I think those farmers will keep those nasty brutes off our backs as they promised, so let's make the best of it – all we've got to do now is reach London and find your dad.'

'You *told* them!' Foster accused her. 'You said Dad's in London, and then you said he's with that Phil. Now they *know*!'

'London's immense, love. A Christian name won't help them.'

'Mam? Has Dad done what they said? He wouldn't never steal no one's dosh or nothing, would he?' He was recalling his own brush with theft, and the dismal feelings it had left him with.

'The dead man must have had a briefcase, even if you didn't see it. I'm afraid your father may have picked it up. I've no idea what he could have been thinking of, but that's why we need to find him.' Dead men, she thought, and London underworld figures, and driving across Wales in a more or less stolen lorry – what has this to do with us? Why us? We don't live this sort of life at all. 'Chin up, that's a good boy.'

Foster was confused and the journey was no longer an adventure. Something had gone badly wrong in the world of his parents, the world he had to depend on, the world where by rights nothing ever happened. He felt sick in his soul, wished they hadn't stopped to eat in that smelly old farmhouse with those rather scary old people. He wanted to be home enduring a normal tedious Sunday, knowing there'd be school tomorrow, knowing Dad would be pottering about waiting for his hand to get better, knowing that if anything did go wrong his dad would be there automatically to put it right. His dad was always the arbiter, to trust absolutely. Foster yearned for a world whose balance was as true and inevitable as the tide. But that world had just gone, perplexingly, without warning and perhaps forever.

'That'd be Phil Thomas,' George hissed suddenly to Gently. 'He's Welsh, isn't he? And a sanctimonious little sod to boot.'

TWENTY EIGHT

'There's a proper mess you are,' Bob Ryman murmured gently, gazing down at the damaged features of his friend. 'I'll come back when you're awake, is it?' Mal Mabey was sleeping. Bob stroked the back of his hand. 'Keep your pecker up. You'll pull through.'

'Close pal, is he?' asked the doctor, raising an eyebrow just enough to be insolent.

Bob thought, What do you mean by that, you smarmy bastard? 'Yes,' he said. He disliked the stink of cleaning fluids, the ranks of empty beds with their mattresses and sheets stacked identically, disliked the bland colours, the quietness, the sense of pain and loss being swamped in disinfectant. If I'm ever poorly, he thought, I'll stay in bed at home. He didn't like doctors. Dr Parry was walking him towards the exit.

'Looks worse than he is,' Parry was saying. 'A splenectomy isn't going to have any long-term consequences. There's some organs you depend on, and others that don't seem to be there for any reason. He won't know it's not there, mark my words. Nobody needs a spleen.'

'Tell me again about Small Derrick, what you said on the telephone.'

Apparently Small Derrick Jones had gone to the hospital bleeding badly from a five inch slash down his calf, and had some glass in his head. Dr Parry laughed as he repeated Derrick's insistence that he'd caught his leg on a fence. From Small Derrick's shakiness and the stench of his sweat it was obvious he'd been beaten up by someone who terrified him.

Bob Ryman wondered if there was a link to Mal's beating, though they seemed to have been hours apart, and Small Derrick's gang didn't go in for mindless brutality, just mindless and often incompetent theft. Another disturbing thing, though, was that Colin's uncle had knocked on Bob's door late Saturday night, to say he'd had his boy in tears most of the evening and had just shaken it out of him: two strangers, big men, reporters, had threatened Colin with a knife, cutting the buttons off his trousers. Now Mal lay in a hospital bed after a cold night at the side of the road, and between lapses into unconsciousness he too had said something about two strangers. So what was going on? Bob Ryman hadn't a clue, except that it was going on in his town, and someone was asking for trouble.

'Only the clothes on him...' Dr Parry pursued, smirking awkwardly, as if this were a delicate matter, but risible. 'When he came in, I mean, what he was wearing was...he's not a bit, you know...bit of a fairy, is he?'

'He's a blummin' reporter, boy! What are you saying?'

'Not my place to judge, don't get tetchy – all I'm saying is, if your pal's one of them, well, with the narrow minds round here what can you expect?'

The penny dropped: 'Good grief, he was at a fancy dress ball last night! What you're...no. And where would Mal pick up filthy ideas like that?'

'It's perfectly all right,' the doctor tried to reassure him. 'They do exist, you know.'

'Queer-boys? Not round our way!' Bob insisted, wanting to throttle him.

The constable had fixed ideas about homosexuality. Until recently it hadn't existed. It was a sign of the times. You got hints in the *News of the World*, and men caught it in cities and foreign ports. Not in Milford. Bob's imagination was consistent with his limited experience. He could easily imagine the fun Mal must have had kitting himself out in petticoats, painting his face – no different from a clown costume, or playing the backside of a donkey for panto. God, he thought, a man should be able to do that without some overpaid smarmy doctor raising his eyebrow. You dressed up to show you liked a laugh and knew what absurdity was. It was being one of the lads. Where was all this filth coming from these days? Poor old Mal deserved better than a doctor in his Sunday golfing gear implying he was a pervert.

'When can I ask him a few questions, then?'

'Not before tomorrow,' Parry said. 'Internally he's a shambles.'

Bob drove back towards Milford with a headache. Small Derrick, Colin, and now Mal kicked half to death, and on top of all that this sick dread that the moral fibre of the community was beginning to fray. Mal had been his friend since they started school together. His best friend. Seeing him so poorly, his head deep in a white pillow, Bob had wanted to scream. He'd also wanted to hold Mal's hand.

What if Dr Parry was the head of a ring of well-educated perverts out to corrupt the entire area? Nothing like that had happened before, but who was to say it couldn't? Even normal sex was something Bob frowned upon. Normal wasn't the word, he reckoned, even when your parents conceived you it was a bit unnatural. His hero used to be Errol Flynn, dashing and clean-cut, until he heard those stories about orgies with young women. He tried to tell himself it was more lies, because Flynn looked so clean and good natured, but once doubt dripped on you you couldn't remove the stain.

Some of the men and women he dealt with were little better than animals, of course, but generally they came from bad housing and weren't typical of anything but deliberate squalor. Trawlermen like John Eakins were Bob's true heroes, natural aristocrats with a rugger player's simplicity and strength.

He was muddled. He reached home and made a pot of tea and took a few aspirins. When Peter Walker came into the kitchen he was staring at a Vernon Ward print of a summery open window and a nice harbour – he'd saved it from a calendar because its lightness reminded him of summer on the Haven, and the flowers on the windowsill relaxed his mind.

'Going all right, Bob?' Peter asked.

'Been out the hospital – did you hear about old Mal? Blummin' doctor there's a funny customer. I fancy he's a bit of a nancy-boy.'

'The doctor! Never!'

'He talked funny. Wanted to make out Mal was one. I nearly strangled the bugger, honest.'

'I seen a queer once,' Peter Walker winced, 'in a picture-house in Cardiff. I'm in the men's having a jimmy riddle and he sidles up and asks if I can help him get his thingy out, bold as brass.'

'Good grief! What did you do?'

'Well I should've hit him, but he had his arm in a cast.'

'In Cardiff, you say?'

'Amazing, isn't it? I says, Do I look like a homo to you? And I get out fast. But it upset me for months, in case there was something the matter with me I never knew of.' He glanced at the Vernon Ward. 'That's a lovely picture, that, we got one very similar in our front room.'

They drank tea and talked for a few more uninformed minutes about the state of the nation. The good thing about sharing prejudices was the bolstered sense of camaraderie. It was helpful to identify an outside threat to straightforward manliness, reassuring.

'Reason I'm calling,' Peter remembered at last, 'is I think you should call round John's. Bit of hubbub last night, then I seen two men up the street later on. Haven't had sight nor sound of John or Rachel all morning. And Foster usually plays with our Petey after chapel. I put my head in and give a shout. Nobody's in. There's a mug broke on the floor. You want to go and investigate.'

'Two men again,' Bob ruminated.

'Could've been pals of John's, I never got a decent squint at them, but he sometimes talks about old pals from the valleys, or from the war, don't he? Mind you, they looked more like tallymen – coats and hats types.'

'No reason to think they was pals of John's at all, then, really?'

Peter Walker looked crestfallen a moment. 'No,' he admitted. 'Don't know what put that idea in my head. But I never seen John all day yesterday, neither. Did he say he was off anywhere?'

'And the house is empty, you say?'

'Which is unusual, at the very least.'

'I agree. Whatever else is going on, though, I can't imagine old John's in trouble, can you?'

'Not old John, no.'

'Well, then.'

Bob Ryman was confident of that, but after he'd confirmed the emptiness of John's house, studied the broken mug in the kitchen, discovered the mess of wallpaper on the front room floor, then found an inexplicable, slightly squashed turd there, he wasn't confident of anything. It was especially disconcerting because less than forty eight hours ago he'd felt so proud: the only recent mystery had been solved: the dead man was a Mr Wary, a London solicitor. His partners said he may have been in possession of some papers relating to projected developments in the area, but he had a weak heart and there was no reason to suspect foul play. If the papers were lost they were lost – there'd be copies of anything important, and nothing in his briefcase would have been worth stealing. He must have wandered around the Point to get nearer the sea. Heart attack. Unfortunate location for it, but these things happened. The body would be returned to London. Bob Ryman had expected to get some weekend fishing in, before all this new stuff.

'I'm beginning to form a picture in my mind,' he said darkly, 'and I don't like the shape it's taking.'

'Is that a dog's mess there?' Peter Walker sneered. 'Only Mrs Eakins won't have no dogs nor cats in the house.'

'Take it upstairs and flush it away, will you?' Bob said. 'It's not the sort of thing they'll want to find when they get back.'

He didn't elaborate on the picture in his mind, mainly because it was extremely dim. There were two irritating strangers in it, a little boy's fly buttons, a hospitalised reporter in girlie clothes, and lots of shapeless innuendoes leering from the margins. Small Derrick was mixed up in it, and John Eakins could be, though John wouldn't have anything to do with a ratty little squirt like Small

146

Derrick Jones. It was a mystery, and Bob hated mysteries, had no aptitude for them.

As he saw it his job was to be a benign presence, capable of force. The area rarely required more from him. Unlike the big cities, Milford had been spared the worst aspects of postwar impatience, so crime couldn't get a grip. He only ever resorted to brute strength when he played rugby, and he was an effective enough second row to have earned the respect of most of the men in town. Consequently, if he needed to stop a Saturday night punch-up, he could do it verbally – Now, now, boys, enough's enough! If that didn't work he'd lay somebody out, and if necessary he could rely on prompt assistance from sturdy men like John Eakins, who were invariably there when called for. It was a good town, healthy, fundamentally decent, not exactly prosperous but not crying out for development and the loss of innocence either.

How could a stray dog have got in, anyway? Anyway, it didn't look like dog's doings. How could a human turd have got on John's front room floor? Some families didn't know any better, but on the St. Lawrence estate everybody was clean, bar the smell of fish. His house and John's were the only ones where fish didn't permeate the kitchen. Sam Niblo's always had that strange niff you got on your hands if you handled chickens... Bob Ryman felt the pressure of thought on his brain. Things were happening that couldn't happen in his neighbourhood, with or without a benignant constable.

Instead of driving out somewhere to fish he sat at home and stared at another favourite painting, a print of a lake with mountains and some ducks in flight. In that world there were no dead bodies or turds. It was natural and safe and the only policeman necessary was God. Bob Ryman contemplated the picture a long time before he realised he was wondering why he was so lonely. He liked to be in the changing rooms after the game, liked the rude humour and unembarrassed nakedness. Did that mean he was sick? It had always struck him as a manly time, and he, with his big body and deep voice, was a man's man, and that was the opposite of queer. And he'd be damned if he was going to stop hanging around with Mal just because of that doctor's insinuations. How did a man like John Eakins find a woman like Rachel and marry her? What was it like, being married? Was it something he should consider? He didn't dislike girls, just hadn't found the right one yet.

It was late afternoon when his telephone rang. Nobody rang on his day off, though he always had an open notepad and a sharpened pencil ready for important messages. Archie Flynn asked when he'd last spoken to Rachel Eakins. The skin under his ears went cold.

Archie wasn't very clear. Something had happened out the far side of Haverfordwest – two men, apparently – several people injured – and Mrs Eakins, it sounded like, had appropriated one of Fisk's lorries – could she drive? – no one knew where she was now – with her son – where was John Eakins? – yes, two big men, violent types – sounded like they was chasing after Mrs Eakins, or maybe John – something going on. Any ideas?

Bob Ryman's hand was shaking when he replaced the receiver. His head throbbed like a farty old engine. The two men had to be out of John's past – he'd never said anything about anyone being after him, but knowing John he wouldn't. If he had a problem he'd sort it out alone. Whatever he'd done was unimportant – there'd be a sound reason. He hadn't asked for help. He'd gone missing, presumably to draw the threat well clear of the Haven and his family and friends. Typical of John.

You got to help him, Bob Ryman thought, and at once the world was clear again. No need to think about anything else.

He hurried to his car and drove to the police station at Haverfordwest, to learn who'd been injured and what was known about the whys and wherefores of it all.

I'm coming, John, he kept saying silently as he drove, and it seemed to him he grew stronger and more virtuous every minute now he had a mission. If this was a private thing, between John and these hoodlums, he might, he decided, have to take a few days' leave – Archie wouldn't worry. Perhaps enlist old Fred Knight – Fred could be useful in a roughhouse. He imagined the three of them, fists at the ready, facing a bar-room full of fighters. It was probably an image accumulated from several old films, the good guys outnumbered but confident, wisecracking while they got to work. It was like being a kid again, full of energy, unconstrained by the dull monotonous routines you fell into in adult life. It was similar to the anticipation he felt before a tough game, as if he were on his way to the crusades or something. John was probably trying to defend the Haven singlehanded, but when they faced the foe side by side... Bob felt righteous and omnipotent. Furthermore, he realised with a rush of pleasure, it was not remotely a sexual exhilaration, because he wasn't moving down there at all. Thank God for small mercies, Bob Ryman thought, I'm straight as an arrow, me!

TWENTY NINE

What sea was that, washing nearer then receding? No sea he knew, with no wind whistling through the trawl-rig and no shrieks from nearby gulls. He was not the body on the rocks, either, though he seemed to be immobile in the same fashion. Couldn't even part his eyelids. Perhaps he had only slept a few seconds, and his body was insisting that he stayed put until it regained some supple slap of life. But it was a new sensation for John Eakins, to be bound into a kind of paralysis of lethargy.

No sea at all, he realised as his hearing attuned itself to the hymns drifting up from a wireless on the floor below. Must be a morning service. Must be Sunday morning proper. Ought to shake a leg.

But he was reluctant. Not comfortable, not even relaxed, but weighed down in a dreariness he couldn't account for. It was as if he'd done a dreadful thing, too dire to face, and would lay here in darkness forever. And there was more: a strange, obviously irrational conviction that if he accepted his fate, stayed still forever, this appalling weight, which managed to pin him down and yet be completely lacking in substance, a great cannonball as hollow as a balloon, this would go, the dull error of intruding on Bobbie would no longer be bothersome, the dreary money would be sorted out – if he could remain where he was, soon these aching hollows would lift off.

Blummin' glad nobody knows I've slipped away, he thought. None of his friends knew he'd sneaked to London. With any luck he could return home and no one would be any the wiser. This trip back had been a mistake.

'Not like you to sleep all day, Mr Eakins.'

His eyes opened before he made a conscious effort, and he was looking up into the soft white heavily-wrinkled face of Mrs Champion, whose eyes were a pale greyish blue, a sea colour, not cold like the sea but lively and youthful and oddly beautiful. Her expression showed gentle concern and he could tell she was an old lady, but at the same moment he could see the strength he'd never before noticed, almost the beauty in her face. To imagine an elderly woman was beautiful came as a shock, since he rarely meditated on such matters, but it was persistent and healing. In another moment he had swung his legs off the bed and was sitting up refreshed.

'What is it, nine o' clock? Ten? A second ago I thought I'd be asleep again by now – now I'm wide awake.'

'Well it's nearly seven,' Mrs Champion said, drawing back and smiling. 'I did knock several times. I was beginning to worry about you.'

I've had a couple of hours, he thought. Never mind, that's enough. Then he sagged briefly, realising his error.

'It's Sunday evening, isn't it?'

She smiled, withdrawing towards the shadow cast by the wardrobe, to the dark door into the hall.

'There's a bit of boiled ham,' she assured him, 'and I can fry up some bubble and squeak if you fancy a bit of supper.'

He nodded. His door closed. He shivered. He felt disconnected from time, but strong enough to do something about it.

The first thing he did was address an envelope to Bobbie. He meant to send her some of the money, as an apology and a reminder that he hadn't stolen it out of greed. As soon as he held one of the plastic packets in his bad hand, though, and had to decide how much to donate, he became perplexed. He could have parted with the lot easily – it would have been a relief – but what would the poor young woman do with so much? It would surely cause more grief than delight. And yet there was so much to be squandered he could slip in fifty, or a hundred, even a thousand, without sacrifice. Or five thousand. Ten thousand – the unreality of it was getting to him. You couldn't be a philanthropist unless you knew a lot about those you meant to help, he reckoned. He found a pencil and scribbled a faint note: Sorry if I hurt your feelings. None intended. This is from a bit of a windfall. Please accept and no questions asked and say no more about it. Sorry to have bothered you. The man from the train. J.E. Goodbye.

Having written it he turned again to the money. Sod you, he grunted, and stuffed what he guessed was a thousand pounds – the contents of one packet – into the envelope along with his explanatory note. The amount he knew was more than generous, but it was also inconsequential and, apart from a mild relief at having rid himself of a small part of the whole, he didn't feel particularly noble.

When he dropped the envelope into a drawer – he wouldn't be able to buy a stamp until Monday – it fell on top of the letter he'd already written to Rachel. That didn't seem right, Rachel's letter being so thin, Bobbie's so fat. Again he had to frown and wish he could think of some way to use his wealth for his wife's benefit. Then he wondered if he could let Mrs Champion have a few hundred, to redecorate. The room smelled damp and the paper was old, worn away alongside the mattress and around the light switch.

Downstairs, Mrs Champion said, 'It's so nice having you back again.' And he was wretched with her loneliness for several seconds, though hundreds of lodgers must have been through since his day.

'It's because I hurt my hand,' he explained. 'Usually I'd be too busy, but I been at a bit of a loose end lately, that's why I come to look up old Phil.'

'I feel forgotten sometimes,' Mrs Champion said. 'I remember my boys, but the years go by and they never come back – no reason to, I know.'

'Well, life goes on, I suppose, and we all move away.'

'But do any of you ever remember? I remember, so clearly.' She wasn't quite looking at him, or talking to him. She was a strange old bird, he thought, and she *was* old, despite that peculiar beauty in manner and bearing. She was very old, frail too, and still carrying her youth around, and all her memories of lodgers who'd never actually been friends, just polite strangers beneath her roof. John Eakins didn't know what to make of her. He wanted to apologise, or reassure her, but it wouldn't have rung true because he hadn't carried her in his thoughts down the years.

'Best go see if I can locate Phil Thomas,' he said, to get away.

'I wish you better luck than last night.'

'Aye,' he said, confused, wondering if she meant not finding Phil or finding Bobbie. 'Thanks.'

It was good just to be out in the street breathing something like fresh air. Around one corner he caught a glimpse of sky, a thin purple cloud fringed with gold. London only allowed bits of the sky; you had to be on a trawler to get the whole cathedral.

The barker outside *Jack Rabbit's Live Girls* was not the man John had spoken to on Saturday evening.

'Great show tonight, sir,' he said, beginning to extend his arm to usher John in. He was wearing a dinner jacket, a frilled white shirt with a bow-tie, and had a friendly, open grin – good-looking, a bit like Russ Conway, so it jarred that he was doing this for a living instead of playing the piano. 'Best dancers in Soho,' he added, urging John to look at the glossy photographs on the display boards. 'Some just go through the motions like they're half-asleep, not these. Our girls go at it like there's no tomorrow.'

In the photographs they weren't really dancing, John could tell. They were holding dramatic poses, one with her fingers parted like a cat wanting to scratch you, another holding her own hips as if her dress wasn't already skin tight. They were beautiful women, wearing outfits normal women never wore, and John didn't mind

151

looking, though they were too sophisticated for his pockets. He grinned, remembering the money.

'Like 'em?' the barker asked.

'That one reminds me of Alma Cogan,' John said.

'She's a corker. Can't sing, but she does a snake-charming act that'll make your eyes pop out on their stalks.'

'Well, another time, perhaps – I'm looking for Phil Thomas. I was told to come back today. Know Phil, do you?'

'You're the Welshman!' the barker exclaimed. 'Thought you talked funny! I just didn't twig it right off – thought you was an Indian, mate, sorry!'

'What?'

'Indians, you know how they talk.' He put his hands together in prayer and started moving his head oddly: 'Oh my goodness gracious, what a silly billy I am, sir!' he said in a thickly accented travesty of Welsh.

'You do this for free, do you?' John said sourly.

'I'm only saying. Don't get stroppy, mate. Anyway, yeah, Phil was here, and he's gone round your gaff – left an address or something, didn't you?'

'He's gone round my place? Mrs Champion's, you mean? How long ago?'

'How should I know? Half an hour, twenty minutes? What's it all about, you buying the club or something?'

'What do you mean? I'm just looking up Phil – haven't seen him since just after the war.'

'Oh, sure!' the barker said sarcastically.

John turned away and started walking back. The man's reactions were peculiar, as if he'd heard quite different things than John had been saying. Clearly someone had passed the message on, though, and that was reassuring. John began to hurry. The barker had looked at him very strangely as soon as he said he was looking for Phil. The Welshman, he'd called him, as if he were someone special, someone everyone was talking about.

Mrs Champion never locked it, but she did like to keep it shut. In the narrow hallway all was quiet, nothing disturbed, and yet John advanced with trepidation, all his senses alert to some unseen calamity. He glanced up the stairs, but again nothing was visibly disarranged. He squeezed his right hand, mainly to flex his good left. His upper body was too tense, as if he expected to be pounced on any second. Something, not quite a noise, drew him towards the back room to check on Mrs Champion.

Then he rushed to her. She was on the rucked-up carpet, and

she hadn't fallen, she'd been hit. Her cheek was swollen and bruised, left eye puffed and closed. She winced as he tried to help her to a sitting position. She'd been clobbered.

'It's all right now, Mrs Champion,' he said as soon as he felt her fear of him. 'This is me, John Eakins. What happened here? I'll call you an ambulance now just, is it? Anything first? What can I get?'

She was weeping. He wondered who could ever be so base as to attack a helpless old lady. His blood boiled. If he'd been in he'd have shown them!

'What have you been up to?' she managed in a quavering voice, accusing him as if it were his fault.

'No, I'm here to help you now. We'll get the police, the ambulance, you'll be all right. Was it burglars? What was it, Mrs Champion? No, don't need to answer. Just stay quiet now. I'll use your telephone.'

'Mr Eakins,' she whispered again, frightened, groaning, 'what have you done?'

'It's not me,' he said, exasperated but full of pity for her distracted agony.

'They've smashed up your room. I said I was calling for the police. Should have done it, not said it.'

'My room? But...' He hovered awkwardly between the prostrate body and the telephone, trying to understand. 'But nobody knows...' His voice evaporated. I was out under an hour, he assured himself. It's not my fault. It's nothing to do with me. There's no way anybody could know I got that...

He made an emergency call regardless. The first thing was obviously to bring assistance to Mrs Champion. For himself he couldn't think clearly and had no time to be concerned.

THIRTY

John Eakins stood his ground, accepting that somehow someone had heard about his money and beaten up poor Mrs Champion just for sharing a house with it. He should have told her, but couldn't have. And as he couldn't have he shouldn't have taken his old room. It was his fault. She was right. How on earth anyone could have known about the money, though...no point fretting. He could have attempted to shut her up, he supposed, made up a story about how the money wasn't so much stolen as floating free, and how he'd meant to use it for good works. But that was unworthy. John Eakins was no liar and Mrs Champion was hurt.

A policeman arrived just before the ambulance and assumed John was a relative or a helpful neighbour – he was just a bobby on his beat, similar sort of bloke to Bob Ryman, getting the essence of the situation in a glance: old girl senselessly beaten by hooligans who probably thought she had a few quid under the teapot.

Mrs Champion heard him speculate and, though not drifting, didn't set the lad straight, reserving that for the long baleful look she aimed straight through John's honest eyes to the shaky navigation system of his soul.

'Tell them what your attacker looked like if you can,' John urged. 'Don't be afraid to talk.'

He wasn't sure why he was saying that, to make her feel he wasn't hiding as much as she feared, he supposed, a way of thanking her for her reticence, a compromise. He could have said something about his room, the money, the reason, and she'd observed his ignoble silence.

'I'll try and visit tomorrow,' he called gratefully just before they drove her off.

When he went into his room he was almost glad to see the mess – bed tipped over, sheets and clothes heaped raggedly, drawers pulled on to the floor. Not subtle thieves, these, but noisy men who didn't give a damn. The money was definitely gone. And he was glad. If he'd been in they could have asked and he'd have handed it over, whoever they were. On the other hand, some of it could have gone to Mrs Champion now, in recompense for being so trusting, for believing everyone as naive as herself.

I'll make it up to her from my own pocket, he decided. And that was right too. He was responsible for her suffering – didn't want to be, couldn't think how it had come to pass, yet should have foreseen it. A lonely old lady who meant nothing to him. Like that old-time king, he thought, Midas, ruining everything he touched. I never should have left the Haven. Never should have picked up the briefcase. Never should have thought of visiting Phil. Never should have come away from Rachel.

At least she was untouched by all this grimness.

A thought crossed his mind and he hunted for the drawer where he'd placed his letter home. The letter was gone – Bastards! he thought – So was the one to Bobbie – at least there was a bit of dosh with that one, but Rachel's was private. So now whoever had it would know where he came from. Maybe they'd try blackmail. Bastards! Just let them!

John Eakins sagged. He'd brought this on himself. He could see that damned briefcase sitting there on the rock, awaiting the tide. He could have left it. Why hadn't he been sensible? Net result: those terrible bruises to Mrs Champion's face, the shock and fear and new distrust he'd forced on her. What a way to treat the elderly – just before you die of a nice rosy lonely old age, Mrs Champion, here's what people are really like, not considerate at all, you've deluded yourself right up to the end, nearly, and now I can disappoint you – serves you right for having such a sad little fantasy life, peopled with ciphers.

Only it didn't serve her right and he felt as though he'd ripped the wings off a butterfly or something. What right had he, or anyone, to intrude on such a fragile old existence? She'd gone on for decades living in the past, and although he found her a bit pathetic he envied her because she'd harmed no one with her life. She should have been permitted to reach the end without this rough awakening. Everyone had that right, surely. It didn't ask much.

John Eakins glared at his right hand, then, slowly, he raised it and made an awkward stiff fist, and slammed it hard on to the iron bedstead. The pain soared through his teeth till they felt as if they gushed red.

That's a stupid solution, he told himself at once, nursing his agony. Wish to God I had some whisky.

Slowly, rooting around in the kitchen downstairs to get a cup of tea, he remembered why he'd hurried back from his brief outing.

Where was old Phil in all this?

Thirty One

Foster pressed until his mother promised they wouldn't stop off to see her relatives in the valleys, and once he believed her he settled into enjoying the drive again. Not the drive itself, which was monotonous, but the thought of getting to London, seeing famous sights and boasting to his pals next week. Relatives weren't bad, exactly – they were good when you visited them at Christmas – but they had squashed old houses full of the smells you associated with places that weren't really yours. Foster's house was new and didn't smell of anything, not like that farm. Those old bodies were just the same as the relatives – old, essentially, and well-meaning. You had to be polite around them. They were in tight with God so you felt like it was Sunday the entire time. Of course today was Sunday too, but it felt like a day that hadn't been invented yet. It was good when those men came in and stopped the bad men. That was like the pictures, except they didn't have a showdown. But those bad men wouldn't be able to catch up now. Foster's mind danced quickly over disturbing patches: London was the main thing.

'Why can't they have a wireless here,' he reached forward and tapped the dashboard, 'like they got in American cars?' That was the best thing about America. You drove these huge cars, shinier than English ones with lots more chrome, and you listened to rock 'n' roll on the car radio. Radio, they called it, not wireless. Wireless was old-fashioned. He mouthed the right word silently, radio, and turned an imaginary dial to tune in.

'I don't think they have them in real life, Foss,' Rachel informed him. 'Where could you plug it in, for a start? I think they want us to think they're really advanced, you know? What do they call it? Science Fiction. You can't have a wireless in a car. You'd crash.'

She was so sensible. So that was too good to be true. Pity. But his mother usually saw through to the truth of things, so she had to be right.

'Are we nearly there yet?' he asked.

'Where? London?' Rachel smiled sympathetically. 'We're still in Wales, love. Long old trip, isn't it? We're close to where I was brought up now, though, so another hour or so and we'll cross over to England. We'll have a break then, is it?'

He was behaving himself remarkably well, she thought. He didn't have a lot to say, but wasn't fractious. Probably the frights they'd had had tired him out. They must have got back on the road by mid-morning, so she guessed it was early afternoon now – didn't have her watch on. No maps in the cab, either. But the main towns were signposted and she was reasonably certain she hadn't gone wrong. Even so it was taking longer than she'd have thought. The lorry rarely climbed above thirty – too many bends to risk it. Handling was easy enough, except when she had to come down through the gears on climbs, and apply the brakes on descents. And they'd have to fill up somewhere, if they could find a garage.

A picture on a white pub wall: a jolly huntsman astride a horse whose body was a beer keg; iron bridges set in rough blackish stone, the battleship grey girders riveted all along, like stitching with golf balls; big long posters: toucans in one, a man carrying girders in another. Guinness, Rhymney Ales – all signs of her part of south Wales. She'd only ever seen them in this area, and in Cardiff, maybe. Never in Pembrokeshire, anyhow. And it was peculiar to be driving by in a lorry, instead of coming by train. Rachel's childhood memories weren't enchanting, but home was home, whether you longed for it or went back just out of duty. Actually, she realised cheekily, it was liberating to pass so close and not stop off to see anyone.

For a while she thought about Ezekiel and his wife, and their strong sons – it was wonderful how they'd turned the tables on George and Gently, so convincingly that she knew there'd be no more physical danger from those two – of course, there remained the worry about John, but she didn't dwell on it. Other things occupied her, like the name of that boyfriend. Odd that he'd come back to mind for no reason, but she'd misremembered the name. It wasn't David Barrington. David Barrington was the name of an English teacher who'd once said she could be a writer when she grew up. He'd meant it. He was the first person to give her any confidence. So why couldn't she remember that boy's name, when she remembered walking with him on the downs so vividly?

It didn't matter. Even to Rachel it had no conceivable relevance, yet her inner life was often crammed with similar minor crises, insistent questions crying out of some dim recess to be her companions. And even while she struggled to recall a forgotten name she was experiencing odd delayed jolts of fear – if John had lost his hand after his accident, if Foster had been prosecuted for thieving – anything, it seemed, but the most recent and real events in her life.

Apart from registering the signs of being close to her childhood she barely noticed the journey. And that intrigued her momentarily. A journey, she thought, is composed of the memories you trawl en route, and some of them might be what you'll remember next-time you think back to the journey.

Ezekiel again. She knew some who'd drifted from the chapel after their experiences in the war years. They felt let down personally by God. Rachel's attendance became more regular. She felt the best way forward would be for congregations of decent people to sit still and have kind thoughts once a week. She supposed Ezekiel would frown at anything so slight. She wondered too about the circumstances in which that poor stranger had died alone on the rocks, wondered if he'd left a widow, and why God had allowed him to pass away amidst harsh elements.

Foster kept asking about London so she began worrying ahead: What time of night would they get in? And where would you park a lorry in London? And where would you find lodgings if it was after dark? Realistically, she knew there'd be no point trying to hunt for John until Monday morning. A new day would make it easier, probably.

Like Foster, who could blot out the immediate past and thrive on what lay ahead, Rachel found herself almost blasé about the panic that had made her leave Milford. Saturday night was an age ago, and even this morning's encounter lay well back. It didn't occur to her that she was being complacent, though, and she couldn't imagine how a time she had put behind her might still be rumbling away, capable of engulfing her.

By the time they approached Gloucester she was ready for a break and asked Foster to keep his eyes peeled for a place to eat. Although most places were shut on Sunday she was so relieved to have accomplished the drive across Wales in safety that she believed a restaurant would turn up on cue. Some things were bound to happen that way, if you were deserving.

Finally she reflected on what she was doing, and why. It was in the contract, she remembered: you marry for better or worse, not in order to keep things as they are. And it's within reason, you don't have to promise any superlatives. Nobody'd marry for worst. It was comparative. David Barrington had taught her things like that when she was a girl. Or was his name Andrew? It was Andrew something. So you marry and contract to make a difference in each other's lives.

'There!' Foster exclaimed. 'Open for afternoon teas – did you see it, Mam? The hotel's up by here, on the left.'

'Well done, Foss. Good boy.'

There was no room for two in the kiosk, but Gently had to dial and be ready with the coins. He was also needed to prod the button when the call was connected. George wedged himself between Gently's broad back and the heavy door, balancing the receiver on his thumb, wishing the lead were longer.

'Mr Gravett!' he said, as if genuinely gratified to have got through. 'This is George, Mr Gravett. I'm sorry I didn't catch you last night. No, I did try. Yes, I expect it was an error.'

Gently was unable to turn around, yet managed to communicate shared exasperation through his immense back. Nothing actually moved, but George was sure of his partner's understanding. It was a gruelling business, having to grovel to Bull Gravett, and for someone who'd just had a hand in wiping out four powerful farmers it was too petty for words. If he'd had a choice he'd have taken it, but things had taken a messy turn.

'No, things are a lot worse than you feared, I'm afraid. We've had all kinds of trouble since we arrived. Yes, of course we were discreet. None of this is down to us, Mr Gravett. These people out here are devious. Seems like the entire area is corrupt, as far as I can understand it. No. Hold on a minute, please – listen, Gently and I have been held prisoner in a barn for two and a half hours. Trussed up like bloody martyrs. Well of course we got out of it, that's why I'm phoning now. Yes, I'm sorry, Mr Gravett. I'm not losing my temper. We're a little put out, Gently and me. We weren't expecting anything so well organised. Yes. Yes. All right, if we've got enough coins I'll explain.' He kicked Gently's heel. Gently said 'Fuck 'im.'

George continued: 'Mr Wary kicked it off, though it's possible he wasn't doing the dirty on you, but dying didn't help. I'd say either the estate agent or Fisk, the chap in the transport business. He seemed wide-eyed greedy enough when we spoke to him, but things have happened since. Well, for a start, when we'd only been in town a couple of hours and talked to three or four of our contacts, we were met by the local team. Yes, they wanted to give us the bum's rush. No, no problem, naturally. But obviously they'd been put up to it, they couldn't have known about us otherwise.

'Next thing is, we pick up a hint that the money Mr Wary was carrying got lifted, apparently by a local fisherman, so we had to check that out. We spoke to his wife, who more or less confirmed that he had it. No, the man himself had left town. I'm coming to that. I didn't altogether trust the woman, so instead of going back to the hotel, Gently and I waited on the road into Haverfordwest – yeah, that's right, only one road out of town. Sure enough, in the early hours along she comes in a lorry, and, get this, it's one of Fisk's fleet. Exactly. We were about to pursue her when a big fellow on a motorbike tried to force us off the road. Yeah, this is a careful operation we're talking about. This guy came from the other direction. She must have signalled him. They know our every move. Yes, he's in the ditch – maybe in a hospital by now, who cares?

'Anyway, that delayed us and we lost track of the woman until this morning. She was hiding out at some farm. That's when we were jumped by four armed men. I'm not exaggerating, Mr Gravett – four of them. They took turns at us for a bit, then tied us up in a barn while the woman went on her way. The good news is we got something out of her before these characters burst in on us: her old man was on his way to London. Probably arrived last night. We think his contact is Taffy Thomas – that's him, Phil Thomas. Well I think it's good news because you may be able to get your money back. No, I know that's only a drop in the ocean, Mr Gravett. I realize the rest of the operation's looking a bit sick. No, Gently and I can't go back now. We had to get a little rough with the local muscle, and there'll be too many looking for us. We're coming back now. I'm sorry, but it's really not our fault. Yes, you'll need to interview all the interested parties, but for my money it's the estate agent or the road haulage fellow. I don't know what they hoped to gain by crossing you – maybe they thought they could get a better deal off somebody else. Shifty, these Welsh businessmen. Yeah, Taffy Thomas and Eakins, John Eakins.'

He pushed the receiver under Gently's elbow, depositing blood on it. Gently backed out of the kiosk and faced him.

'You didn't say you were going to tell Bull Gravett about Eakins,' he challenged morosely.

'Forget the money,' George spat. 'If he gets it back maybe he'll think everything else I said was true, and maybe he won't drop us in concrete. It's called thinking ahead, mate, saving our skins. We were supposed to creep in and out on tippy-toe, remember? Not fuck up the biggest semi-legitimate deal that bastard's ever made. Money's the root of all evil, okay?'

Gently frowned. It was what one of the farmers had told them when they were tied up and obliged to listen.

'You're too old to have served, let alone survived on the Burma railroad,' Gently mused as they trudged back towards their car.

'Maybe I'm not as old as I look. Maybe I look this old because of what I went through. What the fuck did you ever do?'

'I was unfit. Only one good lung. Bullet near the spine. Poor eyesight, too.'

'What's wrong with your eyes? I don't see you wearing specs.'

'I prefer the world the way I see it. I see what I need. You sure you can drive with that hand?'

'Never expected that old man to come at me with a bloody cleaver.'

'Dumb move putting out your hand to stop him, though.'

George chuckled wryly. He got behind the wheel and demonstrated how he could turn it with the heel of his hand. Then he decided Gently was taking the thought of kissing all that money goodbye pretty well, so he confided in him: 'I don't believe John Eakins really has the stuff. That was for Bull Gravett. He'll pull him in, and Phil Thomas too, and that's their lookout. I reckon Mrs Eakins has it. John Eakins stashed it at that farmhouse, then went on to London to set up, I don't know, some deal with Thomas. Why else would she have come out last night in one of Fisk's lorries? I bet it was already on board when we walked by. We needn't have gone up to the farmhouse. We could have picked it up and gone on our way.'

Gently whistled. It was dispiriting, if they'd been that close.

'She's what – three hours ahead? But going about thirty, and thinking she's clear. So she'll stop for a meal. I reckon we'll get ahead if we go flat out. I know where we can wait for her, too. Birdlip Hill, just the other side of Gloucester. Nice deserted spot. Nil desperandum, chum.'

'Cut her off at the pass! I like it!'

George started the engine and shook his head. He couldn't decide whether he liked Gently's gullibility and ferocity or loathed his barminess.

'What?' he asked impatiently.

'It's an expression.'

'The pass? What pass? It's a steep hill for God's sake.'

'It's what they say in cowboys.'

'This is like your Four Stooges thing again, isn't it?'

'I never said there were four,' Gently protested. 'There's Three Coins in the Fountain, Three Steps to Heaven, and Three Stooges.'

George considered this rationale for a moment and thought he might as well go along with it.

'There's Four Horsemen of the Apocalypse,' he offered.

'So?'

He gave up. 'It just popped into my head. Nothing.'

'All right,' Gently said agreeably. 'Let's be them.'

Never should've left the smoke, George thought glumly, trying not to catch sight of his ruined fingers.

★ ★ ★

Bull Gravett was auditioning would-be pop idols. He guessed there was going to be a market for this grating noise because kids today had no sense. He sneered at the poofs in elaborate hair-dos as they struck their guitars and dramatic poses. It was a painful way to make money, but somebody had to do it. George's phone call upset him. He whispered to one of his aides:

'Ask around the clubs, find out if there's been a Welsh bloke called John Eakins asking for Phil Thomas. Find out where he's staying. He may be carrying something of mine. Bring it back. Turn over Taffy Thomas's place as well. Bring both bastards here as soon as you can.'

His aide hurried away. He listened to another baby-faced poof with a sneer he must have secured with paper clips, and the same chord and pose as the last one.

'You're good, kid,' he called out. 'Real American.'

'Gee, thanks, mister,' the kid blushed.

'What I'm looking for is an English sound. Rock 'n' Roll's dead. Piss off back to your bedroom and get an acne cure. You're a disgrace.'

His musical advisor looked worried. Bull Gravett hit him between the shoulders.

'I just had to say it to one of them,' he chuckled. 'Don't tell me he was the best!'

'Well, no, admittedly they're much of a muchness, but if we can get a record deal and a quick film – it's almost a guaranteed return, Mr Gravett, for quite a modest outlay.'

'So you said,' Bull Gravett sighed, leaving his stool. 'Okay, you carry on. And be right.'

On his way out he called over another aide: 'I've got a problem. George and Gently went out of control. I think they've scuppered the oil deals in Milford Haven. A mistake to send them, but I wanted to trust old George. I really thought he could rein Gently in. Sad. Take whoever you need. See if you can do them before they get back. Quick, quiet and permanent. Use a squad car and some uniforms, same as with poor old Midge.'

It saddened Bull Gravett to have to deal with gangsters. He put Frank Sinatra on the gramophone to soothe his sensitive soul. Shickcarrrgo, Shickarrrgo, he crooned appreciatively.

Thirty Three

The girl's heels made attractively plump detonations. A gaudy headscarf didn't quite cover her hair, bleached to a kind of whiteness that didn't at all suggest infirmity; the raised collar of her belted white raincoat didn't quite hide all of a face tanned with greasepaint to a lively plastic shine, then set off with some kind of silvery stardust: she could have been a tart or a showgirl, though she wanted to be an average inconspicuous stroller who just happened to be approaching Mrs Champion's.

The front door, as she'd been advised, was unlocked, so she let herself in and cautiously moved upstairs and then knocked.

'Are you John Eakins?' she asked nervously.

John weighed his caller warily: she wasn't likely to jump him.

'Who are you?' he wanted to know.

'Can you pack quick and come with me? They'll be back looking for you any time now.'

'I'm packed.' He strode over to the bedstead and picked up his duffle. He'd been on the verge of leaving for ten minutes, just hanging on for Phil Thomas or some idea of where to go.

The girl was already downstairs. By the time he reached the hall she was in the street. He followed. She made surprisingly fast progress for someone on four-inch heels. He was hampered by the weight of his duffle, though it really wasn't heavy enough to be an excuse. He caught up.

'You're from Phil, is it?'

'I'm not to say anything.'

'Where are we going? Phil's place?'

'It's not safe. Somewhere else.'

'So are you a friend of Phil's? His girl? You work for him?'

The clacking rhythm faltered, only briefly. John looked up the street in time to see a man pause, glancing their way before pretending he hadn't registered them.

'Damn!' the girl swore, lowering her head between the wings of her collar, as if her face were the only identifiable part of her.

John realised that there weren't many people about, and that slipping unnoticed through London streets on a Sunday evening was probably as difficult as in the streets back home. It was only impersonal to people who didn't live and work in it. The girl might be endangering herself, unless she was drawing him into an ambush – but she was too concentrated and awkward for that.

'That duffle bag's a right giveaway,' she admonished him. 'It's obvious you're a sailor or a soldier or something, slinging that on your shoulder.'

'I'm making you conspicuous? I'm sorry.'

'It don't matter.'

As far as he could tell she was leading him north, parallel with Tottenham Court Road. But they kept making turns down empty sidestreets, so he soon lost his bearings and what little he could see of the evening sky wasn't a great help.

'Okay,' she said, stopping at last. 'This is as far as I'm coming. You carry on up there to the end, go left. After about a hundred yards there's a mews. Go through and out the alley at the back. Wait there and if we haven't been followed your friend will get you after a couple of minutes.'

'Thank you,' John said, hoping he'd remember it all. 'What if he doesn't turn up?'

'I think you're on your own then.' She was about to hurry away, but changed her mind. 'You've caused him plenty of trouble, you know. If you're his pal you shouldn't have done it.'

'Well...' John started, only he couldn't explain what he didn't get.

The girl checked in all directions, then unbelted her raincoat and handed it to John. She had extraordinarily long nails, he noticed, not knowing about stick-on false ones. She picked at the knot under her chin. The nails were a bright red, like her lips. Glossy. Unreal. Rather glamorous, clustering at her throat like ladybirds.

'Here, let me,' he said, reaching up to assist before realising his right hand wasn't sensitive enough. 'Sorry. Can't help.'

She pulled the headscarf forward and let it decorate her neck instead.

'This is supposed to be me Mamie Van Doren,' she explained, unpinning the wig and revealing her real hair. 'Makes us more like Doris Day, don't it?'

'I thought it was genuine,' John said shyly. 'You was stunning in it. But your own hair's blonde anyway, and longer.'

'Not so unusual, though.'

She stuffed the wig into a pocket of her raincoat, then proceeded to turn the raincoat inside out. Clearly the idea was to effect a complete transformation and confuse pursuers, who were apparently non-existent. John didn't say, but he thought she remained just as easy to recognise.

'If I don't see you again, thanks for your help,' he said.

'Phil's been good to me,' she told him frankly.

All the cloak and dagger stuff was somewhat baffling, but John

Eakins didn't question the need, and made his way obediently to the mews. A couple of carts suggested that at least some of the stables still contained horses, but some had been converted into garages and even flats. Londoners, he surmised, were getting desperate for accommodation. On his first stroll to the end he missed the narrow alley completely, but it was there just as she'd said, and at the far end were houses and empty sites – possibly remnants of war damage, though he was surprised. They'd had plenty of time to tidy up.

A couple of young teds were idling around a bubble car, making frequent repairs to their hair with steel combs. John Eakins wondered how long it would be before they wandered across and tried to intimidate him. He also wondered how many others might be on call. It didn't look like a prospering neighbourhood. The teds didn't bother him particularly, though. He was a lot more concerned about the types who'd roughed up Mrs Champion, and they'd be older and less obsessed with hairstyles and hard poses.

'Hey, John!' a voice came from behind.

Phil Thomas was beckoning at the end of the alley. He wasn't in disguise, and looked in good shape. John moved towards him. Phil grabbed his arm and hurried him into one of the mews' garages, dragging the doors shut before giving him a hug.

'Good to see you, boy,' Phil said gruffly, 'despite the blummin' chaos you've brung.'

'Good to see you, too – you don't look hardly no different at all. But this chaos, Phil, I don't get it. What've I done?'

Phil Thomas barked a laugh: 'Same old bloody John Eakins, then!'

'Aye, I don't change.'

'Come upstairs, you daft bugger, we'll have a chinwag. What you been doing with your hand?'

'Just an accident. It's healing.'

'Still punch as good as ever, though? Southpaw – that's right, isn't it?'

'Oh yeah, my left's fine. How'd you remember?'

They went up through the garage into an unexpectedly long and well-lit room. Phil explained it belonged to a friend, a photographer, and forestalled John's queries about the large pin-up photos on display. Phil didn't turn a hair, but John was astonished to see such images where Vernon Ward prints would normally have been. Phil walked over to the largest refrigerator John had ever seen and pulled out four bottles of beer.

'How come you've never come to see me all these years?' Phil asked, throwing John the bottle opener. 'I send you a card every year. Last time I heard from you was four, five years.'

'I never was a letter-writer, Phil.' John sat opposite his friend and picked up a beer from the coffee table. He was relaxed, and didn't feel guilty about not keeping in touch. Already he felt as though hardly any time had passed since he and Phil last drank together. "Sides, my wife disapproves of you.'

'And why's that?'

'Working in Soho – she thinks you must be degenerate, so she's fixed it into her head that I can't really like you.'

'You're so virtuous, is it?'

'Got it.' John grinned. So did Phil. 'What is it you do, exactly? All your cards come from the one club, which don't exist no more.'

'Well they're just cards – had a stack of them. I suppose I'm a sort of promoter – agent, fixer – bit of this, bit of that. Got money in a couple of clubs, some in theatres, a bit in publishing. And, to gladden your wife's heart, yeah, I represent the odd exotic dancer and photographer's model – quite a number of them, actually. These kids get exploited if they aren't careful, but it's a decent life – well, it can be, for some. Most don't have a lot of talent.'

John Eakins nodded, and swigged beer. The world Phil was alluding to was alien to him, and not especially interesting, but he wasn't inclined to disapprove. Phil was a man he respected, and if Phil thought it was a world with good qualities John was willing to believe him. The most significant thing, as far as John Eakins was concerned, was Phil's reassuring presence. As soon as they'd met John had felt at ease, not merely because Phil knew his way around London – it went deeper. Phil, like John, was a man who got on with life according to his own values – he didn't try to get anyone else to join him, didn't make an issue out of surviving, and wasn't likely to fold if things got tough. He was a quiet, solitary but not unfriendly man, a joker who'd seen more than enough madness to know where he should be serious. So what if he consorted with striptease dancers and unsavoury men? Phil himself was funda-mentally decent, and John sensed an immediate old rapport such as he couldn't find back home.

Bob and Mal, Peter Walker, Fred Knight – they were close enough, but none struck him as being essentially responsible. It seemed an odd word, yet apt: *he* was always responsible, for Rachel, too, and it was a burden he hadn't been able to share. Not that he'd resented it, any more than he might have resented being broad shouldered or having a swarthy complexion – it was part of his make up to be trustworthy. Only it narrowed him. And he wanted the luxury of going wrong occasionally, being daft, or at least not being perpetually *there* to satisfy expectations.

'I've got myself in a bit of a pickle, Phil,' he said comfortably.

Outside the evening was deepening, pink and mauve in the clouds, the hesitation before night, the time of starling swarms – at sea a time suspended and reflective, water slapping the hull, lighting the lights, losing the horizon in the east, watching it grow stronger for a while in the west.

He expected Phil to sit back and listen, but his friend said a pickle was an understatement.

'Presumably you've come because Alan Wary died, but you could have used your head, John. Anyway, what's the plan?'

'Mrs Champion's been beaten up. Remember her? Poor dab. I'd like to get hold of whoever did that.'

'In due course, but why did you bring the money back?'

'That's another thing – how did they know? How do *you* know? I'm serious, Phil, I never mentioned I had any money.'

'You got my letter? About Alan?' Phil was frowning, John mystified. 'I wrote. Asked you to meet him. Alan Wary was a fairminded man, he wasn't at all happy about going down to Wales to broker the kind of deal Bull Gravett wants, so I told him you'd help.'

'Me! I don't know nothing about deals. This is bizarre, mun!'

'Your not knowing about this is bizarre. I'm puzzled, John. Okay, I'll explain. Bulstrode Gravett's a greedy sort of bloke. It'll be his people who've turned over Mrs Champion's. Right now they're after me an' all, as your accomplice. You shot your mouth off last night, telling everybody who you were, asking for me, leaving your address – daft, John. Really. About two this morning I got the message – should have come there and then, because I realised you must be in a fix, but I reckoned I'd sleep on it and come about dinner time. Luckily I got the tip-off – one of my proteges was auditioning and heard Bull telling his men to round you and me up – so I had to get out of my own place and find a sort of safehouse before I could risk a visit.'

'What's this got to do with the man who died around Hakin Point?'

Phil shook his head, reluctant to be suspicious, yet unwilling to accept that John Eakins was as clueless as he appeared to be. Patiently, he went through it, his voice monotonous, as if he knew it to be redundant. But John wasn't conning him. No doubt a letter had been posted, it just hadn't arrived. He remembered staring at Alan Wary's dead toes, and it was somehow poignant that he was supposed to have met the man whose money he'd taken.

168

Phil Thomas had had dealings with Alan Wary and – though he regretted it subsequently – introduced him to Bulstrode Gravett. Wary was known as an honest broker. The money was for sweeteners, for several businessmen who'd let themselves be beguiled by Gravett's talk of transforming the quiet Haven into a new Klondike. It all depended on the arrival of oil, of course, but Gravett had reliable informants, contacts with clout, so he was sure of the potential.

Alan Wary was in a bind. He had to use the money, and get the right people securely on the team; mainly, he had to return with deals Bulstrode Gravett could rely on. Phil's suggestion was that if Alan Wary discreetly made contact with John, then John would know who to let in on what was going to happen.

'I reckoned you'd know someone who could sort of circumvent the development plan, if necessary – I mean, Bull's contacts could all be perfectly honest, honourable businessmen, with the good of your area at heart, but if not...'

'I wish I'd got that letter, Phil, but even if I had...' I'd have shown it to Bob Ryman, he thought, and me and Bob could have talked to Mr Wary.

'Well, you must know people. I reckoned on the honest townsfolk putting some moral pressure on these others, maybe ensuring the money was used sensibly. The main thing was to work it so that there'd still be the kinds of expansion Gravett wanted, so he'd turn a tidy profit, but he wouldn't gain control. It's the thought of him having control over a whole town that freezes my blood.'

'Could that happen? What would he do?'

'Well, your wife wouldn't like living there.'

'Right. I see.' John wasn't convinced that he did really see as yet, but in a sense it no longer mattered. 'So now this Gravett chap has got his money back, so what does he do? Start again?'

'No,' Phil said. 'Gravett doesn't have the money. I got there before his thugs – must have just missed you. I took it. I've got it. It's here.'

He didn't produce the briefcase – just as well, John thought, stunned by these revelations. The only cheering note in the last few hours had been his satisfaction at being rid of that money. Now it was back, unnecessarily, stupidly, to haunt him till he confessed and officially ended his life as an honourable man.

I'm damned, he thought, I can't tell Phil the truth!

He couldn't, after travelling to London expressly to unburden himself. But what could he tell him?

Phil, as if sharing his thoughts, looked unhappy again.

'So if you didn't talk to Alan, how come you wound up with the money and looking for me?'

'I think you'd have to call it a lucky stroke, Phil,' John said, tormented by the need to lie to his friend: 'My boy and his friends were out playing when they found the body. They came to me because I'm around the house all day, on account of this bloody hand, see – most fathers are at work. So I was on the scene before Bob – he's our local policeman – or anyone else got there. I looked in the man's coat for identification – lucky I did. Found a few names, including yours. Soon as I saw that I thought you might know what it was all about. All that money – I was afraid it might land you in trouble if it was at all fishy, so I hid the wallet and brought the briefcase with me.'

Phil sat back and sighed loudly: 'Coincidence or what!' he exclaimed. 'That's amazing. Honest John Eakins, eh! Anybody else would have stolen the money, but not you, mate! That's incredible! Anyway, thanks for coming, then, even if you have stirred things up. I was worthy of your loyalty, wasn't I?'

'Absolutely,' John insisted, covering his shame. 'But what's our next move? You say it's here?'

'We'll have to deal with Gravett. It gives us something to deal with. I'd like to make sure something goes to Alan's family. Maybe Mrs Champion as well. But...'

'Whatever you say. If this man's as bad as you say, I don't like the idea of him becoming a big fish in Milford. That's still on the cards, is it?'

Phil shrugged: 'If Alan could have met the right people he'd have returned with a *fait accompli.* Now... I just don't know, John. We're out on a limb, really, you and me. There's some hard men on the streets.'

John Eakins nodded sagely. He'd heard a great deal that was new to him, and he'd scuffed a bit more of his soul, but Phil believed in him and he believed in Phil, and together, even if it was a touch fanciful to imagine, they could make a difference.

'There's some hard men in here, too,' he bragged, and laughed, and was more or less serious.

THIRTY FOUR

'We want a word with the boyfriend, duck,' the man under the stairwell said, ignoring Bobbie even while speaking to her.

Bobbie couldn't see his features, though behind and above him a patch of grass and railing caught the low glow of early evening brightly. Her father had promised to run a lead from the light above the steps – his idea, he'd first suggested it about a year ago – but he was always promising things he never got around to. Her mother defended him, said he was so busy, and she'd have to be patient, and she had no callers anyway, and if a light was only to help her stick a key in the door it was hardly urgent because when was the last time she was out after dark? And didn't he do enough for her?

Bobbie wasn't expecting anyone. She'd been in all day, some of it speculating about why John Eakins had left without a word. The knock had made her think of him again, though there was no reason he should come back and apologise. Nothing needed saying. He was a married man who didn't know why he'd called on her to start with, a stiff, uneasy man, a self-deceiver.

'Boyfriend?' She wasn't sure she'd heard right. She was sure, but it didn't make sense. Husband, perhaps? Or just somebody come to the wrong house, more likely. There was another beside him, scraping against the dustbin. Not much room out there. Glinting amongst the shafts of grass, what, a cap off a pop bottle, ought to tidy that away. Street rubbish. Once she came out to smashed glass, a Tizer bottle someone must have kicked through the railings. And Jenny played out on her hands and knees sometimes. But it was a quiet street, usually, and Jenny knew not to go up the steps.

'What boyfriend?' Probably salesmen, though door to door selling on a Sunday was unusual. Selling bibles? Or faith – a few years ago, after the Billy Graham concert, there'd been a spate of believers knocking and wanting to enlist you on their team. What did they get out of it themselves? she'd wondered. Funny sort of job, conversions. Bobbie had no time. When you've got to struggle to put bread on the table you can't be vexed by trivia.

'Oh, not a memorable boyfriend,' the man scoffed, and Bobbie tensed, realising that these callers might not have the wrong house after all, and might not be harmless. 'The sort of boyfriend who'd give you a grand for no reason – nobody you'd remember, eh?'

'Pardon?' That was a thousand, a grand, that was fantasy money. And Bobbie knew no one in such a league.

'We'll come in and see for ourselves, if you don't mind.'

'No,' Bobbie said fast, 'I do mind,' and tried to close them out. 'Too bad.'

The edge of the door seemed to stab her hand suddenly, and she caught a backhand knuckle slap so hard it sent her across the room. Another shove and Bobbie sprawled on the sofa, too shocked to cry out. They were in and in business, as if they'd made it their place and she was an onlooker who'd have been better off steering clear. One was rapidly checking out the rooms, the other gazing after him, ready for boyfriend trouble. Bobbie's parents had taken Jenny for the day, inviting her, too. She'd made an excuse, as usual, then just sat around all afternoon, wondering about John Eakins, reassuring herself about her modelling – might even get famous – one thing led to another – modelling, acting, need a divorce at some stage, though, and then some wealthy geezer...but a grand, what was that in aid of? Good job Jenny was out, at least. Rough types.

'Cozy little nest,' the sniffer said on his return. He had a few of Bobbie's photographs in his hands. He was shaking his head to say he hadn't found that boyfriend. She'd left the pictures on her bed. He was smirking, holding them up for his friend to gawp at. 'Off the beaten track, mind,' he told Bobbie, and she stared back, assuming she should agree with whatever either man said. 'Where d'you pick 'em up? Can't be many punters round this neck of the woods.' Whitechapel? she thought – he doesn't know history.

'I live here. What are you trying to say?' She knew exactly what he was trying to say, but not how to defend against it. Her cheeks burned. Anger and guilt together. She wasn't on the game. Nothing like that. But a few times – not recently – but what woman in her position wouldn't? You have to make ends meet somehow. And anyway nobody knew. It was hardly a job. But after he'd been sentenced and there was no future anyway, no security. But for her it was a mistake. You had to feel more willing inside. She'd resented doing it, and the payments, slight enough, hadn't seemed like clean earnings. So Bobbie didn't carry on in that line. Even if she had she wouldn't have brought them here, where Jenny lived. This is home. A decent place. And both men making out the pictures were cheap, leering at her, making out she was cheap, thinking they were so much better, so bloody high and mighty, wanting someone to despise, working it up.

'I'm not on the game,' she defended herself. 'I don't have a boyfriend. I'm married. I have a daughter. My parents are coming back with her, any minute now.'

These two, she didn't know it, had come flush from beating up an elderly lady. They had her address on the envelope, along with John's note and more money than one stranger would give another in charity.

'What did you do that was worth a grand? I wouldn't give you five bob.'

'She's turned his head. Simple sailor – promised things his old lady can't do for 'im. Mysteries of the orient, know what I mean?'

'So he'll be back for more. Says he hurt your feelings – likes a bit of nasty, does he? Bothered you. Man from the train. What's that, some sort of lingo you've got? Then a grand. This is all news to you, is it?'

The way they were talking, almost friendly in the mockery, yet edging around, pretending they had something to find out, was not lost on Bobbie. She'd heard men deliberately delaying before, all the time with one thing they were driving at, the explosion of violence. They were going to attack her before they left – no other reason for hanging on. What had she done?

Nothing, and it didn't matter. She could have been somebody else and they'd still want to hit her. This was a sort of foreplay, this lingering in the room. Some of these types carried razors. If they cut me that's the end of the modelling. Bobbie wished she could protect her face. Your face is your fortune, her mother used to tell her. It wasn't true, but an ugly face would be a severe drawback.

'I met this man on the train yesterday,' she said, as calmly as she could, determined not to gabble nervously. 'The sailor, John Eakins. He didn't know anyone in town, so he came over last night, and we talked. He didn't like those either,' she added, nodding at the photographs, trying to bring it all back to mundane reality. 'There wasn't any transaction. If he's written me a letter I'm surprised. If you think he was sending me money I think you're mistaken.'

'A grand, kid, is no mistake.'

'What is he, then,' she laughed, 'an eccentric millionaire?'

They appeared slightly less aggressive already. Bobbie thought she was winning them over.

'My husband,' she continued, 'is a guest of Her Majesty. Wandsworth. He kept quiet at the time, so we're supposed to be protected.'

'Yeah?'

'I'm sure you know how these things work.' She should have mentioned it before they burst in. 'You're working for somebody – have you checked who you're dealing with? I'm not saying my husband was big-time, but loyalty...'

173

Not so much loyalty as being scared shitless – he'd been fully aware that the men he could name had cohorts in prison. Even so, silence was traditionally respected, and these two, unexpectedly, glanced at one another for a recommendation that neither could give.

Bobbie had the advantage. She regained her courage quickly. They were dangerous, but immature. Types who'd overdo the mayhem for kicks, but also to impress. Some of her husband's friends were similar, though he at least had had no violence in him. It was the older men, the ones who didn't look particularly tough, who were truly dangerous, because they were the ones with the organisation, the ones who issued orders. She didn't have to feel inferior to these two, didn't even care to differentiate them – both wore white silk ties, one had a tab-collar and a gold tie-clip, the other a tie-pin; one had a recent welt across the back of his hand; both wore too much brylcreem. Bobbie had as much right to exist as either of them, so she stood up and faced them head on, refusing to be bullied any more.

'We'll be back,' the one who'd spoken initially threatened.

'No you won't,' Bobbie said. 'You'll check and find out you've to leave me be, and if I say you roughed me up you'll have your hands broken.'

She didn't suppose that was remotely likely, but it sounded good, and after they'd left she continued standing there pugnaciously, until she started wondering what had come over her; then she hurried to the kitchen and boiled a kettle and poured enough Camp coffee into her cup to steady the nerves of a regiment.

I was that close to death, she thought dramatically. They wouldn't have killed her, but might easily have cut her badly. She'd heard of such things. Some of the gangs were out of control. Bobbie was impressed by the way she'd acquitted herself, having tended to assume she was relatively feeble. Part of her wanted to collapse helplessly into a protective man's embrace, as if she couldn't sustain her own strength – but she'd always been stronger than her husband, and she certainly didn't want to tell her father what had happened – he'd never supported her anyway. No, she thought, I won't give way just out of relief. Damn it, I stood up to the creeps!

She collected her photographs from the front room, and lay on her bed to examine them. At first she couldn't find anything good about them. The way that young punk had sneered had robbed them of grace – John Eakins had done the same. But it wasn't fair. They were good pictures of her. She was proud, even if other people saw them as dirty pictures. When she'd posed, she remembered, when she'd finally disrobed in the studio and felt the lights on her body, it hadn't been like normal nakedness, more like dressing up. The man who photographed her was a funny little fellow, not attractive, and talked too fast and too crudely, and yet after a while she found she didn't dislike him because he was so enthusiastic. He even showed her how he retouched negatives and prints, obliterating blemishes, getting that smooth shiny grey tone that transformed ordinary flesh into glamour. She always held her stomach in, though she wasn't fat to begin with.

Bobbie knew her talents were limited, but believed they were okay. You had to do something to prove you'd been alive, and she was doing what she could. In the end nothing you did was going to amount to much anyway, so as long as you could face yourself in the morning you were probably doing fine. She was a step up from creeps who bullied their way into people's houses and just went after money all the time. She was a sort of an artist, or an entertainer – people could get pleasure from her work, and that couldn't be wicked.

A thousand pounds, she remembered suddenly. Why was John Eakins going to give her a thousand pounds? There'd been something sad about him, but nothing mysterious. She hadn't met anyone with that sort of money to dispose of, and it was kind of him to want to help her, even if he'd stolen it. The world was changing anyway – everyone was fed up with living drably, and what with worrying about the bomb and so forth it was time for a change – brighter clothes, better music, more fun. She'd often thought that, resented being stuck in a basement flat with Jenny and no chance of a new life, tied to her imprisoned husband who already seemed to belong to a world she'd passed by. So in a way it was appropriate that a total stranger should turn up and ask nothing from her and make her rich anyway. Cinderella story.

Except he hadn't. Somehow what was rightfully hers had been intercepted. And one thing Bobbie knew was that nobody gets a second chance. It was rotten luck that she hadn't recognised good fortune immediately, and made more of an effort, and stayed with Eakins through the night. She had no means of contacting him, either. A sailor from Pembrokeshire, from Milford Haven, that was all she knew. If he wasn't dead by now he was probably on his way home again.

Ships that pass in the night, she thought wanly. Then she thought: I'm not going to go on living as if I'm serving a sentence too – Take the bull by the horns! The courageous image strengthened a vague sense of purpose. Bobbie opened her wardrobe and searched for an outfit she could wear with the same boldness she'd brought to modelling. She didn't know what she was going to do, but she wasn't going to sit around in a basement flat letting the world roll over her. Beauty doesn't last. Nothing else does, either.

The future isn't something that waits there for you to catch it, Bobbie thought, and it isn't something you have to accept on today's terms – you make it now, and if you sit here that's what it will be. Change today. Now.

She was reluctant to be dragged down from her dreams by the return of her parents and daughter. Have a nice day? And what have you done with yourself? No, she thought, this isn't enough: I won't have it.

Her father had found something to grumble about, like he nearly always did.

'Just outside,' he said, 'a Smiths crisps packet, two fag packets, look, Craven 'A' and Churchmans, and a bottle top. You have to take the trouble, Bobbie, when it's on your own doorstep. Otherwise it's like a tide that'll wash over and spoil everything.'

'I didn't go out, Daddy.'

'That's what I'm saying – you don't bother, so you don't even see half of it. It's like you don't care.'

'Oh, come on.'

'I mean, you promised you'd tidy up in here as well – didn't she, Mother? – and look at it! I don't think you live in the same world as us. All you youngsters today. Different when we were young.'

'Did you have a nice outing?' she pointedly asked her daughter, but Jenny wasn't paying attention. Dry ice-cream around her lips, a bag of uneaten sweets clenched in her hand. Jenny preferred her grandparents anyway. Shall I show them the pictures? flashed through, but it often did, and Bobbie never would. Her father was right: her world wasn't his. She was going into the future. He wasn't going with her. He wasn't going anywhere, miserable old sod, and neither was her mother. Bobbie wished there was room to scream and not have everyone staring. John Eakins was a stranger, but not unkind, evidently, and when there were so few options you couldn't be a prima donna.

THIRTY FIVE

Was it the road to Heaven that was paved with Good Intentions? Bob Ryman had an idea it was Hell, but what was wrong with Good Intentions? You couldn't always see them through, perhaps, so they wouldn't be as hard-wearing as Good Deeds, but they ought to be serviceable at least. Some roads were better than others. It depended how frequently they were used. On fishing trips he found wooden bridges with slats missing, tracks with potholes that would cripple a jeep, but they still got him where he wanted to go. Road to Hell be damned, he thought – What a blummin' daft expression!

His powerful urge to rush to the aid of John Eakins should have catapulted him to London in no time, and instead he was witnessing the steady erosion of the urge, and that was as complex as betrayal, He felt uncomfortably like a Judas; ideally he'd have been Peter the Rock

But John wasn't looking for help. Whatever it was, he'd gone into it alone, and no doubt wanted to stay that way. And charging off after John Eakins the way he'd hoped to was, as Joe Davies dryly pointed out, 'a bit gung-ho even for a gung-ho second row'.

Joe Davies was a man you heeded, because he too was in his twenties, but already a detective who'd led two murder investigations. Only a few years older than Bob, Joe had a mind, they said, like a shiv, and the only thing likely to hold him back was his socialism (he didn't hail from the area but, like John Eakins, had drifted over from the valleys, where his father had lived a miner and died at fifty seven of TB – the usual story). Joe wore a Harris Tweed sport coat and a red tie – smart in one sense, but obstreperous in another. After all, not everyone in the higher echelons was going to be won over by the recollection that, until a torn knee took him out of the game, he'd been capped twice for Wales. He'd had the grace of another Don Hayward, in his prime. That made him okay as far as Bob was concerned – the red tie was a wilful eccentricity which added to the man's integrity. He was a man's man and a team player despite his politics. But he wouldn't get many more promotions. Bob was pleased to note that Joe Davies's blonde hair was thinning.

After Joe had taken him through the appalling injuries sustained by the folk of Paradise Valley, and assured him that everything possible was being done to apprehend the two big-time London gangsters responsible, Bob realised that his own plan had been emotional and unprofessional.

'Poor little Malcolm Mabey, too, you say,' Joe sympathised. 'I've met him a few times. Don't worry, Bob, we'll have 'em. As for your pal John Eakins – you're sure he isn't mixed up on the wrong side of this? Certain sure, are you?'

'I'd stake my pension on him, Joe.'

'Aye, well, that's one thing, and it does you credit to think well of your neighbours, but what you wanted to do – it wouldn't look proper, Bob.'

'I realise that, but...'

'I've talked to Fisk. Far as he's aware, Mrs Eakins haven't never drove a lorry up till now, nor had no business taking one out, neither. Now, what she was doing down Paradise Valley with a pair of gorillas from London is any bugger's guess, and until one of them poor sausages makes enough of a recovery to give me a decent statement I'm keeping an open mind about her and her husband. Understand?'

'I do, aye, because it's understandable. Only if you knew John...'

'Well let's hope you're right.'

Bob Ryman knew better than to force his opinions on an impartial listener. Common sense still waved its hands in a general all-forgiving way, assuring him that John and Rachel – and not forgetting young Foster – were innocently caught up in this sudden and ugly mess, but Joe Davies had a balanced overview.

Another thing about Joe that impressed him was the framed signed picture on the wall next to his uncluttered desk. And Bob thought: yes, that's how to live a good life – make a chain of the highlights, and remember your friends, and who you are, and do your work and don't get too big for your boots, and yes, wear a red tie to show you don't care if they stop you rising to the top – insist on it, even, but keep your professional balance.

My duty is to the neighbourhood, and that's bigger than individual neighbours, he reminded himself. Then he stopped off at the hospital, not to get the latest on the Paradise Valley family, but to look in on his best friend. Mal's mother was at her son's side. Bob put his arm around her shoulders. She couldn't understand why anyone should hurt her son, and Bob said she was right not to understand, it was only outsiders would do such things. She touched Mal's forehead, and Bob wished he could do that too. Mal lay so helpless there. I'm not leaving my patch, Bob told himself defiantly.

There's choices you make, and John's gone too far outside. I'll help when he comes back. Meantime I'm here – for Mal, he knew he meant, though he avoided completing the sentiment and allowed the prospect of defending the entire Haven. Joe's not wed, but nobody'd dream of thinking he was a queer. Anyway, he's practically a communist, so he can't be. And Mal just loves to cover weddings, so he's straight as they come an' all. It's just normal all round.

For the first time, and for no logical reason he could come up with, Bob Ryman found himself at odds with John Eakins. Not in any sense he could put words to. He just wanted, for a second, John to turn out bad.

I'm at sixes and sevens, he corrected himself immediately. All this has only happened today, and John only went missing some time yesterday. By tomorrow it'll have blown over, and John'll have nothing to do with none of it. But he should've come to me if it was a danger to Milford he saw. That's what I'm here for. What's he think he is, the Lone Ranger?

'Bob?' Mal whispered, opening his eyes a fraction.

'It's all right, love,' Bob gushed without thinking. That was perfectly all right. Men used the word affectionately in times like these. Sometimes. But he felt his cheeks burn with embarrassment.

'It's all right, love,' Mal's mother said at the same time.

'Aye,' Bob added gruffly. What it was, he couldn't, and shouldn't, leave Mal, even for a day. Now he was watching him it was obvious where he had to be.

You don't have to do what you mean to, Bob discovered in perplexing details like compromises, because you're not necessarily who you think you are. Heroic images dashed in his brains, but probably he wasn't a knight in blazing armour galloping into battle. His strength lay in staying put, like a tower, like battlements, like a rock rooted to the sustaining Haven.

THIRTY SIX

John Eakins retreated to the kitchen and thence to a bedroom. They had Lionel Hampton on the radiogram and girls nodding their heads fast to the beat, concentrating hard, as if endorsing some baffling argument. The girls wore summer dresses and white shoes and strings of pearls; they wore red lipstick and short pastel-coloured cardigans; they took compacts from handbags and touched up lips, eyes or cheeks in the pin-sharp mirrors; they talked about Dennis Lotis, the Planetarium and Scrabble; they talked about polio jabs and how to cover blemishes successfully, Marty Wilde, the Goon Show; they thought Katie Boyle was perfection in poise, smiled readily at John Eakins, but weren't vitally interested in him. They were usherettes, hat-check girls, strippers, bit-part actresses; they were friends, or friends of friends, of Phil. A few of them were accompanied by defensive-looking young men, possessive, claim-staking, not on their own territory.

John Eakins sulked in the bedroom. Phil had said one or two people might pop in, and John had asked if that was a good idea, what with them being in hiding and all. Phil had assured him that wasn't the way it worked, not with Bull Gravett.

John felt abandoned. Everyone seemed to be having fun, but anyone could slip away and inform on him and Phil. So he waited glumly, reconsidering his friendship. Although Phil had sounded remarkably well informed earlier on, it now seemed that he lacked John's sense of doom. John had taken it for granted that once they met he'd have Phil's exclusive attention, and perhaps that had been unrealistic. Even so, throwing an open party when you were in hiding showed a pretty cavalier attitude.

A girl opened the bedroom door and smiled encouragingly. She might have been the one who'd led him to the mews earlier, but he wasn't sure.

'You don't want to be in here,' she told him. 'You're worrying, aren't you?'

'It seems a bit noisy,' he muttered, for her to go away.

'What do you expect? A seance?' She chuckled at her wit and helped herself to one of his cigarettes. 'Phil's doing this for you, you know.'

'I'm not sure he's got the right idea.'

'Phil? You'd be tied up in the back of some warehouse by now.'

'What do you know about all this, then?'

'I go with Nicky Billings – Nicky the Marble.' She paused, mildly crestfallen by John's blankness. 'Well, Nicky's a sort of accountant for Mr Gravett. And he tells me things, and I tell Phil.'

'Does Nicky know you tell Phil?'

'Hardly! Cripes!'

'So how come you tell Phil?'

She drew angrily on the cigarette and scorned to answer.

'Listen, chum,' she said, pulling open the door to go, 'if Phil's on your side you may even get to spend your bloody money, so you don't have to stay in here waiting for the roof to cave in. Trust him.'

John found her fierce loyalty invigorating, and decided it probably didn't matter if Gravett's men found him politely hiding in the bedroom or chatting unconcernedly elsewhere. He sighed, realised there was no point being homesick and longing for Rachel, and did his awkward best to mingle with the party.

Eventually Phil joined him: 'We could be leaving any time now,' he explained, smiling as if he were saying something else. 'A couple of Bull's toadies are in. Soon as they leave we scarper.'

'Whenever you say, but I don't get it.'

Phil clutched his arm for a moment: 'Later,' he promised, and moved on. John observed for a little while, hoping to guess who the toadies were, but he couldn't. Everyone was chatting, laughing or nodding in much the same way. The vibes of Lionel Hampton had been replaced by Julie London, one of the few voices he could identify. At any other time he'd have swooned into it. Julie London sounded both grown up and seductive. He made his way to the radiogram and asked the nearest girl to put her next choice on.

'Oh, but this is so romantic,' she said, swaying to illustrate.

God, John groaned to himself, she thinks I'm flirting. A table-lamp cast a sidelight through her reddish hair and made her right eye uncommonly bright, as if illuminated from within. It was hard not to be transfixed. She was attractive and eager to engage him. Perhaps she'd grown tired of waiting for someone better. He found himself desperately trying to think of any singer's name.

'Got any of Churchill's speeches?' he asked.

'I expect so. But no one else is going to enjoy that.'

'The stuff that was on before, then, the jazz.'

'Are you a friend of Graham's?'

'Who's Graham?'

'This is his place.'

'The photographer?' He watched her fiddle with the contraption for changing records. Her hair was pinned up at the back, her neck beautifully clean and touchable. He wondered why he hadn't felt this spontaneous readiness to grab Bobbie, thought he might even attempt a dance with this one.

'Are you a model?' In response she wiggled her bottom. 'Is that a yes?'

She completed her task and began straightening and turning, but before she could answer a man stepped in.

'You're the Welsh geezer, ain't you?'

John supposed this must be one of the toadies. Am I supposed to be afraid of you? he thought scornfully. The man looked mean, but not substantial enough to intimidate John Eakins, who was at once aggressive and ready for a fight. The girl had been wedged back towards the radiogram, and she was trying to remain pert and good natured while struggling to keep her balance.

'You're in this young lady's way,' John hissed.

'What would you like to do about it? Got a crippled hand, I hear. Want to lay one on me, do you?'

It was evident he'd come over to cause trouble, and quite likely he had his buddy close by with a knife or something. The prudent way would be to withdraw and let the girl topple over if she was going to. John had grown too tense for prudence. People nearby were already hushing and looking concerned. He was out of place. This whole noisy scene was wrong. He didn't need an I'm-tougher-than-you exchange with this jerk, and the crack about his hand infuriated him. Without warning, and at great speed, John Eakins brought his forehead down. The crack was heard around the room. His opponent stayed on his feet for a few seconds, dazed, expressionless, then went down heavily.

'It's how buffaloes fight,' John said quietly. 'Don't they teach that in London schools?'

The girl who'd looked so pretty before now looked aghast. John rubbed his forehead with his fingertips. It was in the war, a G.I. who claimed to be an authentic American Indian told John about buffaloes going for head-on collisions – like a couple of locomotives – bam! – the ground shakes. Why he'd just resorted to it he didn't know. He'd never head-butted anyone else.

'Jesus Christ!' Phil cried, dropping to one knee. 'Graham! You all right, boy? Hey, Graham!'

The girl stared at John. So did everyone else.

'He was trying to pick a fight,' John muttered uncomfortably.

'Graham,' Phil continued, slapping their host's face to revive him. Over his shoulder: 'I should have warned you – he does that, when he's had a few. Just his way of reminding people whose booze they're enjoying – you're meant to back down. I think you've bust his nose. We'd better get him to a hospital. Shirley, call a cab, will you?'

Shirley stepped across the prone form and looked daggers at John.

'Lout,' she spat.

For a moment John Eakins thought he'd like to go berserk and beat up everybody. He was a pariah, but it hadn't been entirely his fault. Nobody cared. Graham was someone they knew. John was a stranger. Phil had managed to get Graham to his feet. A couple of others came and took him.

'I thought he was...' John whispered.

'I know. Good job we're going, anyway.'

'Have they...?'

'Right after you conked Graham, yeah.'

'Look, I'm sorry. Look, we can give him some compensation, can't we? Can't we take a few hundred from the case?'

'Maybe, maybe – not now, though.' Phil turned to the room: 'Sorry about that, everybody. A misunderstanding. He thought Graham was a G-man.'

A G-man, John learned afterwards, was anyone heavy-handed who worked for Gravett. It was a joke. He didn't get it. He thought G-men were American government agents. That was the humour of it, Phil said humourlessly.

They had an hour's walk to their next safe house, and John spent most of it saying how sorry he was, but what he really wanted to understand was why Phil had invited so many people, including these G-men characters.

'What was you thinking, Phil? To me it sounds like the daft stories Foster comes home with after he's been up the flicks.'

'I bet the stories he tells don't get so painful.'

'Good guys, bad guys.'

'Poor old Graham'll think twice before he tries it on again.'

'You see why I nutted him, then?'

'It's not a mystery, John, it's not that – it's just...all these people are my friends.'

'Yeah, I see your side of it too.'

'And you, you're a family man.'

'Aye, well, that's true.'

They paused to rest, John not bothering to lower the duffle bag, Phil setting the briefcase down on a wall. The streets were deserted. No one was going to notice them. Phil explained the geography: nobody connected with the clubs ventured north in search of lodgings. London wasn't really a big city, more a series of routes –

you grew intimate with your patch, and anything outside wasn't interesting or necessary. It was actually parochial, he said, like village life but with entertainment.

'So the thing is,' he went on as they proceeded north, 'Bull wants us rounded up, beaten up, probably – in fact he may be planning to dunk us in concrete, make us disappear forever. There's rumours that's how he operates, but I'm not certain – he's affability itself face to face. Anyroad, I can't be seen to run craven, John, know what I mean? A lot of people depend on me for a living, really.'

'And you trust them all?'

'Not altogether, but I have to be seen behaving normal, like. Shifting places is all right, but...'

'So was that girl who came in the bedroom to cheer me up – did you send her? – was she the one who came to Mrs Champion's?'

'Vicky? No.'

'What about Shirley?'

'No. Shirley's with Nicky the Marble.'

'No, that was Vicky, wasn't it?'

'Have they swapped again? Well, no matter. So we have a little party, and word gets back to Mr G. By the time his people come to collect us we've gone. Now Mr G knows we're around, we haven't been scared off, and he'll start thinking it over. Got to soften him up, John, so he'll be ready to negotiate.'

'Can't we just go and drag him down some alley?'

'I think it's unlikely we'd find an opening. But if we can persuade him his money's safe or, even better, his plans for Wales can go ahead, then maybe he'll come around. You any good at bluffing?'

'Never had a go,' John said, having built his entire life on saying what he meant. But he had lied to Phil about seeing his name in Mr Wary's wallet, and Phil now was being the pal he'd wanted to find, away from crowds, just walking and working at a problem with him. So he was willing to listen.

On Tuesday morning Phil phoned Bulstrode Gravett and told him their misunderstanding needed clearing up. He said nobody'd double crossed anybody, and Alan Wary had given the seed-money to John Eakins because John Eakins was the man to deal with in Milford. But he was an honest man. But, he had a vision of development.

'Now all you got to do is sound convincing tomorrow,' Phil grinned to John when he stepped away from the telephone kiosk.

'My pals, back home...we're all agin it – change, I mean.'

Phil shrugged, not unsympathetically: 'It happens, though, whether you're agin it or not. Trick is, to have an influence.'

'That's a trick I've never had,' John sighed. 'Not so sure I want it, neither.'

'I'm sorry, John, but as soon as you connected me with Alan's money and came visiting you got pulled in. But if you'd had the letter I sent I hope you'd have come in anyway.'

'Rachel thinks we should move away, if they start oil refineries or whatever. Find another unspoilt little spot.'

'They'll be stockpiling oil there whatever happens – that's just the basic situation men like Gravett want to exploit. It's business, John.'

'That Shirley's an attractive girl.'

'Aren't they all?'

John reflected soberly: 'Yes, they all are. It's a new world I'm in, Phil. I don't know my up from my down any more. I feel grubby, like I done something bad, and I'm uneasy in myself.'

'Everybody gets those feelings now and then.'

'Not me. Maybe I've been sleeping all these years.'

'Well, who decides what bad is? What did you do, have a fight with Rachel before you came?'

'Not exactly. She don't know about the dosh, though. She thinks I got fed up and wanted to see you and meet stripteasers and stuff.'

'Don't let it get to you, that makes it ten times worse, and it's only in your own mind in the first place. What have you ever done that's wrong? You're an honest man, John, you can't help it.'

'Yeah, that's the way I look at it. Rachel's the one goes to chapel, not me, and I'm the one feels guilty.'

'Can't you call her up, if you're missing her so much?'

'She should've had my letter today, if those G-men hadn't took it when they ransacked Mrs Champion's. God, I wish this was all out of the way now, Phil!'

'Aye, well, if you can con Bull Gravett tomorrow you'll go back home a saint, I shouldn't wonder.'

'I just want to get back to normal.'

'Where's that?' Phil laughed, and John smiled and tried to fit in.

THIRTY SEVEN

Wednesday the streets glittered silver while a night's downpour slowly dried. Glare tired the eyes, but gave an impression of freshness to Soho. John Eakins had a limited wardrobe: either he wore his donkey jacket or he carried it. Phil had wanted the meeting to be public and neutral – Regent's Park, Hyde Park, Trafalgar Square – but Bull Gravett insisted that the *Listen Ear* was neutral enough, since it lay a few streets outside Soho proper; it was also open to the general public, kids mostly, who'd be in from ten a.m. drinking milk shakes and espressos and listening to young hopefuls singing maudlin love songs or vaguely rebellious threats to rock their lives away. Bull Gravett had some sort of deal with the milk bar, but he didn't actually own the place and it wasn't one of his usual hangouts.

'If we don't pull this off,' John said, 'what's our next move?'

'Leave England,' Phil advised, but broke into a smile again: 'He's not a psychopath. All he wants is to make money – that's why he's spending the morning listening to music he hates. Someone's convinced him there's going to be a big market for English teenage stuff, and not just copies of American styles – God knows where these forecasts come from, but he's been impressed, and it's certain to come out from London, obviously, so he'll be wincing and wondering when he'll hear a new Bing Crosby.'

'You make him sound a real criminal mastermind!'

'Oh, he's dangerous. Five years ago you wouldn't have had any doubts on that score. These days he likes to think he's some sort of an entrepreneur, thinks it's more profitable, long term, but he keeps a lot of the old crew close by, protecting his interests. We can talk to him without getting our knees sledged.'

'I get it,' John nodded. 'Somebody else'll do his dirty work later.'

'Should that be necessary.'

'Nice fellow.'

'He owns clubs, John. He has influence. Don't underestimate him.'

John had little desire to estimate him at all. What he wanted was to get this over with and return home. Meetings with underworld figures had not been on the itinerary when he set off from Milford way back last Saturday morning. And now, though he'd achieved nothing but the waste of more than half a week, he was about to persuade a man who had people killed that he was capable of setting up what Phil called the infrastructure for profitable developments on the Haven. It was like a bad dream. Never should've took that money, he chided himself. And don't think about poor Mrs Champion! If he dwelt on that senseless bit of violence he'd take a swing at Bulstrode Gravett no matter how public and neutral the meeting place was. The man deserved a thrashing.

The *Listen Ear* was as unprepossessing a joint as its name had implied. Sandwiched between a junk shop and a corner fag shop it had old newspaper pages taped over the windows and a narrow door wedged open with a flat iron. The interior seemed dingy and at first completely unlit, but that was partly the effect of the bright wet streets: there were a few lights, under small brown shades, on the tables. Atmosphere, John thought, wanting to get out again as quickly as possible. Lights on tables, and a lovely morning outside. He lit a Woodbine so he wouldn't be too overwhelmed by the stink of stale cigarettes. Nobody was singing, but some youngsters were sucking drinks through straws and calling each other Daddy-o. They were presumably in the vanguard of new musical directions. If there were any serious hard men in the place John couldn't spot them, but he soon picked out Bulstrode Gravett, the only adult there. I can take him, was his first thought, and that was always a relief. Bulstrode Gravett wasn't wearing a suit and tie as expected. He had a pale blue V-neck jumper with the logo of a golf club on the breast. His slacks were cavalry twill. He was jowly and the jumper pulled too tight across the stomach. John didn't mind fat men, but there were ways of carrying extra weight, and Gravett's was the way he didn't like: the belly looked like a pregnancy attached to an otherwise slim figure. He's a creep, John deduced.

'We just had Tommy Steele,' Gravett said by way of a greeting.

'The Bermondsey boy himself?' Phil queried knowledgeably. 'I'd have thought he was too big by now. With or without his Cavemen?' Evidently Phil needed to compete – John reminded himself that Phil was the impresario, and doubtless resented a chancer like Bull Gravett developing this sideline.

'A kid that looked a lot like him,' Gravett explained. 'Teeth, grin, hair, you know.'

'Sign him up?'

'Well, what's it to you, Phil?' The manner had changed instantly, almost furtively, yet for no reason. Gravett extended a hand to shake John's, but withdrew it before John did anything. 'Sorry, you can't shake, can you?'

'No.'

'Please take a seat, Mr Eakins. We'll get to business directly. First, Phil – Philip – What's it all about? I thought I knew you,

Philip. I thought you knew me.'

'I wouldn't try to pull a fast one on you, Bull, and I think you know that. In fact, I was trying to help, and if you're willing to listen I think you'll stop calling me Philip.'

'Okay, Phil, I'm a reasonable man. This place isn't suitable, though, is it? What say we slip out the back? There's a quiet room.'

'This'll do us,' Phil said warily, and Gravett shrugged.

The next singer sounded, his voice so low everyone stifled their nattering. John shifted his chair around to watch. The newspaper-filled windows cast a dead church grey-blue light across everything, with a speckling which almost became a pattern in places. Before the end of the first verse people were resuming conversations, sucking up frothy drinks, drowning him.

'You like this type noise?'

'Huh?' John returned to Gravett, who was ready to get on.

'This type noise, you like it?'

'Can't say I do.'

'Talentless people should be told.' Gravett shook his head. 'I'm going in studios, pubs, clubs, everywhere there's a chance of picking up the new sound. Beginning to think it's a wasted effort. Stick to tarmac, concrete, casinos, crap I know. Now golf-links,' he breathed in and aimed a finger at the design on his jumper, 'that's where there's going to be plenty dough. I see your part of Pembrokeshire ten years from now, Mr Eakins, and we'll have exclusive greens, competition standard, and greens for beginners – I see twenty, thirty, forty new courses: Then you'll be needing decent hotels, and venues to spend money and relax in the evening. Much better road network, of course. Heard about the M1?'

'What's that?'

'Ever get to see the autobahns during the war? Wonderful, right? Well, right now they're finishing one from just up the road to Birmingham. Motorway One. And there'll be more. Now I think, if things go well, we could end up with one running west all the way to Milford Haven. What say to that?'

'Mmm,' John ruminated. 'That's a big thought.' Loopy, he thought.

'I've got big plans.' He suddenly patted himself on both cheeks, such a strange gesture John snorted a contorted laugh. Gravett stared hard at him. 'What type music you like, then? Sinatra? I go for Sinatra. That man has a voice, right?'

'I don't hear a lot of music. I'm not much for it.'

'No? Christ, that's a relief!' He was referring to the retirement of the nearly inaudible but still grating singer. He clapped, once. 'Films, then? Don't tell me – Bible films: *Ten Commandments, Demetrius and the Whosits, Helena Troy*. Am I right? You go for these old-time religious sermony things? Don't tell me – *The Cruel Sea*. Get it?'

'Me being a trawlerman, you mean? Very good. But no, I don't go to the flicks.'

'See, I'm trying to get a sense of who are are, Mr Eakins. I like to know the men I deal with.'

'Sounds fair enough.'

'You don't care for music or for films. Gambling man, by any chance?'

'Not me. Well, the pools, but...'

'Have you got no interests at all?' Gravett sounded personally moved, not quite outraged, but genuinely perplexed. John shrugged, wishing he could be more helpful, but he really was stumped. 'Self-sufficient, then.'

'What's that when it's at home?' He hadn't come upon the expression, and was disturbed to be confronted by his lack of a life. Possibly London was a distorting mirror, and once home again he'd be reassured. When he was working he hadn't needed supplementary interests. He felt like a bumpkin. 'My wife goes up the flicks every week,' he remembered, vaguely hoping that would be satisfactory. 'And my boy, he goes an' all, and what's more he likes all this rock around the clock music. But I, no, I don't.'

'Ah, Mrs Eakins,' Gravett nodded, getting more serious. 'Your wife and your son. Good and blameless people, I'm sure.'

'Well, aye, of course – What? Are you saying something?'

'I beg your pardon?' Gravett was a beat slow in sounding mystified, so instead he sounded tantalising, sinister without obvious substance.

Phil said, 'Stop beating about the bush, Bull – John's not going to leave himself open. He's a family man and he lives in Milford Haven, which you know, and everybody in Milford Haven knows and respects him, and if you wanted to get men in on the quiet to do some business they'd be picked out before they got near him. Christ, you could go down there with tanks and bazookas and get nowhere. It's a community, Bull. The contacts you made won't get the job done because they don't have the weight, and I reckon you suspect that already. Now let's get serious.'

'Cat got your tongue?' Gravett quipped, making himself laugh so hard he started coughing. It was sufficient commotion to bring a large man with a broken nose through from the back. Gravett noticed and waved him away again. Phil and John noticed and exchanged raised eyebrows.

Phil called to mind his talks with Alan Wary before the latter's unfortunate expiry. He guessed a couple of names would add credence to his scam: 'Daniels the estate agent, Jenkins the amenities man, Fisk the road transport chappy – most of the local Chamber of Trade, and good men one and all, Bull, but in Wales business gets done on nods and winks in the right quarter.'

'I know that. What the fuck'd I give Wary forty five grand for?' At once he tried to wave away his anger, which wasn't coordinated with the jumper and slacks. He looked sullen, caught out crude.

'Phil's only telling you true, Mr Gravett,' John said earnestly. 'Your Mr Wary come to see me, soon as he seen how it was. Now I'm not no Fisk nor Jenkins, like, but I do know – no matter what these gentlemen have said to you in the past – that not one inch of road gets laid, not one square of turf, not one brick, and so on and so on – nothing happens to Milford without Bob Ryman says it's a green light. Bob's the law on this, and he's a bloody good rugger player. Now to an outsider like you, you'd think he's only a bobby, just like you'd think I'm only a trawlerman, and Mal's only a reporter on a local rag. It's a question of who to respect in the community. And then of course it's a matter of who's related. Now there's brothers and uncles and nephews and cousins and in-laws and all-sorts to be accommodated.'

'This sounds like the mafia!' Gravett snorted.

'Mafia nothing!' Phil mocked. 'This is Wales, Bull – you tie your shoes in Tonypandy and somebody knows it in Bangor.'

'I'm not saying Jenkins and Daniels and Fisk and the rest can't make a good contribution,' John added, confident now that the whole thing was under way, 'but if Mr Wary had distributed the money right away chances are ninety per cent of your plans would just get bogged down in committee – we got more committees in Wales than voters. Now there's ways of proceeding towards a goal without seeming to, and that's what you got to do. As I understood it from Mr Wary your basic ideas are fine – golf courses, better roads, some good hotels – and we've got plenty of scope with the marina, an' all, and once the ships are unloading all that oil we'll have loads of new jobs, isn't it? – new jobs, loads of new people coming in, pots of money to spend, opportunities beyond!' It amazed him how easily he could translate dismaying possibilities into currents of exhilaration and sound sincere.

'I think you talk my language,' Gravett admitted. 'When you

190

came in carrying that reefer jacket I had serious doubts, I don't mind telling you.'

'So what is it? You saying I can go back home and get down to business among my people? Or you want your forty five back and forget it?'

'I'll be honest with you, boys, I thought things had already gone down the drain. My informants...but that's how these quibbles arise. I chose Alan Wary myself, you know. Not only honest, but shrewd with it, and capable of taking the initiative. Well, the old bugger didn't die in vain, then!'

It was hard to believe this slippery, shallow, inept small-time mogul was the man whose word had been strong enough to give John indigestion the last couple of days. He wondered if it held true of most men in power, that they were inadequate when you got up close.

After a few more minutes of forced mateyness they were ready to leave. It had been extraordinarily easy, the briefcase full of money not even an issue. Phil stood first, and rather than shake Gravett's hand clapped him on the shoulder, firmly. Gravett stood next, then John, and without warning Gravett grabbed John's bad hand and pumped it harshly. The colour drained from John's face and he winced audibly, though he held himself straight.

'Oh my word!' Gravett gushed, letting go. 'Your hand! So sorry!'

He sounded stricken, but must have had it in mind all along. Phil moved to John's side to hold him back. John trembled like a volcano about to blow. Slowly he reached over with his left and took hold of his forearm.

'That wasn't too bright,' he growled.

Broken nose was in the doorway again, and at least one other back in the shadows. Phil took John's jacket from him and moved towards the light, and John followed.

It maddened him to have let Gravett get away with that, but Phil said he was proud of him. The hand and now the whole arm throbbed violently. The man has a grip, John conceded miserably. You can't tell by looking, not about him, not about no one. All you do, you make assumptions, then you find out how wrong you were. Nobody knows anybody, when you get down to it.

'He'll be calling Milford, just to make sure your bobby has the clout you claim for him.'

'I got carried away – I never considered that.' John felt bad – he'd imagined it was all over. 'All right, I'll phone Bob, or Archie Flynn to get a message to Bob, say what's up, and he can call on Mr Fisk and the rest. It's sort of true, nearly, what I was saying.

They'll know Bob, and he is the law, and if he says it's going to be common knowledge they'll be willing to think again, probably.'

'I bloody hope so, John.'

It was a little after midday, Wednesday, the streets dry and no longer glaring, the usual unconcerned bustle everywhere. Phil found him a telephone in the back room of a cafe where he was pally with the staff. John sat at a table, had coffee brought to him, and called Bob Ryman. Bob was at once anxious and impatient, but John said his message was blummin' urgent, so he got Bob's attention and summarised the whole fiasco. He heard Bob's gasps on the other end, disbelief, anger, then determination – Bob said not to worry, he'd have words with the upstanding local business community right away, and he knew who else to tell, to get the thing on the right footing.

'So you coming back now, John?'

'I think I got everything tamped down here,' John assured him, taking a sip of coffee. It was good to be back in contact with home, good to feel confident his friend would go on the warpath. 'Thought I might hang on a day or two, though, for old times' sake.'

'Has nobody been in touch with you, then? Like Rachel?'

'Rachel? Well hardly, Bob, I'm not really on the phone – I mean, this is just a place, I'm not staying...'

'There's things have happened, that's all,' Bob said portentously. 'You best come home now, honest. I can't say more.'

'You don't sound like you,' John frowned. 'What's up?'

'I can't say on the phone, but you need to be here. Look, Mal's in hospital, for starters. Got beat up. Had to be operated on, had a what-they-call-it, hysterectomy.'

'Christ! Sounds grim!'

'Nasty enough. But it's not only Mal. Mal's sitting up now, well enough to listen while his mam ticks him off for a naughty boy – he's loving it. Look, I can't chat, I got to chase up these men of vision who've been keeping so quiet. Get back, John.'

'Well what? Is it about Rachel? She ill or something?'

'Hard to say. Please, now, get yourself home again.'

With that Bob hung up. John couldn't finish his drink. He sat on, bewildered and worried. Rachel's health was excellent. Had Foster got himself into trouble again? That was all he needed, he thought angrily. Then he realised he could clench and unclench his right hand, a fuller movement than hitherto. That's amazing, he thought, it's damn near gone better all on its own!

If I shift I can get a train to Cardiff, maybe Swansea. Get back first thing tomorrow. Then he considered how ironic it was that he'd left Milford to solve a problem in London, and solved it, and should be going back singing, and now here were intimations of dismal news, so he'd make his return in a shabbier frame of mind than his outward journey. I'm like a blummin' shuttlecock, he glowered to himself, a blummin' yo-yo, up and down like a blessed metronome. Never used to be. Wasn't even like that in the war – this is what getting older is, finding you can't carry on doing what you've done for years, meeting people you don't know and doing what they want. It's a raw deal. One of these mornings I'm going to look in the mirror and not recognise the bugger staring back not knowing where he is.

'How'd it go?' Phil asked.

'No problem. But Rachel's got a cold or something, so I got to hurry back.'

'No rest for the wicked, eh!' Phil joked.

'Not if they're married, no,' John smiled wanly. 'But who needs rest?'

And he didn't rest all the way to Swansea, though he leaned back, stretched his legs, and closed his eyes. It was worry all the way, but lacked the hard edges of a subject to worry about – a Rachel worry: illness, injury; a Foster worry: an accident, another bungled record theft – and although John sprawled about looking lazy as a lord, in his mind he was thrashing in dark waters against invisible assailants from the deep. By Swansea he was exhausted, and it was too late to complete the journey anyway, so he found a room and slept, and when he awoke early Thursday there was no less to worry about, so he didn't feel the least bit refreshed.

By nine he'd reached Milford, and he was glad to get to the bridge without encountering anyone he knew. It was an ugly little bridge – he wasn't conscious of having noticed that before. It was short and stocky and quite graceless, the walls either side flat but rougher than sandpaper, dull to look at. Presumably such details were unimportant, but John was in a critical mood. Why did the bridge have to be ugly, and why was his reaction to its ugliness a snorted 'Typical!'? Typical of what? Wales? Underdevelopment? Lack of concern? It wasn't as if he'd noticed any particular beauty in London. Nor did he want to be disappointed in coming home.

He looked over the parapet at the harbour, trawlers tight under the market, gulls screeching as usual, and breathed in the heady stench of fish, tar, oil and salt water. And that was good. He filled his lungs and turned towards Hakin, the tops of a few houses on the estate already visible above the small quarry at the end of the bridge. Five minutes and he'd be indoors, and whatever Bob had hinted at would come clear. Whatever it was, John decided, it couldn't be so dreadful and wouldn't be anywhere near as momentous as the events he'd been swirling in. Home was home, after all.

He climbed over the stile, then over the fence into his own back garden. Foster hadn't cut the grass, then, so that worry about the wallet had probably been needless. The shed door hung open, but he might have left it like that.

Sunlight glinted on parts of Sam Niblo's chicken run – repaired sections, most of the wire too rusty to shine. The backs were tranquil and reassuring, as was the pale blue sky with its scattering of small clouds. It was going to be a fine day. John Eakins felt something between a return after arduous exile and a return after half an hour's stroll, so he was completely unsure of how to act when he went in. Being undemonstrative, he thought he'd make nothing of it, leave all the responding to his wife.

He dropped his long white duffle bag in the kitchen. The money was inside, but no longer needed hiding. Since his interview with Gravett all that had changed, and the money was for the consortium now – all they had to do was become a consortium, whatever that was.

The air had something dull in it, he noticed, and if air could hold absence, that was what it had done. Not quite stale, but still, as if nothing and no one had breathed or moved it in days. When he called his wife's name the noise went into that same air and vanished. He called again, louder. Went upstairs slowly, to confirm what by then he knew: no one was home but him, and by himself he didn't fill the place.

He opened the front door and brought in four days' milk, opening a bottle at random – fresh enough, the days not yet hot enough to turn it. He filled the kettle, made tea, drank tea, didn't explore other rooms, noticed the stains where someone had spilt a drink, was unable to think anything through. Only he realised things must be a lot worse than he'd feared, and in a few minutes he'd go across the green to Bob's and learn how bad. Before that, though, he stayed with the sufferings of the returning exile who hadn't been greeted: So where do I fit in? he asked sourly, sensing all around the inhospitable answer.

He was tired, worn out, and believed he had a right to something near a hero's welcome, but he also understood he deserved no such thing and this drabness was about right.

They won't be back while I fret, he reckoned. That was it, he was going to have to work for the right kind of outcome. You think you done enough, but you kid yourself – you got to go off again and go and see them where they are and let them know you'll protect them and be reliable and true. You got to set the world to rights, John, he encouraged himself, though he wasn't thinking of a world any bigger than his wife and son.

THIRTY EIGHT

They put tiny little carrots and peas on the plate, with some other green nosh that he didn't even know what it was – cauliflower or lettuce or some such, but greener than the green they paint drain-pipes and gutterings with, and tough like the card on a Shredded Wheat box when he halfheartedly ripped his fork through – but his mam was in such fine fettle she said even before he tucked in he didn't have to eat nothing he didn't fancy. She wanted him to enjoy the experience, and was keen to get the most out of it herself, because neither of them ate out hardly ever – well, never, in Foster's case, and only a couple of times in Rachel's – never before with herself in charge. So he had chicken and chips while she had chicken and potatoes. The tablecloth was white and stiff as a piece of tarpaulin, and had no stains or frayed holes in. They sat by a window and all the tables had places set though there was only one other family eating and they were right over near the silver trolley which had great big cakes on, which Foster kept his eye on, too, fearful it would get wheeled away before he had a choice.

When they'd finished his mam told him he had to place his knife and fork side by side on the plate, and screw up his napkin and drop it on the tablecloth, then the waiter would come back and ask what else they wanted. They had a list of all the food you could have, and they had separate sections for lots of ice creams and lots of different cakes, and even a selection of cheeses; then they had a whole pile of soft drinks. Foster was impressed. He couldn't make up his mind whether he wanted an ice cream or a slice of choco-late cake with whipped cream. Then again, he could have an apple pie. The waiter didn't rush him, seemed amused and pleased he was taking so long, and Rachel finally said he could have ice cream *and* chocolate cake, and finish off with a coca cola, as long as he thought his stomach could cope. He did. He wished he could take that giant folded list away, to show Petey and the others eventual-ly. They'd never believe it without proof. They were just about in England, that was why his mam was so happy – she'd brought him right across Wales and it was safe now and the journey was near-ly over and she was proud of herself. Actually, Rachel said, they were only roughly halfway, it just felt that most of it was behind them now.

She was in no hurry to move. The spacious, genteel restaurant was both relaxing and invigorating, so she had energy to spare, but the atmosphere was worth soaking in a little longer. If there were places like this in Milford or even Haverfordwest it was a shame John hadn't taken her, but possibly he wouldn't feel comfortable in a sophisticated setting, and she wouldn't dream of going alone. This way it was excusable – they had to eat, and it might as easily have been a transport caff full of lorry drivers and fat smells. Gracious living, she thought, is for me. But she knew she was kidding herself and it was unfair, when she and her husband always worked hard for their money. And the furthest they went for a proper summer holiday was Tenby, unless they stayed with relatives. It was money, but not only money, that restricted their lives; it was attitude as well – habit and small expectations. But when you're forced to flee, she thought, you find out it's not so hard to get to somewhere else and have a fine dinner like this, and really it's not exorbitant, and a little luxury isn't cheating anybody.

She wondered if she'd made her life less memorable than she should have, and if she could change from now on. It would be a hard thing to discuss with John. They were both set in frugal ways, and sensible with money – that came from growing up through lean years before the war, making do, learning to despise fancy things as wasteful; it came from chapel, too. And here it was, a Sunday evening, and she wasn't even dressed right, and had no qualms about missing an evening service on top of the morning service she'd already missed. God, Rachel believed, was with her on this trek, and he understood and sympathised and knew she was trying to do right. She was also trying to be nice to Foster, because he'd been a very good companion on the whole, a lot more patient and pleasant than she'd have expected.

At last they returned to their lorry, which Rachel had filled at a pump just before they parked. Everything was working out well. The light was beginning to go, but they'd have at least another hour before dark. She couldn't decide whether to go all out for London, arriving late in a big strange city and then having to find a bed and breakfast, or to stop in an hour or so in some small town. Unfortunately she wasn't sure of the best route. Having come this far, though, Rachel was confident enough to leave the details to be decided by circumstance – if they found a nice market town with a respectable hotel, maybe they'd halt the night; if not, there'd surely be somewhere in the city, it was mainly a question of not being intimidated by the anticipated scale of the place.

'That waiter called you Madam, didn't he, Mam?' Foster remembered as she shifted gear to begin the long climb uphill into England proper. 'Madam,' he repeated, wriggling in the soft warmth of the cab. The waiter had also called him Sir, once, and he'd tried not to laugh aloud or in any way let on that he wasn't used to it, but it had been like being somebody else, a famous person, and he'd felt a twinge of excruciating pleasure in his willy, one of the first.

'It's nice to be treated courteously sometimes, isn't it?'

'That chocolate! Mmmm!'

'We'll have another meal like that in London, tomorrow night.'

'Cor! With Dad an' all?'

'Yes, even if we have to frogmarch him into the stores to buy him a jacket and some new trousers.'

Foster chuckled because it sounded funny, frogs marching, and he could imagine his dad protesting, but in that soft way he sometimes had, which meant he didn't mind and was only playing reluctant for them to feel stronger.

'He could have a tie an' all, and them shoes with pinholes in them.'

'Brogues – yes, I can just see your father in a polished pair of brogues, wearing a good jacket and a tie! We'll make a point of it, Foss. I bet he won't look half bad, either. He's a good looking man, you know, your old Dad.'

Foster chuckled again and nodded, but less easily. It was slightly embarrassing to hear her say things like that, not what parents ought to say. And aside from that, there was the disloyalty. That woman in *The Kentuckian* had civilised big Eli Wakefield and turned him into a sissy, in looks at any rate, and you couldn't do that to heroes. But she hadn't understood that, he recalled, she hadn't felt what little Eli felt at all, yet that was what the picture was all about. His mother had risen in his estimation throughout the day, but she was still only his mother.

The hill rose ahead of them and to their left, but off to the right the land fell away and spread out into the greying indistinct dusk. You could still see details, hedges, trees, buildings and some lights, but for the most part it looked like an undiscovered and potentially vast new country. It was England, Foster realised, and he wanted to stop and take a longer look. He'd always had it in his mind that England would be in bright sunlight and covered in orchards, branches bowing under buxom apple blossoms, swallows darting overhead, and there'd be huge cart-horses drawing haycarts down the lanes, and you'd see oast-houses like they had in a book somewhere. It was disappointing to be entering this world just before nightfall and missing the full experience.

'All right,' Rachel said to placate him, but also because she was down to first gear and unhappy about the way she was handling the hill. It wasn't the lorry's fault: she'd messed the changes and couldn't seem to correct the thing. It was virtually grunting and sweating. 'There's a bit of a lay-by on the other side, look.'

But before she reached it she noticed a gap in the hill just ahead on the left, and turned in gingerly, and found a sort of quarry space with plenty of room to turn and park, and no risk of accidentally shooting over the edge. The lorry was out of sight of the road, but Rachel was no longer worrying about being pursued. Foster was, though. Suddenly that apprehensive tension in his belly had returned. Could have been the dinner, he supposed, but he was imagining those two men again, more threatening than they'd been in real life. Time had lapsed, and the actual encounters were comparable, in the anxiety they'd provoked, to a previous fear. Years back. What was it called? *Beyond Mombasa.* Or something like that. Supposed to be a jungle flick, like Tarzan, but it turned out to be more to do with ordinary people who are out driving when these angry black men come out at them. They were called the Mau Mau and they were against the white people, and Foster had suddenly become aware that he was a white person, and that even though it was a film the Mau Mau were real people, and the fear they caused was a real fear. And it was that feeling he had when the man took his mother into the front room, and the same feeling he'd had the day he had to tell his dad he'd been caught shoplifting.

'What's the matter, love?' Rachel asked. 'Tummy queasy already? Bit of fresh air should help.'

They walked out from the quarry and crossed the road to look over the edge and out at the view. Miles and miles spread away below, and Foster saw how his bad feeling had arisen: England, that dimming panorama, reminded him of Africa, in sunset pictures on the back page of *Eagle*, then that made him think of the Mau Mau film – not think of it exactly, but have the feeling come back without knowing why – and so inevitably those two men re-entered his thoughts. Foster worked that out all by himself in a flash of wisdom, and it pleased him but wasn't anything he could explain to his mam, because although she was right there next to him she hadn't shared any of what he'd just been through. It was possible she'd had equally exciting things going on inside her, but unlikely. Foster didn't credit grown ups with doubts and fears. Being grown ups they obviously knew what was around the next bend.

Higher up the lay-by a van was parked, and there was a wastepaper bin near it. The van, Foster realised, was a special kind he hadn't seen ever before: it had glass side windows that slid open, a light in the back there, a man waiting for customers – it was a sort of shop, a van selling ice cream and soft drinks. A coal lorry came around the estate selling coal. A Johnny Onion man wheeled his bike around selling onions; the chimney sweep came on his bike too. But a real ice cream van – that had to prove they were in England. They moved closer and he saw a sign for a soft drink. The bottle in the picture was green, and it drew him like gold, because if he could discover and taste a new drink before his friends he'd have something they'd never have. But the name was written in such a way he couldn't be sure how you were supposed to say it. The first letter looked like a number, 7, but you couldn't make a word out of a number, so it had to be a quirky way of writing Z, and the drink must be called Zup because you couldn't say 7up, you had to say the number and then it would be two words, Seven Up, which didn't sound likely as the name of anything. Foster worried over things like that, which seemed to make the world unnecessarily involved. Just when you thought you understood enough to get by you'd see something illogical and be made to feel you were just a baffled little kid again.

'Mam,' he wheedled, 'they don't have that one back home. It looks like a good one.'

The lighted windows of sweetshops and toyshops were still magical to him, and the bright colours of advertising signs often made him dream of paradise. Rachel was somewhat less receptive to light and colour, and found her son's sudden enthusiasms bewildering. A soft drink was a soft drink, and it wasn't long since he'd had two big beakers of coca cola.

'You'll be sick,' she promised.

'Aw, please, Mam!' He really wanted to ask if he could look in the wastepaper bin as well, because you never knew what you were going to find and this one had bright packaging promising undreamt-of treasures – Foster had faith in the potentiality of unprepossessing things, as long as they were new to him. If the man in the van had said everything was free he'd have been overwhelmed, but not incredulous. If they asked directions and the man said London was just around the bend there, and his dad was expecting them and had a nice room all ready, he'd have been ready to believe it. Things turned up, not on a regular basis, and not when you expected, but at odd times, like now. This quiet evening on a hill he hadn't known about before, seeing England going dark in the long silent spread of limitless fields, and one or two stars already out almost directly level with his eyes – we're high as the stars! he gasped. So marvellous, and the coolness coming in flurries up the long grass from England, and the warmth of the lorry waiting to enfold him a hundred yards downhill, in the quarry place. But he guessed she'd say no.

Rachel pointed to the picture of the drink and the man said 'I was about to close up for today – not much traffic now', and Rachel agreed and he opened the bottle on a special bottle opener fixed to a cupboard.

'Ask him what it's called,' Foster hissed anxiously. The man heard him and grinned indulgently: 'This is Seven Up,' he said. 'You'll like it. It's good.' And he popped a couple of barber-pole straws in the top and handed the drink down, leaning right over to reach Foster's hand with it, Rachel stepping aside.

Rachel realised she was spoiling her son, but it was only this once and as long as he knew it wasn't going to become a habit there shouldn't be much harm.

'He was a nice man,' she mused as they strolled down the hill, keeping to the gravelly lay-by even though there were no cars. There *was* a car, but so far down it would be a couple of minutes before it reached them.

It was funny, she thought, but as soon as she'd started tucking into her dinner, appreciating the weight and quality of the silverware, she'd stopped worrying about whatever it was exactly John had gone and done. There was all that to go, and some of it might be unpleasant, but for now she was able to retain this overview, the serenity of being with her son in safety on a high hill way above the land, and she believed they'd pull through any difficulties, she believed in John's fundamental strength and decency, she believed in herself more than ever, and she believed that the surrounding quietness made the natural world a church whose benign leader smiled on her like a whisker of breeze.

The car had its light on full, and it came up very slowly, hardly seeming to ascend at all, but that was deceptive.

'Don't dawdle, love,' Rachel said, momentarily apprehending something her common sense wasn't registering. Would anyone in a car that far away be able to see two people against the darkening sky? 'Foster, finish it in the cab.' Going fretful again, he noted with disappointment – the best view ever, and the drink was all right even though he shouldn't have tried it so soon after the others, but she couldn't just enjoy the moment, and that was her problem. He sighed and let her hurry him away from the flurries of wind. His dad, he bet, would have said it was like being out at sea, just you and these fantastic expanses, and no women being sensible and saying it was time to come in just when you were beginning to feel part of the universe.

'If anything should happen,' Rachel said, 'you do exactly what I tell you, and if I say anything, even if it's not true, don't contradict me. This is important, Foss. Are you paying attention?'

'Aw, Mam,' he grumbled.

She shook him roughly and the bottle slipped and smashed, losing half his drink.

'Just follow my lead,' she carried on, ignoring his temper. 'And Foster,' she said, leaning close suddenly, 'I love you, and I love your daddy, and remember that.' She had no time to tell him what was racing through her mind, and scarcely knew herself. 'If I have to say or do something...there's times sometimes you have to act in a way...like in the pictures, Foss, when they're acting, and it's not really real.'

She tried to start the engine and stalled. She was agitated. Foster was mystified. Then he had that Mau Mau dread come on again and thought it wasn't fair when they'd come so far and had such a good time the last couple of hours. At such a moment, he thought, his dad ought to turn up out of the blue – or the greyish black, to be more accurate – that was what ought to happen, and you'd go all warm and know you were safe.

'Go, you buggering nuisance!' his mother swore at the steering wheel, and it was so unlike her to curse that he felt almost as reassured as if his father were with them after all.

The broken shards of his green glass bottle became illuminated before his eyes, sparkling on the gravel like a wonder. But his mam hadn't turned the headlights on yet. He raised his eyes to the rocky gap and the road.

THIRTY NINE

'Missing, Bob,' John repeated crabbily. 'Why can't you say it so it sounds worrying, depressing like, which is what it bloody well is?'

He'd heard it first from Bob Ryman, then, with more suspicion in the eyes, from Joe Davies in Haverfordwest; from Peter Walker, who was appalled and sympathetic to begin with, letting his fascination seep in only after a couple of minutes, and now from Bob again – Missing, as in No honest woman goes missing. As in Disappearance is unusual, and what's unusual is unwelcome and probably underhanded.

'All I'm saying,' Bob said, trying to reach the opposite of what he was thinking, 'is you mustn't give up hope. I'm not saying she've fled the country or nothing.' He paused, but couldn't look his friend in the eyes. Peter Walker was nodding sagely and imagining it would be quite exciting if she turned up in France or Spain. 'You know me, John,' Bob added, more with bemusement than conviction, 'and I know you. And Rachel. And your boy. I'm on your side. It's difficult for you.'

'What about Rachel? She'd contact me if she could, Bob, so the fact that there's been nothing...What your buddy Joe bloody Davies is saying – she took eight hundred quid from Fisk's safe, like that makes her Houdini, the Wizard of bloody Oz or something...' He shook his head in desperation.

Bob Ryman was caught between admiration for a superior officer and years of friendship with John and Mrs Eakins. His problem was he *could* imagine Mrs Eakins doing something against the law – something about her had always rung false, he now believed. Like how she thought she was a cut above her neighbours on the estate. Smart office job. Never went up the bingo. Not a mixer. Truth be told, he'd only tried to make allowances because he liked John, and now John had turned out disappointing and Bob remembered he wasn't born local. Be as tolerant as you like, but these things would make a difference sooner or later. Which was a shame, because John had seemed like the exception that proved the rule. But what had he come home with? He hadn't saved the Haven from development. Possibly he'd given them the means to defend themselves against the worst of it, but it would happen, and the money he'd brought only confirmed how imminent changes must be. Bob reeled in his line and examined the bait, then cast again, unable to concentrate.

'It's our savings she took, mun, and that's all,' John insisted, and he'd already tired of repeating the same honest facts. 'I told him, we got our savings account there. Rachel handles all Fisk's money, thousands, wages, purchasing, the lot, and she've never took a far-thing in her life. But he don't hear me. He listens like a filing cab-inet listens. It's all in there, in his mind, all worked out neat already. And he's barking up the wrong tree. And you think he's right, don't deny it. And you tell me he's one of the best. I'll tell you one thing for free, he's not like no bloody socialist I ever met.'

'It won't do no good having a go at Joe, John. His record speaks for him. Anyway, then there's the lorry.' He had to put that in, heavily, with regret. 'But we're treating it as missing persons, doing everything in our power to find her, if she wants to be found or not.'

'Find those gangster-types – they seem to have left a trail of bro-ken bones. Rachel's trying to keep out of their way. They're after her. I'd have thought that was the only way to look at it.'

'Well, you see, aye, in one way, but...well, they don't have no reason to go after her, isn't it? Anyway, they're missing an' all. Nothing since Paradise Valley.'

Fisk's lorry had been found as far back as Monday, parked in some sort of a quarry outside Gloucester. No damage. Full tank. Keys in. No signs of struggle, no handbag, no shoe, no note, nothing to say Rachel and Foster had ever been there save their fingerprints.

On Tuesday a waiter had said a woman and child answering their description ate in his restaurant early Sunday evening. Not extravagant, he said, but celebrating something – the boy's birth-day, he'd thought, or a piece of good news, like maybe they were about to come into an inheritance (In possession of it, they'd have made better use of the menu. The waiter was a bit of a sleuth, like all waiters). And Sunday, Monday, Tuesday, Wednesday, John had been unaware, his wife and son safe in the house all that time. It made his frustration deeper, as if his ignorance implicated him in whatever they'd suffered and rendered him ineffective as an advocate for their obvious innocence. In his mind they'd been safe. So much for that.

Peter Walker spat into the dark water below. 'We knew there was something wrong, didn't we, Bob?' he purred.

Bob Ryman flashed him a warning look. 'Aye, well, it's all police business now, so we best not discuss it.'

Peter Walker took that in slowly, wanting to boast of how he'd been first to notice, resenting being shut up for no good reason. But he wasn't going to get on the wrong side of Bob Ryman, so he changed the subject. 'So what's his game, then, this old pal of yours? Stripteasers and such, is it?'

'Not exactly,' John growled.

'See any shows, John? These glamour girls, what, friendly girls are they? Bet you liked being off the leash a few days!'

'Peter, my wife and boy have disappeared, and you want me to talk about blummin' pin up girls! You want me to chuck you in on top of that flob of yours? Because I bloody will, if you don't bloody grow up!'

'Aye,' Bob said. 'Show some respect, mun. John never said he saw no dirty shows. Not like that, are you, John?'

'Good God!' John exclaimed in disgust. 'You boys want to hear yourselves sometimes. It's like you're in short trousers, like you live in never-never land. Phil Thomas is an agent for artists, entertainers, and there's nothing wrong in it. He's a respected man in London. And I didn't see no bloody loose women, but what of it? What if I had? I'd still be the same man, wouldn't I? People aren't mucky when you know 'em, whatever they do.'

Peter Walker was confused. He'd been envying John's independence. Bob Ryman was just glad the topic had shifted. He'd given John most of the salient details – Small Derrick Jones getting a beating, young Colin tormented, Mal having to lose his spleen, then that incredible slaughter out at Paradise Valley – all disturbing, grisly stuff; but he'd carefully omitted any reference to John's house, and with good reason, the same reason he'd had when omitting the reference in his conversations with Joe Davies: he'd told Peter to flush away that turd, never imagining it could be a piece of evidence. He'd been hasty and inept, so part of him wanted Rachel Eakins to have masterminded something, just as part of him resented John and needed him toppled. It was unfair blaming John for his own mistake, and unavoidable.

'I'm tired of this,' he said, reeling in. 'Think I'll go see how Mal's doing. Coming?'

Peter said he would. John declined. Company annoyed him. He walked part way back with them, then cut up to the St. Lawrence and let himself into his forbiddingly empty house. He didn't particularly want to stay, but had nowhere to go outside. He felt completely useless. Even in his chair by the wireless he couldn't feel properly at home any more. And there was nothing on that interested him anyway, until the shipping forecast. A couple of months back there'd have been sports reports about now. The rugby used to give him a sense of contact with the whole of Wales and, particularly, the part he'd grown up in. That was because one of the reporters hailed from the valleys, Newbridge, same as John himself, and it was like a shared language, that simple link, because although Bill Watson must have been a good ten years older his litany of names and places would have been the same. Even rugby enthusiasts like Bob couldn't fully understand what it had meant to grow up in a mining town in the twenties and thirties, and get news of Newbridge's triumphs through the war years. Glory days, glory days, John mused, sitting beside the silent wireless as a wind picked up outside and the gloomy room grew gloomier. Never much of a player himself, he carried with him nonetheless a picture of the pitch, the crowd, the great slag heap behind the ground, the warming together of the community, and for him it was stronger than anything he'd found or made in Hakin, and perhaps it was a rule of life that you never felt the world you got into as an adult was as real and mythic, as rich in true values as the world you lost once childhood waned. He'd wanted to be a man like the men he still looked on as his only heroes, and Bill Watson's voice could confirm its continuing existence, somewhere across the airwaves and the hills, back there, back there. Newbridge only lost three games in the four seasons from 1940 to 1944, going undefeated for two consecutive seasons – knowledge like that could carry you through heavy artillery. At the end of the war Newbridge was the first club to tour France, and bloody triumphantly, since 1939. Later, players like Gore the hooker, Gale and Don Hayward, both forwards, were capped – Newbridge bred legends.

The shed door was knocking in the wind. John Eakins tried to stay inside the memories which made him feel he had a strong past. He smiled, recalling an accidental meeting in Cardiff. He'd been with Foster when he spotted Joe Erskine, the boxer, and he'd been so excited he ran after him, poor Foster clinging to his hand. 'Joe, Joe!' he called, and when he caught him he didn't know what he wanted to say, so he asked if he could have an autograph for the boy. Big Joe Erskine, a shy giant of a man, looked bashful, as though no one had ever requested his autograph before. And he was already talking to somebody – Bill Watson, John realised, who was already doing his five minute rugby reports then. And Joe Erskine bent to peer at Foster, grinned shyly, straightened to his full height again, mumbled, 'Well, as it happens...' and reached inside his jacket and pulled out a batch of postcards of himself in a boxing stance, already signed. It was slightly embarrassing, but nice. John wanted to say something to Bill Watson, like I come from Newbridge too. You used to play, didn't you? You went to France with the team, didn't you? Your mam and dad ran the con club, didn't they? Do you remember...? Did you ever go to...? But he thanked Joe Erskine for the signed picture and led Foster away from the two men, and then he laughed because he was as happy as a kid on his birthday. And Foster said 'Who was it, Daddy? Was it friends?' and he said, 'No, they're men I don't know, but you can talk to them – good, isn't it? Joe's a great boxer. The other man just comes from where I do. You keep that postcard safe now. You'll be proud of it one day.' Foster said, 'Can I have some bubble gum?'

John Eakins pulled out a handkerchief and blew his nose. Then he moved around to stop himself dwelling on the past because he didn't like sentimentality in himself or anyone else.

In the evening he heard a car pulling up outside and went to look: it was only Bob Ryman's Standard Vanguard – he could have walked across the green just as quickly.

'Getting lazy, Bob?' John said as he opened the door.

'Going on over Haverfordwest now just. Bit of news I thought you might want to hear. The car our two gangster friends were driving, the Cresta, it's been found near Oxford.'

'Rachel and Foster?'

'Nothing yet. But the lorry was miles from where the Cresta was.'

John wasn't sure what he should make of that. If Rachel and Foster had been pulled from the lorry and taken for a ride in the car it didn't mean much to have found the car.

'There's bullet holes in the windows. Blood on the front seat. Looks like they met trouble. Joe says if it's in-fighting between gangs we may never find the bodies. Whatever weapons they were carrying have gone with them. No prints from Mrs Eakins or your boy in the car, you'll be glad to know, so I don't know, John – the mystery continues.'

'I want to *do* something,' John said urgently. 'How can I set about finding them when I don't know where to start? You feel so blummin' useless in a situation like this!' That wasn't the half of it – he felt as if the quietly fulfilled life he'd led ever since moving to the Haven had turned out to be made of paper.

'One thing,' Bob said, ignoring his plea for sympathy. 'When Mr Wary spoke to you about what he was meant to do with the money, why didn't you come and tell us straight away? Why go off to London with it?'

'Him keeling over seemed to confuse it all, Bob. I should've, looking back. I wish I had.'

'Aye, fair enough. This Gravett – we've tried to see if we can connect him to those two blokes, but he's clean as a whistle. The money's all from proper investors...'

He didn't have anything useful to say, and although he was doing his best to be friendly there was something lacking and John felt the only way of getting back what had gone would be to have another chance at the last week or so, find the money again, tell Bob immediately, and work it from there. Failing that, what Bob and the others needed was for someone to stop the future coming, turn away the flood of change. If I had a brain, he thought, I'd find the answer, but my brain's mush and I'm no help.

There were rocks that rose stubbornly from the sea and withstood its ceaseless battering, gaunt and hostile as the sea itself, and in some of these dangerous, useless presences caves, comforting no living forms, echoed damp ringing sounds of the brief intruder. Eakins had heard of these strange places, but never approached. Now, he thought, his house was such a sequence of mockeries of rooms, tricked out with reminders of Rachel and the boy.

Asleep, or awash in darkness and uncertainly awake, he awaited an outcome.

Bobbie was not the unexpected caller he'd been anticipating. She'd come – she wasn't sure why she'd come – perhaps because he promised a way out for her, because of the money he'd so generously sent. She was nicely dressed and very polite, very anxious not to intrude on his wife's domain. She understood immediately that he couldn't put her up in the spare bedroom because it was Rachel's office. They talked about her portfolio, and he studied the pictures sympathetically as she explained how she'd nearly modelled for Jean Straker, and how Pamela Green was willing to consider using her in *Kamera*. Bobbie said women were coming into their own through art like hers, which insisted on the body's beauty. A new age was dawning, of appreciation and celebration, of simple honest pleasures. But he didn't intend to sleep with her in his marriage bed. That just happened out of kindness, really, Bobbie being so alone. Odd the betrayals of grief, he thought.

Ragged sails circled the peripheries of his dreams, every forward run soon merging into a backwards trace, nothing getting anywhere.

His hand was well enough. He could go to sea as soon as he liked, and would have to soon, to go on making his living. But why? he thought. Why make a living when you can't say what you're living for?

He spoke to Bob Ryman again. Mal was recuperating, but out of hospital, and Bob was more relaxed. He tried to be philosophical.

He said, 'Places change,' in a resigned voice. You couldn't stop places changing, he'd realised. All you could do was move on once they were spoilt.

John said, 'Places only change on the surface. Down in London, it was different in some ways, but I found my way to where I wanted to go, so it must have stayed pretty much the same. No, places only change on the surface, in small details – old rows pulled down, new rows put up. We change, Bob. That's the pity of it. We change underneath more quickly than we do on our faces. We look like we looked last year, but underneath we've had things happen.'

'Aye, that's true.'

'Places outlive us, anyhow, so what's it to you or me if they alter a bit while we're still able to tell?'

'Mmm,' Bob ruminated. 'It's people that matter more, I suppose.'

'I'm not saying that,' John said bitterly. 'I don't think nothing matters, not in the long run. Damn sure I don't!'

'I wish to God that blummin' Wary man hadn't've gone and died round here. We never used to talk like this before.'

'Mmm,' John ruminated. In his mind he was already rescuing Rachel once again, complicated this time because Bobbie was actually with him as a friend Rachel would have to get used to. They were going to take flowers to Mrs Champion.

Trawlers still lined up in the Haven, the water glinting silver, men still unloaded the catch; the trains still left when it was dark; gulls lined the long roof; summer crept in. The same real world went on with its business outside the house, and John Eakins was conscious enough that it existed, only he longer existed as a part of it in quite such an easy way. The yearnings of loneliness, the powerful, vitiating sense of incompleteness, made him question the simplicity of life. His frequent speculative dreams weren't part of that sunny reality outside, but nor were his flashes of actual memory, when he would hear Rachel's voice calling him as clearly as if she were in the kitchen again, or when he would kiss Foster goodnight rather brusquely. When he was remembering them, who was remembering him? Where where they? And if he no longer lived in their unbidden thoughts, how much of him lived at all?

He went down to the docks, met men, made arrangements. It was good to stand on board again, getting his hands dirty, getting ready to put to sea. It was also all he could do. Carefully he cut a couple of snapshots to a size he could carry in his wallet. He couldn't swim, yet rarely considered he might drown. When it entered his mind he was easy about it because drowning at sea seemed a lot more natural than drowning on land.

FORTY

We can't leap from a moving car, Rachel reasoned, not even if they mean to bump us off when we stop.

I could put my hand on his eyes, Foster thought, yank the wheel when he tried to pull me away, make us crash. We might be hurt. We might have a chance. Will I? Won't I? Dad would know what to do.

We say, We got the woman and the kid, Bull. Bull says, Why? What use is that? He's seen Eakins, he's got his dough back, he's made other arrangements, he smiles and later on has us killed discreetly. Why? Because we're a bloody embarrassment now. George sneered at the road ahead. Whichever way he looked at what they'd done, they hadn't had a choice, so it wasn't his fault they'd wound up driving home with a stupid woman and a stupid kid who'd probably be the death of them. Be easier in some ways, he reasoned calmly, to chuck them out, reverse over the bodies a few times. Except for one thing: If Bull *hadn't* netted John Eakins yet, if Eakins was on the loose and carrying the briefcase, yeah, *then* it made sense. Give us it and you get them back safe and sound. A simple transaction, and Bull need never hear a word. But everything depends on so many other things. You try to go in a straight line after the thing you want. You can't. The thing shifts.

I have to remember his name, Rachel realised, thinking again about that walk on the south downs, the very English boyfriend, the glorious sky, the crashed aeroplane. She caught herself fretting and found it strange to be worrying over a detail with no relevance to the rather dire situation she and Foster were in. She couldn't even see Foster. They'd made him sit in the front, next to the dead-looking man, who was the driver. If she craned slightly she could catch a glimpse of some strands of her son's hair, sticking up. Water wouldn't keep his hair in place. Nor would brylcreem. You could paste it down with spit; it would spring back again in minutes. Poor Foss – thought it made him look babyish, because adults' hair never seemed to have a life of its own. She was so glad to be able to see those few strands and know he was there. But did he have any idea how evil these men were, how real were her fears? She wished she'd never left the house.

George knows what to do, Gently thought complacently. He was mildly vexed because the woman had attempted to flirt with him back in that quarry. Possibly she'd hoped they'd let her go, but he doubted she was that smart. One of those he'd heard about – like blokes to rough them up – must have got a kick out of what he'd made her do the night before, dirty cow. She looked prim and proper enough, but that was typical. He didn't like having to sit next to her. He wanted to wash and cover himself in talc. He was afraid he might be sweating. He felt her knee touch his thigh on a bend, and hated that. If she wanted him to talk he'd smack her in the chops. George knew best. George said they were hostages to a fortune. That was the thing to remember. Gently planned it first, but George was seeing it through.

You feel as if the night's going to go on and on and on, Rachel sighed to herself, as if you're trapped in this inordinate pause before they finish with us. But it's not so. We're moving constantly. We're alive, and that's why it's impossible to believe we'll soon be dead. You can't imagine being dead. The effort of it is an effort of thoughts and feelings. Oh, his name was Guy! That's better. It makes no difference, but it's such a relief. Guy! You're my little colleen, he said. No I'm not, you told him, I'm Welsh. He blushed in that helpless way he had, but persisted anyway: Well you can be *my* colleen, how's that? What a snotty young man he was, thinking of you as this simple country girl he could enhance himself by adoring. Bloody fool! He was, though, even though he died at sea. Guy, a nobody, but walking up the steep side of the hill towards the beaming sky that day, that was good – like being the girl in a film, wearing quite a cheap frock, come to think of it, cotton, a flower print, snagging it on some gorse, and goldfinches suddenly flushed from the gorse higher up in a whirl of yellows and reds into the blue you dream of.

They had a school trip to *Moby Dick* when it came to the Astoria, because they filmed it just a few miles away at Fishguard and one day lost their model whale at sea. The film was hard to follow, but it was scary when the man got into bed and had that savage man already there. And then he turned out to be the best friend, the loyal silent one. Foster saw himself like that, not the hero but the hero's devoted friend, savage and skillful with a harpoon, profoundly trustworthy. And it was the whalers who'd founded Milford Haven originally. Whalers from Nantucket. And when the original, real Buffalo Bill came from America with his Wild West Show, where did he land? Milford, of course. And Nelson was connected too. It was a great place, Milford, where real things and film things got all mixed together. It would be good to get back home now, and tell Petey and Dewi and Colin about all this. They wouldn't believe it, not at first, but it would be in the papers, how Foss and his mam turned the tables on the baddies.

'Company,' Gently warned George from the back seat – he'd been watching the headlights reflected off George's bald spot for a while.

'Already seen 'em,' George replied laconically. His terseness was the only clue to possible agitation. Whenever a threat loomed he appeared unconcerned because he was all brain. For Rachel he said, 'This could be where you earn your keep, darling.'

'Say the wrong word and I'll break your neck,' Gently added confidentially.

It seemed to be a police car, content to trail along behind them. George guessed it was unlikely they'd know what had happened to those idiots at the farm yet. Even if the balloon had gone up, why should they be looking for a car this far into England? So he told Gently to be ready but be calm. If they were stopped it might be routine.

Rachel didn't dare look behind. If she had she might have glimpsed a second car, without lights, close behind the police car. No one had seen it. She shifted to the edge of her seat and reached out to touch Foster's shoulder. His cold hand grasped her fingers. Gently watched, decided to let her remain in contact with her son, as long as she didn't flaunt herself at him again. He busied himself with a couple of guns, readying them for firing.

Foster was excited. A police car. If only it can make us stop! He wanted to communicate this to his mam. He squeezed her fingers. She pressed the top joint in one of his, but he wasn't sure she understood the situation. His dad would have. He'd have had a plan all ready. This would be a good time to force the car off the road and make sure the police came to see. But he didn't want to touch the thin man's eyebrows with his bare fingers.

The police car put on speed. The unlit car fell back into the darkness.

'Bugger! He's pulling us over!' George said. 'Play it by ear,' he warned Gently. 'I don't want us killing coppers unless we really have to.'

The cars slowed gracefully and stopped. Two men in black rain-coats got out of the police car. One started walking back. George wound down his window. 'Anything the matter, officer?' he asked innocently.

'You're all right, sir,' the policeman said, 'but we noticed one of your rear lights is on the blink. Just back there it went out alto-gether.'

'Really? That's a nuisance.'

The policeman came right up to the window and rested his

gloved hand on the wing mirror, obscuring any view George might have had.

'I've got to wee,' Foster gabbled, throwing open his door and scrambling free before anyone could prevent him.

Urgently, Rachel said, 'It's all right, I'll get him back. Please!' and she struggled with her door.

Gently moved to stop her, but George said 'Yes' firmly, so he let her out. It was a gamble, but she wasn't going to risk her son's life. She knew how dangerous they were. One word to that policeman and they'd had it. The second policeman was now coming towards the car, standing directly in front of the headlights. He saw Rachel and Foster. Foster was veering towards him. Suddenly he swiped out and the boy tumbled aside, Rachel diving to save him. The swiping arm came right back and pointed at George and was a gun and fired at George's head. At the same time the men from the darkened second car arrived, unseen and unnoticed, and shot Gently through his ears.

'Quick!' Rachel hissed, dragging Foster into the police car. These weren't police officers, she'd realised, but they'd left their engine running. Not all of them could give chase – she didn't work that out, but it was true nonetheless. George and Gently had to be disposed of. Not that only having one car full of killers made getting away any more plausible. She didn't pause to think of the chances. You spin on the chance or slip away.

'I thought it would be Dad,' Foster grumbled.

Rachel ground the pedal down as far as she could. Astonishingly, they were screaming away, spitting rubber and road, and avoiding gunshots.

'I think we must be dead,' she murmured, and then giggled.

'Cor, Mam, you can't half drive!' Foster admitted, clenching his toes.

It seemed more mad now than when they'd been helpless hostages. She was clinging to the road by something other than skill, anticipating calamity every second, yet unable to level off, slow down, apply rational thought, do anything consciously at all. Like dreaming, like flying, like being a spirit.

Odd way to pass through a Sunday night, she thought dizzily, and then thought for a moment of John, saw him plainly, sitting at a table in a night club, laughing with his friend. They had drinks before them and were watching a floorshow, some woman in spangles and feathers. It was black and white, out of a film, but it was John enjoying himself, and she didn't mind.

There'd never been that kaleidoscope of colours, like the

goldfinches, nothing like that with John, no rainbows, but he was a solid man and she'd get back to him, no matter what he'd done to bring on such a slide from sense and balance.

'That must be a town,' Foster said. 'The lights. Is it London, Mam?'

'As long as it's got people it'll do for us,' Rachel hoped.

'I never needed a wee,' Foster boasted. 'I tricked 'em, didn't I?'

Rachel murmured something, concentrating now on getting them safely into the lights, almost allowing herself to breathe with relief, almost ready to believe the miracle of continuing to live.

★ ★ ★

'You can't honestly think she done something she shouldn't!' Mal reproved his friend. 'You've known her for years, boy!'

'Aye, but Joe Davies, he's more objective, see.'

'Rachel Eakins? Never. Either the poor woman's been murdered by them maniacs who set on me for no reason, or she's tied up somewhere, starving to death for all we know.'

'Between you and me, we've been keeping an eye on John all this time – Joe thought he'd lead us to her, but poor old John's in the dark. You're probably dead right, Mal, and it's just a shame and it don't make no sense.'

They were standing on the clifftop walk out by Hubberston fort. Work had started, inconspicuously, over the other side of the Haven. You couldn't hear a sound, but if you kept watching you'd see earth on the move as they levelled the site. It was almost like seeing one of those trick films that show a painting coming into being, shot from behind glass. You can't see the strokes, only the results. A dull yellow field was becoming a strip of brown. A grey line was appearing apparently on the water. It was a long way away, as if it was happening on another day and wasn't going to touch you at all. But clearing the ground and putting down temporary tracks was only the start of it. Not even the start – it must have started weeks ago, and they hadn't expected it to start over there so nobody even noticed. It wouldn't remain so insignificant as time went on. Bob felt foolish because all the time he'd fantasised about buying up land on the Haven to prevent this he'd never even considered buying it on the Angle side. He couldn't have afforded the purchase anyway, but it was depressing to be outwitted even in a daydream.

'Times are changing, eh, Mal?'

'Aye.'

'You want to be writing up the story, boy – how they come and ruined our beautiful Haven!'

'Aye.' Mal nodded. 'I'm not so sure it's the job for me,' he added regretfully. 'Reporting – what you're doing, you're saying what's been done, see what I mean?'

'Bit deep for me, boy. You like weddings, though.'

'Aye, weddings are happy. But then, look at old Beverley Walker!'

'That's a turn-up for the books,' Bob agreed. Beverley Walker had left her husband, simply telling him she had no more use for him. A removal van turned up. Off she went with little Petey, no goodbyes, off to live in Scarborough with a man who sold jukeboxes for a living. 'Old John Eakins said it's people that change. Time was, nothing never changed at all, isn't it? The place couldn't change, and if you knew somebody you'd rely on it. Nobody never changed when we was youngsters, Mal. They was characters.'

'I think that's true.'

'What's gone wrong, then?'

Mal started to shrug, then winced slightly. 'They got a jukebox now in that new cafe in Hakin, on the bottom there. What's it called? *The Moon and Sixpence.*'

'I seen it, aye, and they got a real sixpenny piece nailed up for the "i" in sixpence, did you see that? Jukeboxes! God! What next!' He liked grumbling, but there was something else he was anxious to get off his chest. A delicate matter, because he wanted Mal to remain his best pal regardless. 'Mal,' he asked tentatively, 'you ever thought seriously about getting married yourself?'

'What brings that up?'

'Oh, nothing. Nothing really. There's no rush, though, is there?'

'I haven't even got a steady girlfriend. I used to go courting that Mary Jones with a bad leg, remember? She was a nice girl. That must be five years ago.'

'These nancy boys I keep hearing about,' Bob plunged deeper, 'you don't get much idea there's any of 'em round here, do you?'

'Fairies?'

'Queers, aye. Don't laugh, mun, I was wondering about it just the other day, you know, thinking it over, like, and I thought, you never hear what it's like from their side, do you? I mean, do they know they're sick or what? Do they *like* it?'

'Sounds like a funny thing for you to think about, Bob!'

'It is, really. But it was your doctor bloke up the hospital, Mal – now don't get mad, he made this remark concerning how you was dressed when they took you in, see...'

'Aw, Duw, I know what's coming!'

'I nearly knocked his block off, but since then I've been thinking about the way he was saying it, like maybe it's something you can't help, if you're like that, and it's not like being dirty on purpose, not even a sickness. What I mean is, we all laugh at them, the idea of queers, but we don't know any. And maybe they're almost like normal blokes in some ways, like me and you. Maybe we shouldn't be so quick to take against people we don't know.'

He stepped away deliberately and gazed out towards the mouth of the Haven, wishing he hadn't said anything, convinced he'd said far too much.

Mal bent down and tugged at the tough grass for a while. He was thinking of moving away, now he didn't want to go on working for the local paper; but where to go, what to do – he couldn't seem to get a fresh idea in his head. He felt sorry for Bob, standing with his back to him looking so big and capable. Poor old Bob was making an obvious effort to adapt to change, but it didn't suit him. He wasn't cut out to have weird notions.

'If there was any queer-boys round here I don't think they'd last long,' he said pleasantly. What he wanted was to reassure his friend, although he didn't feel especially confident himself. It was nice Bob was trying to say they'd still be pals even if Mal was a fairy, but it wouldn't stay true, he thought. Bob would slowly distance himself. Any man would, for fear of contamination or something. 'Nothing against them personally,' Mal added emphatically, 'but they better not try it on near me, that's all I can say!'

'Aye,' Bob was swift to agree, turning back. 'That's just the way I look at it. Good.'

And he found he was glad, after all, to have cleared away the possibility. It was good they could go on as if they, at least, were ever-unchanging, a permanent testimony to innocence and clean air.

★ ★ ★

Foster could see his dad in the distance, outlined against an enormous sweep of sky. He wanted to run to him, but a dim painful memory made him linger as if he'd been jilted. He could hear his dad going 'What d'you call that?' and laughing derisively as he kicked a sandcastle into ruins. But that wasn't where the pain lay. 'Tide'll be over it in a couple of hours anyhow,' John justified himself against Rachel's anger and Foster's hopeless tears. The tone of that, his own dad justifying himself, sounding craven in his bad temper, sounding let down by his family, sounding anything but heroic, that was the disappointing core of the memory. His own little castle didn't even matter. It was the failure of magnanimity or something, and it was a fearful thing because it threw away the supports you needed to get by and left you knowing the truth too young. But what you had to do, what you did, was pretend it never happened like that. You had to stay with him, you had to help him feel better. It was love, to force it to be the way you needed it to be. It didn't just come by itself like summer.

★ ★ ★

John Eakins had dug out his old copies of *Picture Post* that he hadn't looked at in years. He stood in the doorway of the shed, sheltered from the breeze, hoping Peter Walker wouldn't come over whingeing about the madness of blummin' wives again, watching Sam Niblo trying to blow up a Lilo in readiness for the summer. He turned the pages until he reached the pictures he wanted to see once more. Only one, really, a group of soldiers grinning – not exactly a group, and not all grinning. They were just hanging around on a nondescript back road. John Eakins had been with them, and he remembered the man with the camera. He could have been in the photograph himself if he'd wanted, or if the photographer had turned another twenty five degrees south. In fact he had – John remembered a few seconds before, or after, grinning at the camera, but that mustn't have made such a good picture for some reason. It was a peculiar thing, though, to be nearly in *Picture Post*. John had made a face at those two, the two who were laughing at something. He'd made them laugh. Probably they were amongst those who'd died the following morning, but he'd never know for sure. He liked the picture. The men were ordinary men, not heroes, and another man, also not a hero, had thought it worthwhile to take a few snaps. It was hard to see why. It didn't mean anything.

Wish I'd asked Phil about that gold, he thought. Then he put the magazine away and wheeled out his bike and cycled up to the top of the St. Lawrence estate, making his way out to Hubberston fort to be alone.

★ ★ ★

Rachel could see John in the distance, outlined against an enormous sweep of sky. It was almost too little, after so much, but looked at in another way, perhaps nothing much had actually happened, only a series of fraught moments. You can't blame people for what they don't know anything about. Nobody's responsible for these things, they just happen if you happen to be unlucky. You can't say when your luck's going to change. You could go on being unlucky indefinitely, though you never do. The important things are elsewhere, the stable things. You have to think the best of other people, otherwise you only make it painful. And life's too short. You go on, holding yourself in check, keeping it all together, and now and then you have those nice little moments and they're all you need, and more than some people ever have anyway, and that's enough, you can keep them, like Foster's bubble gum cards, and they're the collection of your life, and they don't get torn or lost, and they'll never diminish. But God, those lobsters that day!

★ ★ ★

'How do!' John called brusquely, wheeling his bike towards Bob Ryman and Mal Mabey. He hadn't thought to find them on the headland.

'John, how's it going?' Mal greeted him. Bob only nodded.

He dropped his bike and went to stand with them. They chatted inconsequentially for a time, unhappily resigned to the activity on the Angle side of the Haven. It was a glorious afternoon, like high summer except not warm enough, but bright and scented, redolent of promises none of them felt eagerly responsive to any longer.

'No,' John said to something Mal had asked, 'I'm off in the morning, for about a week, I expect, but after that...'

'What? You can't just leave the trawlers!' Bob said, not wanting John around but reluctant to think he might go away for good.

'I'm not forty yet – I can do a different job. There's jobs around. It's being in the house now, it's not what it used to be. And I feel like I let everybody down somehow, an' all.'

'Never!' Bob said staunchly. He's right, he thought.

'Not being here when all this nasty stuff happened. You know.'

'Aye, but fair does, you couldn't help it, boy. You wasn't to know.'

'Thought I'd go back over Newbridge way, see what's going off.'

'Not a lot, I shouldn't think,' Mal said. 'It's just the colliery, isn't it? Wouldn't appeal to me, all that coal dust.'

'Maybe I'll go back over England, then. I don't know.'

'Who's to say what's right and wrong?' Bob Ryman asked unexpectedly, partly as if he were responding to John's continuing depression, partly pursuing his own line. 'Is it lawyers, or doctors, judges, MPs...? It's not like it's written on stone or nothing, is it? Your little boy, he tried to pinch a record that once, aye? And that seemed terrible, but how can you measure that against what those buggers are doing over there? And yet that's not wrong at all. Nobody gets punished for that. Buggers make fortunes, and we wring our blummin' hands over every little thing like it's the end of the world. And what did you ever do, Mal, to deserve that beating? Bloody nothing, that's what! What I'm saying, there's no scales to weigh nothing.'

'It's all in the past,' Mal said soothingly.

'Yeah,' Bob murmured, still frowning, worrying at something. 'But I think I feel the same like John does. Like we been cheated out of something, like we lost it, whatever it was. And I don't *know* what it was.'

John Eakins said nothing, in anger. He knew what he'd lost. Bob Ryman had no idea. He couldn't carry on living in the same community as friends who thought they understood the dark shining caves he inhabited now.

Mal Mabey was all right, though. He'd changed, become more grown up, less boisterous. But Bob was a big fidget.

Mal was looking inland, behind John. He wasn't looking at anything in particular, just letting himself drift away from the dreariness of the conversation temporarily. But then his attention was taken up and he glanced at John and Bob, both too shut in on themselves to be distracted. He looked again, hardly believing his eyes.

'Good lord,' he said softly. 'Look who's here, John!'

John Eakins shivered all down his back, and didn't move, felt he didn't dare. It was the wonder in Mal's voice that made him imagine what he might see once he turned. It was the bleakness of an almost certain mistake that rooted him to the sight of grey, blue-streaked water and the silent rearrangement of the shoreline under the dull low hills on the other side. At the same time he saw, or didn't quite see but felt himself into the memory of an hour ago, making faces at the boys, picking up whatever he had to carry, and setting off again, after that unexpected and unexplained period of waiting, trudging dutifully along a road they were only on because they'd already been on it for hours, not knowing if they were heading anywhere in particular. He wasn't there, but it was like that. The weariness, the obedience – he couldn't say the faith, there was only perseverance, and that because you had no option. And at least you were all in it together.

'Damn me!' Bob said, and barely held back from giving John a hug. He squeezed his arm: 'Bloody Tinkerbell!' he muttered, not quite making his meaning clear. Damned if he'd say he believed in fairies, even to make a feeble joke!

'God alive,' John Eakins faltered at their amazement. But he couldn't turn yet. He weakened and slid his gaze towards the open sea. He took in a deep breath and all the low full sea and high huge sky could offer. Without knowing why it was so, and certainly without wishing to question it was so, he knew that in a moment his existing could be transformed into life, life that counted and he could regain a meaning and a value. Or nothing. And there was nothing for it but submission. The sailor closed his eyes humbly and turned as if to pray. You had to allow for remote possibilities, even when you were trudging down the road with sore feet and aching backs and not really caring what explosions might be up ahead.

Nothing extraordinary, no miracles, only permission to continue as we were a while longer. We won't be long. We can't go far.

They mean it when they say it, so you cling to the words for dear life, after the words have faded, only their warm tones wafting like August evening air amongst your thoughts, your heart, your pulse.

THE AUTHOR

Robert Watson was born in Gwent and brought up in Pembrokeshire. He studied at the London School of Film Technique before becoming a teacher. He now lectures at Bretton Hall College in Yorkshire. Robert Watson is the prize-winning author of three previous novels: *Events Beyond the Heartlands, Rumours of Fulfilment* (also available from Seren) and *Whilom*.